LOVESTRUCK MAGGOT

JARRETT BRANDON EARLY

For Mom, who dedicated her life to teaching children how to read and write while showing them the magic of books. And who also hates the title of this novel.

For Dad, the original space cowboy.

For Natthi, without whom I wouldn't understand the meaning of being lovestruck.

For Alex Beam, just because she's the coolest person I know.

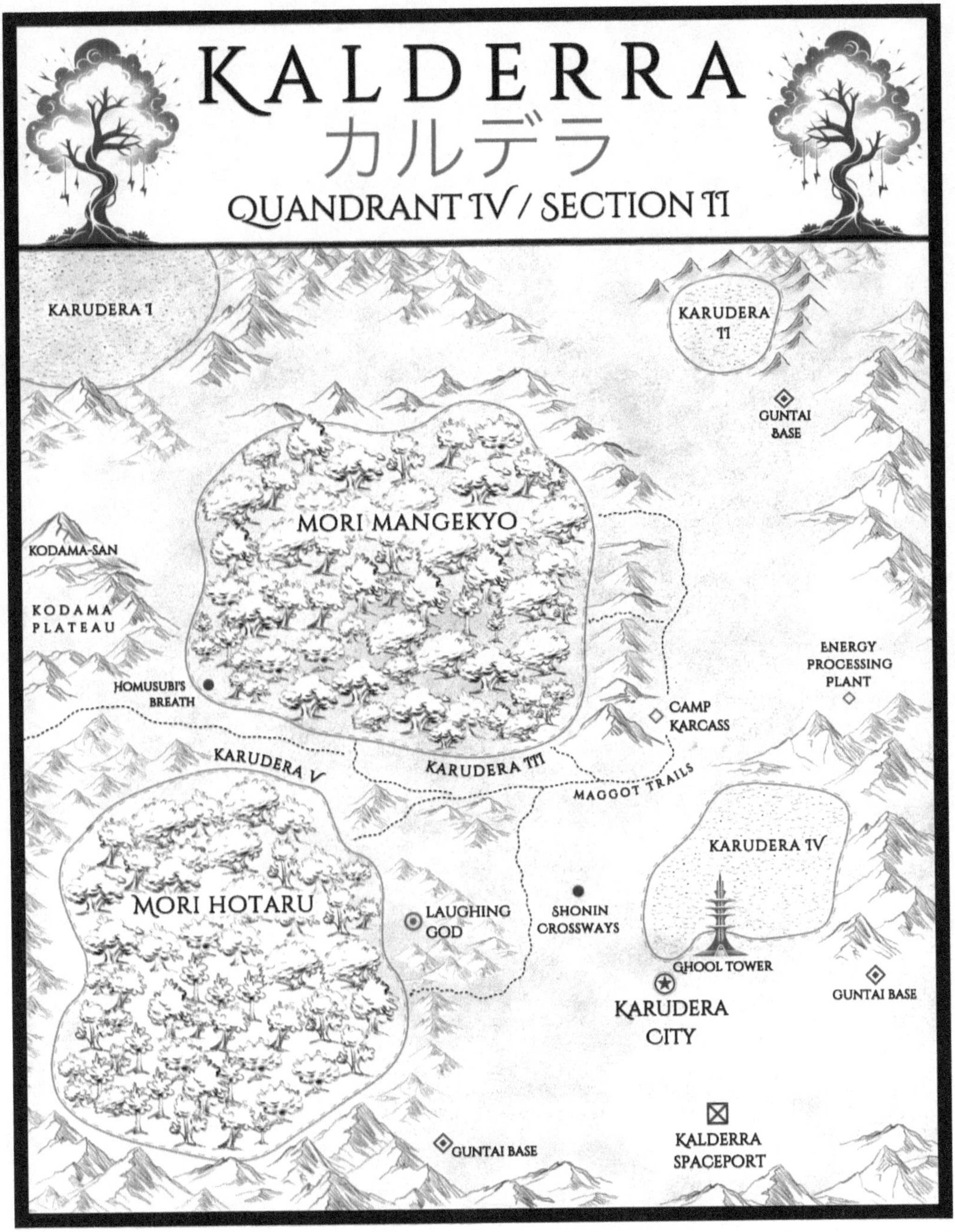
KALDERRA
カルデラ
QUANDRANT IV / SECTION II
KARUDERA I
KARUDERA II
GUNTAI BASE
MORI MANGEKYO
KODAMA-SAN
KODAMA PLATEAU
ENERGY PROCESSING PLANT
HOMUSUBI'S BREATH
CAMP KARCASS
KARUDERA V
KARUDERA III
MAGGOT TRAILS
KARUDERA IV
MORI HOTARU
LAUGHING GOD
SHONIN CROSSWAYS
GHOOL TOWER
GUNTAI BASE
KARUDERA CITY
GUNTAI BASE
KALDERRA SPACEPORT

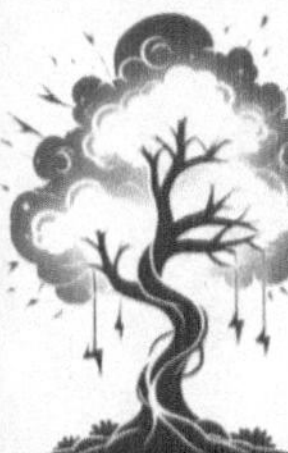

PLANETARY REPORT
KALDERRA

*T*he *below initial findings are based on studies paid for and conducted by Morishita Galactic Corporation.*

Wakusei 364.12.12865.5, for the remainder of this report referred to as Kalderra, is a terrestrial planet in the Kawatare System, located in the Scutum-Crux Arm of the Milky Way Galaxy.

Morishita Robotics drones have visited Kalderra on four separate occasions over the past thirty-five years, collecting data on atmospheric properties, geological composition, and indigenous flora and fauna. After significant analysis (at substantial cost to Morishita Galactic), four outstanding characteristics best define the planet. They are:

i. Kalderra orbits a Type A star labeled Hoshi 364.12.12865.0 that burns at 8,400 K and appears blue to the human eye. While Type A stars are not ideal for supporting life on orbiting planets, especially given their relatively short lifespans (a few hundred million years), intense temperatures, and high radiation output, Kalderra (1 of 6 system planets) is uniquely positioned in a thin slice of habitable zone.

ii. Orbiting Kalderra is a single moon labeled Tsuki 364.12.12865.5.1, which has numerous distinct attributes. Tsuki 364.12.12865.5.1 is massive, representing more than 71% of

Kalderra's size, but is far less dense given that the majority of the moon is water ice, with little rock to be found. Tsuki 364.12.12865.5.1 shines bright violet on Kalderra and has major effects on the planet. Most critically, its gravitational interaction with Kalderra directly maintains the planet's strong magnetic field, providing superior protection against radiation.

iii. Once a desolate, mountainous rock planet, Kalderra experienced a time of tremendous volcanic activity several thousand years ago (estimate). The simultaneous (generally speaking) eruption of more than five stratovolcanoes across Quadrant IV / Section II of the planet transformed the region, with each Plinian eruption emptying magma chambers and collapsing volcanic roofs, leaving massive craters—known as calderas—ranging from 50 to 200 kilometers in diameter.

iv. The eruption of these stratovolcanoes and their subsequent collapses shattered surface rock and churned the ground. There is no current evidence of mineral rich deposits (reluctant to use the word "soil"). In two of these calderas (Crater 3 and Crater 5), vast forests have (surprisingly) appeared, dominated by massive crystalline (and glowing) "trees" with "wood" that is interspersed with veins of striking purple, blue, and pink. These "trees" exceed 275 meters in height and 25 meters in diameter, dwarfing the revered "Redwoods" of Chikyu, once known widely as Earth. While small amounts of liquid water have been detected beneath the surface of Kalderra, no precipitation has been observed by various drones over several years. The appearance and continued growth of these forests remain a significant mystery.

v. In a most unusual discovery, the atmosphere of Kalderra (at least as of the creation of this report) is found to be conducive to human habitation. The planet has maintained (over the past 35 years) an atmosphere of approximately 75% nitrogen and 20% oxygen, with requisite amounts of carbon dioxide and other trace gases. Unfortunately, there has been no adequate data-supported explanation for this. We hypothesize that the "trees" of Kalderra behave similarly to those of Chikyu, releasing oxygen into the atmosphere.

Summary of Findings

Given the record highs of extraterrestrial timber (refer to the recent ¥2.73 billion acquisition of a Reyylorian Monarch Desk by Nataar Rentorii) and the generally acceptable "human-habitable" conditions on Kalderra, one could safely assume that it would be remarkably profitable to establish a colony on Wakusei 364.12.12865.5 for the sole purpose of harvesting this ultra-rare timber. In examining this endeavor, however, two things must be considered.

First, while Kalderra's unique moon helps shield the planet from the worst of its sun's radiation emissions, it is impossible to predict the long-term (or even short-term) effects that colonizers may experience. Moreover, the unusual UV spectra released by Hoshi 364.12.12865.0 and reflected (perhaps altered) by Tsuki 364.12.12865.5.1 could affect human colonizers in unpredictable ways.

Second, while expansive searches have been completed on the surface of Kalderra, little is known beyond its rocky expanses (that constitute most of the planet) or bioluminescent forests. No probes or drones have been sent lower than 7 meters. Although nothing is predicted (or expected) to be discovered beneath the surface of the planet, this study would be remiss not to highlight this fact.

OFFICIAL RECOMMENDATIONS

Establish an exploratory colony on the planet to ascertain human reaction to atmospheric variables, radiation levels, and UV exposure on Kalderra. Target participants for the colony could be drawn from ostracized, fringe, or unpopular religious groups, hazardous political parties, or criminal populations. Exuberant explorers, scientists, and philosophers should also be considered.

Once the sustainability of human life has been established, a dedicated team of kikkorii (expert loggers) from Morishita Timber Limited can take control (utilizing or removing the colonist population). Although estimates of cost cannot be given via this study, the general value of Kalderran timber has been estimated using recent comparable transactions and market values. Using conservative estimates (which are assumed to rise given the increasing demand for extraterrestrial timber), the value placed on Kalderra's "wood" lies (conservatively) around ¥1.2 quadrillion.

In short, this report finds that the planet referred to as Kalderra is a worthwhile investment and should be considered a "high priority."

- Secret Encoded Message Within Report -

Lord Itsuki, it's Manni. If I had expressed my true feelings in the report, you would be fighting for your life all the way from Chikyu to Kalderra. While I know that ¥1.2 quadrillion seems like a crazy number... my Lord... it's closer to ¥120 quadrillion. The timber is that good! I've never seen its equal. And I'm the one who found the Milk Forest in Reyylor! I couldn't even begin to imagine the wondrous creations that your master Sashimonos could craft from such material!

Forgive me, Lord Itsuki, but I find myself unable to contain my excitement. I was beginning to lose faith that I would discover anything more for you in my galactic searches, particularly given my increasing age and failing health. But I have! Kalderra will give my Lord the materials with which he can finally express the godliness of the Morishita Clan in permanent physical form. It is all that I have ever hoped to give you.

I must also admit, Lord Itsuki, that I may have purposely understated some of the risks associated with Kalderra, particularly regarding its potential climatic effects on a human body. You must know that I'm not being inhumane in this regard, my Lord. I simply DO NOT KNOW. I've never seen such a planet, with such a moon, orbiting such a star. The effects could be nothing. Or they could be significant. Either way, I find any sacrifice (or lack of one) well within the acceptable range.

I want my Lord to know that I didn't fully bury these concerns in the report because I didn't want to leave you open to attacks by those who already dispute the validity of our studies. How much more can you and your family give to humanity to prove your love for them?! I mean, a Morishita discovered the secret to traversing the galaxy! Such an ungrateful group of children, unaware of where their meals come from night after night. But apologies, my Lord, I digress...

Kalderra is what you (and your forebears) have been looking for. Despite our advances, my Lord's human form will remain fleeting—unsatisfactory given your impact on the galaxy. But this wood! And the permanent, invaluable things it will create! Oh, my Lord! You will live throughout the millennia through this wood! And all who stare upon its brilliance will remember the Morishita Clan. And most of all, they will recall Lord Itsuki Morishita, the man who made a lowly local botanist his Galactic Shokubutsu Gakusha.

Take this planet, my Lord! Take it, and let the roar of your voice echo across endless generations! And damn the collateral damage! All are worms beneath your greatness!

CHAPTER 1

LOVEBIRDS

Mona Ripple's left hand gently stroked the beautiful head on her lap. Meanwhile, her right hand moved in a blur, deftly folding the thick red paper it held. Sharp creases were made at various angles, corners bent back and tucked away. Mona's eyes, one a dull brown, the other a digital blue, narrowed as her will fought the material's natural tendencies.

A soft moan from below stole her attention.

"Something the matter, my love?"

The young man rolled onto his back on the bed, his painfully handsome face coming into view beneath a veil of blonde hair.

He smiled weakly. "Oh, nothing. Just imagining our life finally free of these walls. I swear the barracks get smaller as each day passes."

Mona pushed Darien's hair to the side, his too-green eyes appearing, twisting the knife that had found permanent purchase in her chest.

As always, she noted the stark contrast of the aging flesh of her hands, acid-marked and scar-riddled, against his newborn-like skin.

Mona bent down and let her dry lips run across the man's unlined forehead before placing a soft kiss in the middle, right where she imagined Darien's third eye lay hidden, always searching the depths of her soul.

Her right hand resumed its delicate work, the metal tip of her index finger flattening a raised edge, as Mona finally responded.

"I know what you mean. I've been here for more years than I care to admit, and it's never felt like home."

"You mean Camp Karcass or Kalderra?" Darien asked sleepily.

"Both, my love. Neither. But I've never had a home, so what the heck do I know about it?"

Darien nuzzled his face against Mona's wrist. "I've never had one, either. But we'll find it together, won't we?"

Mona's right hand fumbled the paper momentarily as her heart jumped. "We will, my love. A few more scavs and I'll be able to buy out both our contracts. Then we'll be truly free."

"Where do you want to go, Mona?"

"Anywhere you want, sweetheart. As long as I'm with you, I'll be happy." A pause. "Have you given any thought to where you'd like to go?"

Darien mulled the question before answering. "I have… but I'm embarrassed to say."

"Nonsense. Just say it, and I'll make it happen."

"I was thinking… Osaka."

"On Chikyu? Why would you want to go to that dreadful planet?"

"Nippon is still really nice."

"Well, of course it is. It's the bloody heart of the Morishita Syndicate. The largest concentration of wealth in the galaxy. But don't let the bright neon and high buildings fool you, my love. Beneath that veneer of class, Nippon is just as rotten as every other kuni in Chikyu."

"And how would you know?"

Mona began forming a response but stopped and swallowed the words. A beat later, "Just trust me, love."

Darien released a long, disappointed sigh. "I knew you wouldn't understand."

Mona's stomach tightened, threatening to release the contents of her meager dinner. The red paper almost fell from her grasp.

"No, no. I'm sorry, my love. Don't listen to this old fool. Forget what I said. Tell me more about Osaka. What's there that you choose it over anywhere else in the galaxy?"

"You'll think it's stupid."

"I won't."

"You will."

Mona's left hand raced down to Darien's ribs and began to dig in.

"Do I have to tickle it out of you?!"

The young man twisted back forth in a fit of giggles. "Stop! Mona, stop!"

"So, you'll tell me?!"

"I will! I will!"

Mona slapped the young man's taught belly before resting her arm along his chest, feeling it rise and fall rapidly as he recovered from the loving assault.

When Darien found his breath once more, he responded. "There's a fashion designer in Osaka. Her name's Tsumugi, and she's reinventing men's fashion in ways that haven't been seen since Yorl Yeng Yoshiro."

"How do you know all this?"

Darien shrugged. "You have your hobbies. I have mine."

"My only hobby is working to get us out of here. Now, what do you want with this Tsu…"

"Tsumugi."

"Right. What do you want with Tsumugi?"

"I don't know. I thought I could apprentice with her. Or maybe be a model in one of her shows. Or maybe partner together on a new men's line. Or be like her muse—"

"Her bloody muse?! Oh, I don't think so, Darien. In fact, I'm gonna take a special trip to Osaka to let this bitch know—" Laughter from below interrupted. "What's so bloody funny!?"

"Your jealousy, of course, Mona. Tsumugi isn't a person. She's the most advanced ARTist on the planet. You know... A- R- T-. Artificial artist? She's just a digital construct. She doesn't even have a synth shell."

"Well, I'm still gonna have a chat with this bitch, even if it ain't exactly woman to woman."

"You're too much, Mona. You know I only have eyes for you."

Butterflies fluttered through the middle-aged woman. "You better. And speaking of having something for someone..." Her right hand swung down.

"Benten's grin, Mona," said Darien as he accepted her creation. "It's beautiful."

He spun the origami heart in his hands, marveling at the intricacy of the folds, the way space and depth and emotion were conjured from mere paper.

"And you did this with one hand? Remarkable. No wonder you're the best Kisser there is... magic fingers."

"But still just a Maggot."

"As am I."

"For now., my love."

"Yes. Just for now." Darien sat up and carefully placed the origami heart on the bedside table. He spun back to Mona, a mischievous sparkle in the pools of his eyes. "But you're not the only one with magic fingers, Mona."

"Oh, really? And how would I know that, Darien?"

"Because I'm about to show you," replied the young man, pushing Mona playfully to her back on the bed.

An instant later, and Darien's lips were on her neck, his tongue searching her ear, his palms caressing her breasts. Mona's eyes unfocused under a tsunami of serotonin as her lover's fingers traced a path south from her belly button, tactfully jumping the thick, jagged scar that ran across her abdomen. Her pupils widened as the young man's long, slender digits finally reached their destination.

Mona inhaled deeply, Darien's floral scent threatening to drown her in ecstasy.

"Do you believe me now, Mona," the young man whispered into her ear.

"I do," she exhaled. "Oh, I bloody do…"

Mona Ripple lay in a dreamy, post-coitus haze, her mind drifting to a beautiful near-future, the antithesis of her first forty-six years of life. She mindlessly rubbed the hairless arm draped over her chest before stopping abruptly. She glanced down through the slits of her eyes, concerned that her sandpaper palm may have irritated Darien's soft skin.

It had not. But Mona still didn't resume her caressing.

Releasing a deep sigh, Mona finally closed her eyes to let sleep envelop her, hoping to drop into a new dream. And not an old nightmare.

Just as the fragments of a lovely vision began to coalesce, Mona was ripped away, the loud signal of an incoming call echoing throughout the small room.

"Oh, Fujin's ass," the woman complained, shaking the mist from her mind. Then to the ceiling, "Accept!"

The hidden speakers in the room came to life.

"Ripper, it's Toro."

"I know who the heck it is, Colonel. There's only one prick on this shit hole of a planet arrogant enough to think that it's ok to contact me on my day off. *My day off, Toro!*"

"Were you busy, Ripper?"

"Getting some much-needed beauty sleep, Colonel."

A moment of silence. Toro didn't rise to the bait.

Benten's grin, this must be serious.

"Apologies, Ripper, but you're needed."

"For bloody what?"

"We've got lume."

"Meeba-lume?"

"Benten's grin! Ripper, don't be daft! Of course meeba-lume! We need you on this one."

Mona shook her head despite Toro not being there to see it.

"No, Colonel. My team was up two scavs ago. Colby's unit got the last one, and now Vasily is up. Lord knows that ragtag crew could use the scratch."

"Exactly."

Mona frowned. "Exactly what, you bastard?!"

"Vasily's got a ragtag crew. And he's a ragtag Kisser. They won't do. We need the best."

"Why, damn you?!"

A brief pause before, "Ripper, it's a class IV."

Mona jolted upright. "There is no class IV, Colonel."

"There is now. That's why we need Karcass Five on this. That's why we need you, Ripper, on this." Silence. "Ripper, do you know how much this will be worth?! Can you even imagine the yennies shoved into our accounts?! Can you—"

"Shut up, Toro! I can imagine more than you can imagine. Karcass Two is going to be pissed. Vasily Pappas is already no fan of Karcass Five. And do I have to remind you of a certain someone who punched a certain someone in the face?"

"Leave that to me, Ripper. I'll spread a little love their way. Maybe give them a week off to spend at Shonin Crossways. All expenses paid. That should shut them up."

Mona's mind reeled. *Class III kameeba are rare enough... and extremely volatile. One wrong move and the scav is gone, along with an entire Karcass team and scores of metric tons of Kalderran terrain. A class IV? That could take out a fifth of the entire mori. The Kodama wouldn't like that one bit. But why should I care? I'll be long vaporized by then. In fact—*

"Ripper!"

Mona jumped at Toro's voice, anxiety bleeding through the colonel's usually apathetic demeanor.

"Where's the meeba, Colonel?"

"Mori Mangekyo. Sector E5."

"Fujin's ass! Toro, the bastard barely made it out of Homosubi's Breath!"

"I know, Ripper."

"How long?!"

"Less than you think. The bastard's lume was so strong, the sats spotted it even before the damn thing expired. We got a jump on it."

"Bloody heck, Toro, it's gonna take us a while to get to it."

"Then you'd better get to, Ripper."

"Place is going to be crawling with rotters, Toro. All kinds."

"Then you'd better make sure Mickie is your Keeper."

"Don't tell me how to run my squad, Toro."

"Of course not, Ripper." Another tense silence. "Time *is* of the essence, Ripper."

"Like I don't know that?! Benten's grin, Toro! You want to tell me about my wrinkly skin and droopy tits, too!"

"Never, Ripper."

"Good! Send it through. And if our dear Countess wants to see a single yenny from this, I suggest someone phone ahead to the Guntai to make sure that the western southern crossing is open and kept that way. Any of those goons impede our path, and I'll have Brass gun them down. It's the only thing that junker's good for."

"Understood, Ripper. And now, may I suggest that you get moving. With extreme haste."

"One more question, Toro."

"And what is—"

Mona cut the feed by blinking hard, having reestablished the connection between her GLIM and the K-Nex network during the charged conversation. The woman sat in frozen silence for several seconds as all information captured on the class IV kameeba was quickly downloaded and made available to her very human, very limited brain.

"Benten's grin," Mona quietly said to herself as she internally viewed the data within the GLIM in her right eye socket. "That's a massive flesher. Full of power. Too full. Too, too full. It's not worth the risk. Too much could go wrong."

Darien moaned and turned on the bed next to her, his thin, muscular back calling to Mona as the ocean would a lonely desert dweller.

The woman better known as Ripper reached down and gently shook her lover.

"It can't be morning already," he groaned. "I feel like it's been only minutes."

"It has, sweetheart. But we've got to go to work."

"I thought it wasn't our turn," Darien said into his pillow.

"It's not, my love. But this is a big one. The biggest ever seen. And they need us. And we need it. This is our ticket out of here, my love. The collection from this scav will be enough to buy out your contract."

Darien sat up at that. He shook long blonde strands of hair from his face. "You think so?" he asked as he wiped the sleep from his eyes.

"I know so, baby. So get dressed. And quickly."

"Do you really need me, Mona?"

"What's that?"

"I mean, it's supposed to be our day off and all. I guess I'm not obligated to work. And do you all really need me? Honestly, I feel like I get in the way more often than not."

Mona took the young man's face between her hands, all thoughts of sandpaper gone. She kissed his plump lips.

"Don't say that. You're a big help."

"The others hate me."

"They don't hate anything. They just can't appreciate beauty like I can."

"I still think it would be best if I stayed behind."

Mona shook her head. "You can't, my love. You're a member of Karcass Five, which means you have to come. You have to come so I can pay off your contract. And then we're free. Free to go to Osaka. Free to start our new lives. Free to be happy forever."

"Ok, Mona. If you say so."

"I do, sweetheart. Just this last time."

"Ok."

"Ok, then. Get ready, please. As quickly as you can."

Darien nodded and spun off the bed to retrieve his clothes. Mona waited a beat before slamming the large red button affixed to the wall. A loud siren screamed across the barracks. Mona let it go for several seconds as she ran to the wardrobe, pulled free her armless skin-suit, and began slipping her naked body into it. As she carefully zipped the front over her breasts, she mentally instructed her GLIM to cut into the speaker system.

The siren volume decreased.

"You know that sound, Maggots! It's go time! Get your shit, and get ready! We've got a class IV! You heard me, Maggots! The first-ever class IV! That means danger! That means riches! And that means get your bloody heads in the bloody game! I want everyone decorated, present, and grinning at the Nest in ten! I don't care that it's your day off! I don't care if you're hung over! I don't care if your willy gets caught in your zipper! Anyone late will have to flash fists with me after! You Maggots want fame?! You Maggots want fortune?! Well, so do I! I'm either gonna get it by scavving the largest kameeba ever… or by carving out an organ from every last man and woman who didn't do their part and selling them on the Dark Tide! The choice is yours, Maggots! See you in ten. Or not."

Mona cut the feed and looked to Darien as he stepped into his grav-boots. He offered an amused smirk.

"Too much?" she asked.

"They'll be ready, Mona."

"Good, then let's go, my love. Can't make threats like that and then not be first on the scene."

Darien spoke over his shoulder as Mona pressed him out of their shared quarters. "Even if your threats were so outlandish as to be hilariously unbelievable."

Mona smiled at her lover's back as the door close behind them. *Good. He doesn't truly know me, yet. But when he does...*

Mona arrived at the Karcass staging ground with Darien in tow. She cursed under her breath when she realized that they somehow weren't the first to the Nest. She cursed again when she saw who had beaten them.

Mickie Brass smiled brightly as he stood at mock attention. As usual, the man was wearing his stupid black hat—an *Akubra* he called it, as if anyone knew what the heck that meant—adorned with an animal skin band decorated with the jagged teeth of unknown monstrosities.

"Perfect timing, Mona," Mickie commented in his strange accent as Mona and Darien approached. "I just happened to be out here working on that dead krawler. She's running great now if you want to take her out on the scav."

Mona glanced down at Mickie's hands, blackened by grease and almost as torn up as her own. She could barely make out the large star tattoo adorning the top of each hand.

"So that's how you spend your day off, Junker? Elbow-deep in a rover's guts?"

Mickie shrugged his broad shoulders and spoke through his thick salt-and-pepper beard. "I treat my machines like I treat my women, lass. When they need a little TLC, old Mickie's there, rain or shine, day off or not."

"How lucky they must feel," Mona quipped as she walked past to inspect her second-in-command's work. "I thought the capacitor was fried. Worse, I thought it shorted all the other electronics."

Mickie wiped his greasy hands on his skin-suit. Like Mona, the Maggot had cut off the arms. But where Mona had done so for purely utilitarian purposes, she was sure that Mickie Brass did it simply to show off his massive, deeply scarred arms.

Typical junker.

"It was. It did. But I told you, lass. There ain't nothing that I can't fix, rebuild, or recycle."

"So you've told me. Every bloody chance you get." Despite her dislike of the man, Mona couldn't help but be impressed by his work. Mickie had done in a day what would have taken the Karcass maintenance crew a week. And without all the complaining. She stepped away from the rover.

"Nice surprise, Junker. I thought we'd have to make do with two krawlers but three is ideal. When the team gets here, I want as much firepower as possible loaded onto one. That'll give us more space to maneuver on the other two if we have to shoot our way to the kameeba."

"Class IV, huh, Mona?"

"Class IV, Junker."

"Where's it located?"

"Mangekyo. E5."

Although Mickie's grey eyes widened a bit, the man did well to hide his surprise.

"Gonna be rotters for one that size, lass."

"Yeah, Junker. Gonna be swarming with them."

"I'll start loading the krawler then."

"Good idea."

Mickie turned toward the armory, punching Darien in the shoulder as he passed. The young man yelped.

"Ow, that hurt, you big galoot."

"Come on, boy. Make yourself useful, and come with me."

"Don't call him that, Junker," Mona snapped. "But go with him, Darien. Do as he asks. Quickly now!"

Darien offered a frown before chasing after Mickie, who was two-timing it down the service path.

As she waited for the others to arrive, Mona made her way to a locked door at the end of the Nest. Placing her GLIM against the scanning device to the right of the door, she blinked twice. An audible *click* was heard before the thick metal slid smoothly to the side.

"Good evening, Kisser," said an automated female voice as Mona stepped into the storage room.

"Yeah, yeah," replied Mona as she looked around.

"May I be of any service, Kisser? What class of kameeba are you scavenging this trip? I can make some suggestions based on that knowledge."

"It's a class IV."

Silence for several seconds.

"I do not have records of a class IV kameeba. Perhaps you misspoke, Kisser?"

"Nope," stated Mona as she sifted through the delicate instruments laid out on shelves to her left. "Class IV. First of its kind."

"I'm afraid I won't be able to make many concrete recommendations based on incomplete data, Kisser. The best I will be able to provide are suggestions based on limited forecasts."

"You and me both, sister."

Mona picked out an array of strange-looking tools, including some of her old favorites, placing them into various pouches on her tool belt. She then turned forward, where rows of unusual boxes had been neatly laid out on a massive, rubber-covered table.

Of varying sizes, each box was metal-framed and paned with a translucent material that danced with color, confounding the eye. Staring too long into its swirling light show would force most people's heads to swim, causing nausea and loss of balance.

But Mona Ripple was not most people.

The woman moved to the far right end of the table, where the largest of the boxes sat.

"Which of these TRAP cubes can contain a class IV meeba heart?" asked Mona.

"None have been tested on a class IV, Kisser."

"That's not what I asked."

"The TC-4500a has proven most reliable at storing high energy levels. Although no tests have been completed, numbers suggest that it could safely contain 350 quintillion joules."

"And unsafely?"

A pause.

"Breakage could be safely assumed at 500 quintillion joules."

"Not good enough." Mona pointed to the box in the corner. Unlike the others on the table, this one was not a cube but a twelve-sided icosahedron. "And this one? I've never seen it before."

"That is the TCx-8708o. It arrived from Morishita Galactic Corporation several days ago."

"Tell me about it."

"It is an experimental TRAP. It has been tested at 400 quintillion joules but projections show that it could hold up to 800 quintillion joules."

"Safely?"

"I didn't say that, Kisser. It is an experimental TRAP. It has yet to be tested in the field."

"But that didn't stop them from giving it to us Maggots, did it?"

"It doesn't appear that it did, Kisser."

Mona sighed. "Screw it. I'll take them both. Maybe the TCx won't be needed."

"That seems a most prudent decision, Kisser."

Mona grabbed each TRAP by its metal handle and hefted them from the table. "Yeah, well, prudent's my middle freakin' name."

"I don't have a middle name on record for you, Kisser. Would you like me to rectify that and correct the error?"

"I would not. Any last words of encouragement?"

"Be safe out there, Kisser. And please be gentle with those TRAPs."

"Why?" asked Mona as she made her way out of the storage room. "Because they're each worth more than I'll make in a lifetime?"

"No, Kisser. Because they are the only thing between you and a catastrophic detonation."

"You need to work on your encouragement, sister."

"I'll review my protocols now, Kisser."

"You do that," Mona stated flatly as the metal doors slid closed behind her.

Making her way back to the upper portion of the Nest, where Maggots had finally begun to assemble, Mona found herself moving at a much more gingerly pace, increasingly concerned about the TRAPs in her hands.

She muttered under her breath. "Who needs enemies with bloody friends like that?"

Mona carefully put down the TRAPs and spun to face her Maggots, who had paused their hasty preparations and now stood at attention. She nodded before speaking.

"Good. I see you're making up for dragging ass on your way here. The first class IV kameeba has been spotted. And spotted early. They could see the lume long before the bastard even croaked. That's the good news. Now for the bad. It died in Mori Mangekyo, Section E5. That means we got a bit of a haul. That means, by the time we get there, the place will be crawling with rotters. That means you Maggots better bring your A-games!" A pause. "Now, I don't need to explain the dangers to you because you're Maggots—*my Maggots*. Rotters aren't the main danger; it's the bloody corpse containing enough energy to power an industrial planet for a bloody Chikyu year. But that's my job. *Your* job is to do *your* jobs and buy me the time and space I need to safely yank this bastard's ticker out." Another pause. "Maggots. We're staring at the biggest payday in Kalderra's history. Want to buy out your contact? You'll be able to. Want to travel to an exotic world on extended holiday? You'll be able to. Want to blow it all on Teelani snatch? You'll be drowning in it!"

"There you go, Bedford," laughed a tan-skinned woman near the krawler.

"One time, Neela! One time and now that's my thing?!"

"One time… for three damned days straight," added a slim, older man whose face was half-covered in burn scars.

"It was two days, Milton, you old bastard! And if you didn't spend so much time willy-watching, then you—"

"Enough!" shouted Mona. She took a calming breath. "Look, I need everyone frosty on this one. One slip up and none of us is coming back. Understand?!" Silent nods were returned. "Good. Here's the game plan. Brass, you're Lead Keeper. Take Bedford, Baft, Sheppard, Saddler, and Milton." Her head swivel slightly. "Neela Patel!"

"Yes, Ripper," answered the woman.

"You're Lead Karver. Take Chance, Maddox, and Hinch. Now, the ticker is paramount in this operation, so cut me a tunnel with enough room to move and then get the heck out of my way. Join the Keepers—they'll need the backup—until I exit with that sweet lume. Then—and only then—can you resume your carving duties. I can't have shit shaking and swaying on this one. Understood?"

"You got it, Ripper."

Hinch, his bald head and face covered in tattoos, spoke up from the rear. "Who's serving as Second Kisser?"

"Darien will second me." Concerned faces turned to look at each other. "Any Maggots got a bloody problem with that?!" Silence. "I didn't think so. So… why are you ugly bastards still staring at me like I'm a go-go girl with her knickers over her head? You have your orders. Now execute!"

Karcass Five exploded into motion. Guns and ammo were loaded onto krawler three, alongside both TRAPs, which were strapped down in the center of the vehicle. Cables were removed from all three rovers and returned to the charging stations. Maggots checked and rechecked their equipment, helping each other haul oversized packs.

Amidst the organized chaos, Mickie Brass sauntered over. The man walked as if he was about to leave for a dinner party, not a potential suicide mission. Mona rolled her eyes.

"What is it, Junker?"

"No one's ever cut clean a class IV ticker, Mona."

"That's because there ain't been one."

Mickie leaned in. "That's what I mean. We don't know what to expect, lass. You might have to adjust on the fly."

"And your point?"

"You need a trustworthy pair of hands next to you, Mona."

"I trust Darien more than I despise junkers, Brass. And I really despise junkers."

Mickie held up his hands in mock surrender. "Poor choice of words, Mona. I meant a more seasoned pair of hands. Let me be your second. You know my hands don't shake when things go to shit, lass."

Mona shook her head as she responded. "Rotters are gonna be everywhere. For all your poor qualities—and there are too many to count—you handle a weapon better than anyone else here. And for some reason the Maggots rally behind you. I need you buying me the time I need."

"Ok, I can see that. Then take someone else as your second. Anyone, Mona."

"Anything else, Junker?"

Mickie open his mouth to speak, showing several gold teeth, but closed it almost immediately. A strange shadow settled on his grizzled face.

"No, I suppose not."

"Good, then you have things to get done. And quickly." Mona looked around the large man and yelled across the Nest. "Ninety seconds! You Maggots have ninety seconds! I dare anyone not to be geared up and on a krawler in ninety seconds! I have no issues removing several tickers this night!"

Mickie stepped away, calling out orders and encouragingly slapping helmets as he made his way through the throng.

"What was that about?" asked Darien as he sidled up to Mona.

"Nothing, my love. Absolutely nothing. Are you almost ready?"

"I think so."

Mona checked over Darien, fixing various straps and belts that he had put on wrong.

"Mona."

"Yes, my love," she replied as she made adjustments.

"I'm scared."

"Don't be, sweetheart. Just do exactly what I say, when I say it, and you'll be fine. Don't think about what's to come." She put her hands to his face. "Close your eyes." Darien complied. "Imagine our future. Imagine what you'll become. Imagine a life of possibility. Now open them." Mona's breath caught when the young man's green eyes popped open. "Where did you go?"

"Everywhere. Everywhere that wasn't here."

"Good. We're gonna make that happen. But first, we gotta earn it."

Mona hooked her acid-burned arm under Darien's and pulled him toward krawler one, calling out as she did.

"Colonel Toro demanded Karcass Five for this mission! Do you know why?! Because we're the bloody best!" Mona slid into the rover's seat. "Maggots! Let's ride!"

The Nest's bay doors opened, and the three krawlers took off into the Kalderran night.

As they left the safety of Camp Karcass behind, the Maggots were bathed in the soft, bright, violet light of Kuyomi as the giant ice moon powerfully reflected the rays of its distant sun named Anohoshi.

Despite Kalderra's mildly reduced gravity, Mona bounced as the krawler's six oversized wheels, supported by sophisticated hydraulics, sped over the planet's mostly barren, rocky terrain.

"Baft!" Mona called out to the driver. "Biggson Baft! You no-talking bastard!"

The giant, mute black man turned halfway, keeping his dark eyes on the Maggot Trail while letting his boss know he was listening.

"Yeah, you hear me! Cut the grav-pull by twenty percent! These Maggots don't need to see my titties shaking like this! I need their heads in the game and not on my supple bosom! And that goes for you, too, Patel!"

The Maggots on krawler one laughed as Baft slowly turned a knob on the rover's dash panel. The dramatic bouncing eased.

"That's better," muttered Mona as the three krawlers sped south on the narrow Maggot Trail, which slowly curved west around one of the many massive mountain ranges that surrounded each of the sunken karuderas.

The krawler's motion now reduced to a gentle sway, Mona hooked her arm under Darien's and laid her head on the young man's shoulder, nuzzling his neck to breathe in his youthful smell.

Mickie stole a quick glance from across the krawler before turning his grey eyes to the violet moon. The other Maggots, meanwhile, smirked to each other, sharing silent jokes that they dared not voice aloud.

Several minutes later, Biggson half-turned once more from his perch in the driver's seat.

"No, not this one, Baft," said Mona, replying to the massive man's unspoken question. "The big bastard didn't make it far from Homusubi's Breath. Take the second trail. I don't want to be in Mangekyo any longer than necessary tonight."

Biggson simply nodded and directed the krawler straight when another portion of the Maggot Trail broke north.

Mona placed her head, one of the few not donning a helmet, back on Darien's shoulder and rested. Or at least tried to.

Some time later, she was shaken from her half-dream by Mickie Brass's annoying accent.

"Mona. Mona. Mona!"

"Fujin's ass! What, Junker?!"

"We're at the crossing."

Mona immediately lifted her head to see several hundred meters ahead, where the Maggot Trail descended into a strange glow.

The area just before the Trail disappeared was filled on both sides with Guntai—Morishita foot soldiers who occupied every planet claimed by the Syndicate, enforcing rules both fair and, mostly, foul.

Mona snarled as the caravan of krawlers approached the crossing's checkpoint.

"I swear to Izanagi, if these fools try to stop us…" Mona leaned forward to call out. "Baft! You don't slow down; you hear me?!" The driver nodded slowly. "Junker!"

"Yes, Mona," answered Mickie.

"Put a bullet in the knee of any Guntai stupid enough to step in front of us! I'll deal with any consequences!"

"Understood," said Mickie as his fingers absently stroked the outside of each thigh. Like Mickie's sleeves, the skin-suit had been cut away there, two squares of material hacked away to reveal metal beneath where flesh would normally be found.

Mickie spat over the krawler's edge and tipped his ridiculous black hat up a bit, intently studying the scene before him as it drew closer by the second.

The Guntai, dressed in their usual all-black uniforms with red accents, appeared to be in heated discussion, with one soldier even stepping into the krawler's path before being yelled down by a senior officer who had lifted her face visor, an ostentatious red plume on her helmet denoting rank.

Mona could feel the lead krawler slowing, if only by a bit.

"Baft! If I have to tell you to floor it again, you're going to wish you could speak so you can beg for your life! Understand?!"

Biggson's response came in the form of the krawler lurching forward, sprinting toward the two groups of Guntai who now stood in formation, blasters drawn, on each side of the Maggot Trail. Despite the unnecessary show of force, the way was clear.

Mona couldn't help but release a small, satisfied smile.

"Ok, Baft! They get it! Drop her down a bit, you big bastard. No need to send us flying into the bloody mori."

The krawlers slowed incrementally as they passed through the Guntai Crossing Guard, the Syndicate's muscle shouting insults—some more entertaining than others—at the Maggots as they rolled past.

Mona looked out into the sea of Guntai and caught the eye of the female senior officer. The woman offered a strange nod as the krawler cut through the sentries. Mona returned a scowl, unable to mask her disdain.

She turned to Darien. "Hold on, love."

Moments later, the krawlers dipped low, and Maggot eyes narrowed as Karcass Five plunged into a kaleidoscope of color.

"Unbuckle and spin. Stay focused, and keep your guns at the ready," Mona told those in her krawler. "I shouldn't have to tell you this, but I will anyway. Double check that your beams are off. Physical rounds only. And I don't have to repeat why. We should be fine for a while, but this big bastard is gonna attract a shitload of rotters. Of every bloody sort."

The Maggots nodded and followed Mona's command as the krawler leveled out, Kuyomi vanishing under an unnaturally bright canopy.

Karcass Five was a unit of relative veterans, with most Maggots having entered Mori Mangekyo at least two dozen times. But one would have never guessed by looking at their faces.

As the krawlers penetrated the inimitable forest, eyes inexorably rose from the broken, pebbled flatness of the ground. They found the impossibly large trunks of subarashi trees—giants that appeared more god than plant. The glowing, crystalline wood was veined with lines of blue and pink and other colors not yet named. Nervous eyes continued to rise, higher and higher, as massive trunks broke off into equally impressive branches, which continued to split and divide in an endless array of angles and distances.

These relatively smaller branches exploded with even more color, studded with bioluminescent leaves and flowers, each the size of a personal hovercraft. The blossoms, in particular, swam with intermingling waves of varying shades and hues, looking like satellite images of a million-year storm on a distant planet. They audibly hummed with the sounds of electric current, throbbing with such power that they seemed to breathe, reminding each Maggot that these were no mere trees they were traveling beneath.

Maggot fingers rubbed against triggers as eyes that should have been studying the ground continued to scan the rainbow canopy of Mori Mangekyo. Only Mickie Brass seemed unshaken, the large, grizzled man calmly studying the unlit cigar twirling in his star-tattooed hands.

Mona rolled her unmatched eyes. *Is that cigar from Chikyu? How much would that have cost? A month's salary? What a ridiculous expense. Damn irresponsible Space Cowboys! How did I get saddled with one?*

"Junker!" Mickie's cigar twirling ceased as he looked over. "Eyes on the bloody ground, if you don't mind."

Mickie shrugged. "If it's truly a class IV, Mona, there'll be no rotters on our route."

"And why would that be, Junker?"

Mickie picked something out from between two of his many gold teeth. Mona shuddered.

"Well, because they're already at the scav site. Or on their way, at least. We're all on the same highway, Mona. All going to the same destination.

All hoping to cash in. All hoping to consume. At least for this short while, we're aligned in a goal. I actually think it's kinda heartening. Species alien and human alike moving forward as one…"

Mona's eyes rolled back so hard, she feared her GLIM would disconnect, rendering her useless for the upcoming scav.

"Well, let me tell you something, Junker. If—"

Lightning shot out from somewhere high above, streaking over the caravanning Maggots to briefly connect two subarashi on either side of the small forest path, causing their trunks to flare and alight like a small nuclear detonation.

The Maggots, including Mona, immediately raised their arms to shield their eyes, the heat of raw power washing over them.

When the Kisser finally dropped her hands, she took grim satisfaction in seeing Mickie Brass no longer carelessly spinning his victory cigar. Instead, the junker was facing out from the krawler, gun in hand, singed retinas readily scanning ground, treetop, and everything in-between.

"I thought there was nothing to worry about, Junker," Mona gleefully teased.

"Fujin's ass! From the rotters, lass! Nothing to worry about from the rotters!" Mickie shouted over his shoulder from across the krawler, refusing to tear his now-intent gaze from his surroundings. "I didn't say anything about these bloody suba-steps! Bloody Susanoo himself couldn't predict why and how and when this infernal lightning will appear!"

Mona laughed again, not noticing Darien cowering in his seat.

"Then all the more reason to stop acting cool and start acting like the bleedin' Lead Keeper!"

Mickie grunted but didn't respond otherwise, which Mona took as a win in her never-ending verbal war with the Space Cowboy. Grimly satisfied, Mona spun back, placing her knees on the seat and chest against the krawler's exterior railing, allowing her GLIM permission to scan the mori as they delved deeper into the karudera.

As the glowing subarashi flashed past, every Maggot's eyes peered up nervously. They knew the terror that could rain down upon them at any moment.

Everyone had heard the tales of the first regiment of kikkorii—imperial loggers—who had traveled across the galaxy on command from Morishita Timber Limited to harvest Kalderra's lone valuable resource. Before their dozers and laz-saws and power axes could down the first subarashi, lightning descended from the trees, burning skin from flesh, boiling brains in skulls, and, eventually, incinerating bones.

None survived. None were spared.

Five full subsequent regiments were lost before the Sindo-Emperor finally ceased his logging attempts, right around the time that the Kodama, Kalderra's native humanoid population, made themselves known.

When the Syndicate's top researchers figured out that the subarashi were not simply reacting to environmental threats—that they were actually controlled by the Kodama—another layer of complexity was added.

With the initial settlers of Kalderra having gone quiet for hundreds of years, presumably killed off by the native Kodama, the Sindo-Emperor's top advisors advocated for the immediate nuking of the planet from orbiting warships. As far as the Syndicate was concerned, any kind of opposition could only be dealt with one way—total annihilation.

But the sitting Sindo-Emperor refused.

The Kodama lived beneath the planet's rocky surface, cave dwellers in every sense of the word. To destroy them would require massive firepower that penetrated deep into Kalderra, sending shockwaves across the surface and placing the subarashi squarely in the crosshairs of destruction.

Something the Sindo-Emperor was unwilling to do.

And so, the elder Morishita decided to abandon the planet—for a time—until better plans could be laid or the Kodama naturally died off.

The Morishita clan had been in control of the galaxy for hundreds of years and would be in control for thousands more. They were nothing if not patient. The Sindo-Emperor could wait. His sons' or grandsons' or great-grandsons' ultimate success would be his own. His was a vision not limited by the span of one life… but by scores of generations.

But then, just as the strategic abandonment of Kalderra was about to take place, another option fell into the Sindo-Emperor's lap. A bizarre occurrence that none could have predicted.

Orbital surveillance spotted a strange creature squirming out from one of the many caves that lined the two subarashi-filled karuderas. Large and incandescent and throbbing with barely contained power, the monstrosity snaked its way through the mori before suddenly dropping dead, evidenced by the sudden shift in readings.

The glow within the dead creature increased twofold, threefold, fivefold before suddenly dimming, Kalderra's mori absorbing unmeasurable power.

A seed was planted. An idea slowly formed. A plan was put into action. Potential casualties fell within acceptable ranges.

Many died at the beginning. But not from the Kodama-controlled subarashi's lightning attacks. Many died because they didn't know what they were dealing with. They didn't know what they were doing.

The Sindo-Emperor demanded that this be fixed.

And so the Karcass regiment was created. And so the Maggots were born. And so the greatest collection of Maggots yet assembled now sped toward the biggest scav ever recorded.

"Three clicks," announced Betsy Sheppard as she spared a moment from studying the charged canopy to look at the tracker on her forearm. The handsome woman's head, blond hair cropped close to her skull, shot up a second later, her blue eyes glancing from one subarashi limb to the other.

The two following krawlers bounced noisily in the close distance as weapons were checked—again—and deep breaths taken.

A fit-looking young man spoke from the front of the krawler. "Fujin's ass! I can already see the lume! What's waiting for us up there?!"

"A big-ass kameeba," snapped Ricksin Hinch, a perpetual scowl etched onto his tattooed face. "What did you expect, Chance?"

Marshall Chance's face swung forward once more. He answered over one broad shoulder.

"Big, sure, Hinch. But this is something… something dangerous."

Hinch snickered. "It's just a meeba, you coward. And a dead one at that! If the sight of lume is enough for you to shit your britches, then I don't need you standing next to me!"

"Are you seeing this lume, Hinch?!" Chance shot back.

"It's just a dead kameeba!"

"It ain't just a kameeba," Mickie Brass cut in, his voice immediately silencing the other two men. "Listen closely. Tune out the krawlers."

A beat passed.

"I don't hear shit!"

"Rotters," stated Mickie flatly. "A lot of the bastards. Get ready. We come in hot."

An even more uncomfortable silence fell over the Maggots.

"Heck of a pep talk, Junker," said Mona to Mickie.

"Better ready than dead," he replied calmly, annoying Mona to no end.

Five minutes later, the head krawler rounded a particularly massive subarashi, and Baft motioned from the nav seat.

"Maggots!" shouted Mona. "We're here!"

The krawler drove into a large clearing and was immediately bathed once more in Kuyomi's violet gaze, the oversized moon staring down through the break in the canopy. As the rover decelerated, every Maggot's eyes— even those of Mickie Brass—went wide.

In the center of the empty space, sitting heavy and dead on the grey, rocky ground, was the kameeba.

And it was larger than any Maggot could have ever imagined.

The kameeba was the length of four krawlers and the height of two stacked atop one another—at least twice the size of any other in the species' admittedly short recorded history.

More expected was the general look of the thing. As all kameeba, it was a gelatinous blob—as if a giant slug, fat with water, had been rendered almost invisible.

But deep within that thick, translucent body sat the prize—the core of the kameeba, the ticker. This ticker, in particular, shined especially bright, causing Maggot eyes to circumvent its exact location to avoid retinal damage.

The insane level of luminosity represented power. It represented danger. It represented well-found fear.

But it also represented a ridiculous amount of shitayen—yennies. And Mona Ripple needed every yenny to ensure a perfect life for her and Darien.

"Oh, dear Izanagi!" cried out Darien, still strapped to his seat.

"Shit in a bag," added Hinch, his beady eyes studying the kameeba as they raced toward the expired creature. "It's crawling with rotters! We're too late!"

"It's carrion by now," bemoaned Sheppard, a hint of relief hiding beneath the display of disappointment.

"Fujin's ass, it is!" screamed Mona. "That bastard's flesh is thicker than Hotei's belly! Will take the rotters an hour to ruin the take! Junker?!"

Mickie didn't hesitate. "Agreed, lass. We can still take her. Take all of her."

"Then everyone quit your crying and start your trying! And my promise still stands! Anyone who doesn't pull their weight will get their ticker pulled alongside this meeba! Understood?!"

"Yes, Kisser!" came the unified response from the others in the vehicle.

As the krawler roared forward, Mickie stood and swung a heavy leg over the guardrail, straddling the thick metal as the rover bounced beneath him.

"Hope you don't want kids, Mickie," joked Sheppard as she pivoted on her knees, lining her weapon up with the scavenger-covered kameeba.

"Balls of steel, lass. Balls of steel," responded Mickie with a wink before letting loose with his Howa 500 automatic rifle.

Muted bangs barely registered against the roar of the krawler thanks to the Howa 500's innovative suppressor. This suppression did not affect killing power, however, as three flesh beetles were torn from the kameeba's back by Mickie Brass's uncanny accuracy.

One massive flesh beetle, eating its fill of kameeba meat one second and having its insides liquified by a tatsumaki bullet the next, fell forward, slipping from the carcass to crash loudly onto its armored wing case. Its six crystalline legs and half-meter mandibles shook in the air for a beat before its meter-long body went still, the churned organs within slowly leaking out from the entry hole.

"I didn't realize I was the only one who enjoyed offing rotters," called out Mickie between bursts, which sent the other Maggots, who often found themselves dumbly watching the Space Cowboy's shooting displays, into action.

All fired as one, and those in the following krawler joined a moment later as Peetso Maddox, piloting the second krawler, flared out to the right to avoid crossfire.

More flesh beetles flew or slumped from the giant carcass as gunfire assaulted the scavengers. Although most of the bullets found their mark or flew harmlessly wide, a few sank into the kameeba.

"Stay clear of the meat, you dumb bastards!" cried out Mona. "There's a bloody nuclear reactor in there, in case you might have forgotten!"

"Yes, Ripper!" came a roar in response, adrenaline now flowing like the great rivers of Chikyu once did.

Mona rose and scampered up the middle of the krawler, careful not to knock the firing Maggots. She leaned in toward Baft so the large, silent man could hear her clearly.

"Go in hot, Biggs. Slam on the brakes even with the meeba. I want a distance of ten meters. I need some space to work."

Biggson Baft refused to take his bulbous eyes from the path ahead but nodded his understanding.

Mona returned the nod and headed to the back of the krawler, passing by Darien, who remained strapped tightly to his seat. Reaching the back, Mona waved, motioning the trailing Maddox, who saluted in return. Mona pointed to the right of the kameeba, held her palm up toward the driving Maggot, and then held up three fingers.

Maddox saluted once more. Mona wanted to smile but refused to show it.

"Ok, we're set," Mona announced as she returned to her space, muted bangs surrounding her voice. "We go left, krawler two goes right. Ten meter perimeter. Dispose of any rotters still on the meeba then turn your attentions to defense. As soon as the meeba is clear of flesh beets, Karvers go to work. And work bloody fast! Give me a tunnel a little larger than usual but stay farther from the ticker than normal. I don't need you butchers sending us all to an early grave."

"Not so early for you, Mona," said Mickie between rounds.

"You're one to talk, Junker! I've seen fewer greys on a Vicurion wolf-dog! And better teeth!"

"Yeah, but mine are more expensive," shot back the junker, grinning to show his many gold caps.

"Enough! Here we go." A short pause. "Maggots. Tonight we get rich together or die together! Who's down with that?!"

"We are, Ripper!" came the group's reply—minus Darien, which wasn't missed.

The Howa 500s went quiet as the krawler abruptly shot out to the left to run parallel to the kameeba, which laid cocked toward the center of Mori Mangekyo, as if the creature had tried its best to return to some home it had never seen.

Meanwhile, the second krawler rounded to the right while the third krawler, occupied solely by the enigmatic gypsy Ellis Saddler, followed Mona.

"Down! Brace!" called out Mona. The Maggots fell into their seats, wrapped their Howa's protectively in one arm, and grasped the railing with the other.

The krawler skidded to a stop on the torn, grey Kalderran terrain, settling perfectly in-line with the kameeba. A beat later, the gypsy Saddler cut his krawler hard to the left, fishtailing so its nose barely missed the lead rover while the back end swung to the right, creating a 45-degree angle between the two vehicles.

Maggots leapt out, some resuming their assault while others ran toward Saddler's krawler.

"Fujin's ass, gypsy!" Mona called out as she descended from the krawler and noticed the scant distance between the rovers. "Cut it a little close, didn't you?!"

Saddler grinned under his thick, curling mustache before hopping out.

"I think necessary, no? Extra protection, no? Big job needs big moves... no?"

Mona rolled her eyes, sending her GLIM into a momentary glitch.

"Big moves get us killed, gypsy. Especially on this job. Help distribute the weapons. When you're done, grab you a ground canon and two auto-mounts. You'll be guarding our six alone. You like big moves?! Well here's your bloody chance!"

Saddler bowed to his Kisser. "A great honor, Ripper. I guard the six like my life depend on it."

"It does, gypsy."

"Then even more reason."

"Just get to it, curse you."

"As you command."

Mona was about to shoot back another response, but the annoyingly accented, deep voice of Mickie Brass stole the opportunity.

"Let's go! Let's go!" the large man roared as he backpedaled to the carrier krawler, blowing a flesh beetle free from the kameeba every few steps. "You know where to be, Maggots! I want the Keepers set up with auto-mounts and shoulder-turrets within the minute! You think this is a rotter pack?! You haven't seen shit yet! The best is yet to come, Maggots. And that'll require the best of you! Bedford!"

"Here!" answered Amos, the too-tall, wiry Maggot with dark skin and dreadlocks, as he rounded the kameeba at a full sprint, coming from krawler two. He leapt over one downed beetle and deftly dodged the snapping mandibles of another—this one much more alive—before sliding to a stop before the Lead Keeper.

"Get loaded first, mate! Sheppard! Help him get his backpacker on and haul an auto-mount for him."

"You got it, Mickie," the blonde-haired woman responded, already lifting an auto-mount from the krawler.

"Bedford, you got the twelve on your own. It's a shit detail, but I know you're up to it. I'll put Biggs on the ten so he can float over as needed."

"Oh, I see! Put the two black men together in the most dangerous, under-guarded area of the whole damn scav," said Amos as Sheppard labored under the weight of the shoulder-turret she was lifting onto the man.

Mickie cocked his head in confusion. "Black men? What two black men?"

Bedford slipped both arms into the straps and hefted the shoulder-turret onto his back.

"Me and Biggs, you gold-toothed, metal-thighed junker!"

Mickie easily tossed a few heavy auto-mounts to Maggots, who nearly collapsed under the sudden weight, before responding.

"You're black, Bedford?"

"Fujin's ass, Mickie, you know damn well I'm black. What else would I be?"

Mickie shrugged, placing his unlit cigar in his mouth. "I always thought of you as sweet, sweet caramel."

"That's the damn same!"

"You think the ladies, especially those dark beauties from Solandaa, think it's the damn same, mate?"

"Well, of course not. But—"

"Then get out there, and keep those rotters from our twelve. You beautiful, sweet-skinned bastard."

Amos Bedford smiled as he rolled Mickie's words around in his mind.

"The twelve will be clear, Mickie."

"I know it will, Amos." The Maggot, Sheppard in tow, turned to leave. "And Amos!" The dreadlocked man turned back. "You won't be in the most dangerous part of the scav. I will."

Bedford offered a small grin before spinning back and double-timing it toward the rear of the kameeba.

"Sheppard, you get back here quick!" The woman, struggling under the heaviness of the auto-mount, simply nodded her buzzed head in return.

Mickie turned back to find the massive Biggson Baft before him, the dark-skinned giant shooting him with a look of curious anger.

"Ahh, you know Amos needs a little lifting before every bang-on, mate. You know you're beautiful, too, you gorgeous bastard! Come here!"

Mickie pulled the man close and planted a kiss on his dark cheek. Biggs playfully pulled away, crooked teeth showing through a wide smile.

"Now, think you can keep him alive? He was right, you know? Lot of rotter pressure's gonna be coming from the twelve."

Biggs nodded in silent response as he slung a Howa 2600 over his shoulder and hefted two auto-mounts.

"Need help with that, big boy?" Biggs cocked his oversized head once more and Mickie laughed. "Rhetorical, mate. Merely rhetorical."

As Biggs trotted off, Mona cuffed Mickie across his Akubra, the metal tip of her index finger banging loudly against the man's head.

"If you're done flirting with the staff, Junker, I think there's work to be done."

Mickie's gold teeth made another appearance.

"Of course, Mona." He turned to the other Maggots scampering around. "Chance! Take as much as you can carry and join Sheppard at the three.

The krawler there's got most of the stuff, so don't kill yourself on the trip. There's plenty of time for that."

The man shot upright and offered a sharp salute. "Yes, sir!"

"All right, lad. I'm a Maggot, not an officer. No different than you. No more important than you. My life's no more valuable than yours. Understood?"

"Yes, sir!"

"Good. The three's gonna be a bloody mess, Chance. But the Karvers are gonna be working at the nine, so we have to prioritize that position. Hold off for a while. Bending's ok. Breaking's not. Once the Karvers are done, I'll have them join you. Then you'll have the firepower you need to blast those rotters back into the mori."

"Yes, sir!"

"Lad…"

The young man's soft hazel eyes finally rose to meet Mickie's. "Sir?"

"You don't break. But you don't die, either. The time comes, you bail and get back to us. Understood?"

"Yes, sir."

"Good lad. Now on you go. Fast like!"

"Pep talk done, Junker?"

"For now, Mona."

"Then let's get to it. This bastard's not gonna gut itself."

"Ok, Mona."

Within seconds, the loud, constant bangs of the auto-mounts began, the mindless machines sweeping left and right, firing upon anything moving before them. Shortly after, the deeper drumming of the Maggot-aimed shoulder-turrets joined in, more carefully selecting their targets. After several waves of gunfire, everything went silent.

"Alright," called out Mona. "Perimeter's set. Karvers! Go to work!"

Neela Patel stepped forward, the athletic woman carrying a heavy light-saw with ease.

"You heard Ripper! We're on! Set your saws to seven for the first three cuts. Then dial down to four for the next two. We'll go at one from then on. I want a tunnel three meters wide by two tall. We'll adjust as we go deeper. And stay well clear of the bloody ticker! I'll do the fine tuning myself. Maddox, take the left. And watch that damn hair of yours as you go in!" The slim Asian man simply nodded. "Hinch, you take the right."

"Understood," replied the ruffian through a mask of tattoos.

"I'll take the middle. Milton, you haul the meat out as we go. Sorry, but you're already old and scar-covered. A few more won't hurt. The rest of us got future modeling careers to consider."

This brought a laugh from the tense group, none more loud than Milton himself.

"Ok, then. Let's carve a tunnel in this bastard!"

Maddox moved toward the kameeba, his light-saw activating, a thick cylinder of shimmering color emanating from the metal laser tube. The man hesitated as he closed the distance."

"Jeez, it's so bright!"

"Then put your helmet on and the damn shade down, idiot!" shot back Neela. "They put 'em in there for a reason, you know."

Maddox shrugged, pulling his helmet on over his spiky hair. "Never needed it before, Neela."

"Well, you bloody do now!"

Maddox raised his left hand and touched a button at the temple his helmet. A slim pane of tinted polycarbonate smoothly slid down over the Maggot's squinting eyes.

"Oh, that's better," commented Maddox.

"No shit, Peetso. Almost like they were made for that purpose," said Neela as she and the other Karvers lowered their own shades. "Anything else you need to do your job?"

"No, that should do it," answered Maddox as the man stepped forward, stabbed his light-saw into the clear flesh of the kameeba, and sliced a neat line down to the grey ground.

Milton did the same three meters to Maddox's right. Neela Patel, standing between the men, made series of downward cuts off of theirs, kicking up a bit of stone from beneath as her saw struck the ground.

Every now and then, a light-saw would hit an invisible pocket within the kameeba flesh, sending a spritz of acid onto the Karvers' skinsuits. More often than not, the suits were thick enough to neutralize the acid before it reached skin. But every few splatterings…

"Fujin's ass, that hurts! This bastard's got more vinegar in it than most!" cried out Milton as he took a brief break to vigorously rub his left thigh.

"Just keeping carving," shot back Neela. "With the yennies from this scav, we'll all be able to fix our ugly mugs. Well, maybe not enough yennies for yours, Milton." More laughter. "Speaking of which… you're up, Milt! Got some meat for you."

The veteran Maggot sprung forward, deftly moving between the Karvers, raising his arms to pull free massive chunks of meeba flesh. Wrapping his long arms around the firm but gelatinous bricks of meat, Milton would scurry back, careful not to knock into his preoccupied teammates, before rushing to place the the valuable meat into one of several barrels placed a few yards away to the side.

Although the old Maggot's face never changed, the acid coating each piece of flesh slowly made its way through his skin suit, eventually gnawing at his weathered arms. And while Milton's progress never stalled, the old man knew that a complete skin peel and regeneration, at least two layers deep, would be required.

If his arms could even be saved.

But on Milton went, a Maggot to the core. Money over health. Team over individual. Return over risk.

And bit by bit, piece by piece, the barrels were filled with kameeba meat, that rarest of substances that—properly processed—could be transformed into creams that decelerated aging, serums that promoted muscle growth, oils that facilitated psychedelic trips, and medicines that allowed a human to live well beyond their natural shelf life... if one was ultra rich, of course.

As the Karvers advanced toward the ticker, Mona Ripple made the rounds, Howa 500 tucked neatly against her shoulder, filling in where needed.

She fired off a few rounds at the six to help the gypsy, Ellis Sadler, deal with a burst of flesh beetles. Then she checked on Darien, whom she had positioned at the nine, closest to the Karvers, ensuring that the young man was at least looking helpful. Finally, she rolled to the three, where novice Maggot Marshall Chance and Betsy Sheppard, along with three auto-mounts, were holding their own against a wave of flesh beetles.

Once Mona joined the fight, a row of gutted rotters were left twitching on the ground within minutes.

"Well done," said Mona as the noise died down. "How're the nerves, rook?"

Chance considered the question for a beat, thoughts racing in his handsome head.

"I... I don't feel any, Ripper. I... I feel–"

"Alive," the Kisser finished for him. "Fighting to stay alive will do that to you. Enjoy it. Most people never experience this. They're too busy *slowly* dying to know the joy of battling *sudden* death." Mona turned to Sheppard. "Betsy, how's he doing?"

"As good as he looks," responded the woman, her blonde head still pivoting back and forth as she scanned for more targets.

"Then he's doing a damn fine job. Keep it up, rook."

Chance awkwardly saluted, his weighty shoulder-turrets preventing a clean motion. "Thank you, Kisser!"

Mona chuckled. "At ease, Maggot. Save that juice for what's to come."

The young man's brows furrowed. "What's to come, Ripper?"

Mona's GLIM scanned deep into Mori Mangekyo, seeing farther and clearer than any human eye.

"Rotter hell is coming, Chance. I suggest you be ready for it."

"I will, Ripper." No salute followed this time as Chance's blue eyes focused ahead, searching the spaces between the hypnotizing subarashi trees.

Mona continued her counter-clockwise trek around the dead kameeba, assisting Amos Bedford and then Biggson Baft. Although the rotters, currently comprised only of flesh beetles, were thickest here at the twelve, the two talented Keepers were more than enough to keep the swarm at bay.

Coming around to the nine, Mona was both relieved and annoyed to find Mickie Brass roaring with laughter and bellowing insults as the Space Cowboy-slash-Keeper let off round after round, each tatsumaki bullet finding a home in the soft insides of a flesh beetle.

Darien was stationed next to the junker, the vast majority of his shots missing their marks.

But her love was trying his best. And though Mona Ripple would never admit this, there was no safer place for her sweetheart to be than next to the insufferable Mickie Brass.

Salty Milton ran past with an armload of meeba meat, depositing it into a nearby, almost-full barrel.

"Hanging in there, Milt?"

"We're getting there, Ripper. One more pass and she's all yours."

Mona glanced at Milton's arms. The sleeves of the old man's skin-suit had been completely eaten through.

"How're the arms, Milt?" the Kisser asked, unable to hide the concern in her voice.

Salty Milton looked down for the first time in several minutes and saw only raw flesh and yellowish fat staring back at him. The man began to respond but, after seeing Mona's own deeply pocked arms, simply shrugged instead.

"They still work, Ripper. And there's still meat to haul."

Mona forced back a tear.

"Damn right, there is. And don't you worry about those arms, Salty. We'll get them tip-top no matter what shape they're in. I'll make sure Colonel

Toro takes care of anything beyond the usual coverage." A pause. "And if that fat bastard doesn't come through, I will."

Milton's weathered face twisted into a grin. "Thanks, Ripper."

"No, Maggot. Thank *you*."

As Milton resumed his hauling duties, Mona slid next to Darien, removing a few flesh beetles from the equation in the process.

"How you doing, my love?" she asked under her breath between shots.

"Ok, I guess," replied the young man, the barrel of his Howa 500 shaking as it pointed out into the swirling color of the mori. "Are we almost done?"

"Not even close, my love."

"Benten's grin, Mona! I thought I was going to be next to you. Not on the front lines with…" Darien's voice lowered. "With this gorilla!"

Mona laughed. "How do you know about gorillas, my love?"

Darien let off a shot that missed its intended rotter by a meter.

"I read! I'm read! I watch things! Unlike these brutes!"

Mickie Brass's head, despite the surrounding noise, cocked a bit at that. Mona yanked Darien further down the line.

"These *brutes* are working their asses off… no… risking their asses to help us get the shitayen we need to start our new life together! Can't you see that?! Can't you appreciate it?!"

Darien's face scrunched. "Why are you yelling at me?"

Mona almost released a sharp-edged reply but pulled it back under the gaze of the young man's too-green eyes.

"I'm not yelling at you, Darien. Just please understand that nothing is free. Our future isn't free. And these people are helping us pay for it."

"I suppose…"

The heat of anger fell over Mona, but before the woman could release the accompanying harsh words that she would inevitably regret, the voice of Neela Patel cut in.

"Karvers are finished, Ripper! Should be a good tunnel for you!"

Mona peered over and nodded at the woman as she exited the hole in the kameeba, silently thankful for the save. She turned back to Darien.

"Come on, my love. We're up. Let's earn our new lives."

"Anything to be away from this madness, Mona."

Oh, but wait until you see what new madness we enter, my dearest.

At krawler three, Mona studied both TRAPs for a moment before peering back at the meeba carcass. The heart of the creature raged within, pulsing with power and tossing terrible brightness from the newly created tunnel.

"Screw it," Mona sighed, forgoing the traditional TRAP cube for the untested TCx. She lifted the large icosahedron, its prismatic walls causing her GLIM to readjust, and shoved it toward Darien. "Take this."

The slight man's shoulders dipped.

"It's heavy."

"Gonna be heavier with that ticker in it. And a shit load more valuable." Her brown eye and GLIM met Darien's green orbs. "Don't drop it."

"I won't, Mona."

The woman nodded in return before sliding an elastic band over her head, positioning the patch attached to it over her natural left eye.

Mona then rummaged quickly through a bag, pulling an item free. She placed a pair of DIGIrims on Darien, checking that they sat nicely on his perfect nose.

"Here, put these on. And don't look directly at the ticker any longer than you have to. One this size could burn your retinas, and I can't have those baby greens getting damaged."

Mona removed several other instruments from the bag and spun to face the kameeba, the cacophony of Howa, auto-mount, and shoulder-turret blasts resuming.

"Let's see what we're working with, my love. Stay close."

Mona paused for a moment to examine the tunnel—the Karvers did a nice job—before plunging into the dead meeba.

The noise of gunfire was immediately muted as Mona and Darien became surrounded on three sides by thick, jelly-like flesh. A flash of pain assaulted the Kisser before her GLIM adjusted to the searing light in front of her. Several steps later, the ticker came into full focus behind a meter of meat.

"Put down the TRAP, and hit the button on the top. You'll have to hold it down for five seconds."

Darien did as he was told. Five seconds after his thin finger depressed the button, a digital display appeared on one of the TRAP's twelve faces. In addition to a capacity reading, a thick line slowly began to crawl from left to right.

"Should take five to ten minutes to boot up. It'll be ready when I am. Now, let's clear this meat away and see what kind of hornet's nest I'm about to stick my bloody hand in." Mona crept closer to the end of the tunnel. She studied the area before her as she spoke. "Darien, hand me my slicer."

"Which one is that again?"

"Yellow handle!" she snapped, more harshly than intended.

Darien, after some frantic searching, handed over the instrument. Mona set the cut length to half a meter, fired up the laser, and quickly started drawing clean lines across the flesh separating her from her prize.

Chunks clear flesh were tossed back down the tunnel, one piece smacking Darien clean in the helmet, almost knocking off the young man's protective lenses.

"Ouch, Mona! You hit me!"

The Kisser didn't respond, the woman completely locked into her task. More strips of meat fell away. The slicer's cut length was reduced. More flesh came away. The slicer was placed on its lowest setting. Slivers curled back and dropped.

And the ticker finally came into full view.

Mona blinked three times in rapid succession, bringing up the GLIM's full range of readings. She leaned forward and examined the exposed ticker, now behind only a thin layer of flesh.

"Fujin's ass!"

"What is it, Mona? Is it bad?"

"It ain't good," she replied as studied the shocking scene, trying to formulate solutions to a possibly unworkable problem.

Truth be told, very little was known about the kameeba—what they did beneath the surface of Kalderra, what purpose they served… how they even existed. Just as little was known about how they functioned as an organism.

A thick tube, or vein, transparent like the rest of the creature, ran from the "head" of the kameeba to the ticker. From the top of the ticker, small arteries reached out, branching out into hundreds, then thousands, then tens of thousands of arterial vessels that spread throughout the body of the kameeba.

Usually, six main arteries could be found coming off the ticker. In larger kameeba, there could be as many as twelve.

This one had more than two dozen.

"Fujin's ass!" Mona repeated. Then she watched in horror.

At the point of expiration, all the power that each kameeba contained was held in its ticker. As the minutes passed, however, that power began to leach out through the connected arteries. Once that power reached the arterial branches, the process sped up dramatically, sending once-centralized joules throughout the carcass. At this point, not only was the power impossible to harvest but also the valuable kameeba meat.

It would be a total loss.

And should those rushing arteries criss-cross or draw too close together? There would be a crater where Karcass Five now worked.

"No, no, no!"

"What is it, Mona?!"

"It's starting to run!"

"Already?" Darien rose as high as the tunnel would allow and peered over Mona's shoulder. "Benten's grin, Mona! Ebisu's luck is not with us today! We should go. We should go now!" Silence. "Mona! It's too late! We need to—"

"Quiet!" barked Mona, her GLIM analyzing run-rates and arterial ordering while calculating total loss and terminal detonation statistics. The Kisser digested a seemingly endless procession of numbers projected atop the swirling, raging ticker.

"I can still do this," she whispered.

"What? Mona, it's not worth it."

"The heck it ain't. I can do this. Give me some space."

Darien gladly took two steps back, unaware that they would make no difference should any number of catastrophic events take place. Nor would ten steps. Or a hundred.

Mona took a deep breath, steadied her nerves. *I can do this. I just need to be fast. And careful.*

Mona loudly cracked her knuckles, removed a small instrument from her belt, and held up her right hand. The metal tip of her index finger folded back, revealing a base embedded with two small lenses, each less than one millimeter in diameter. Her GLIM reacted to the opening, highlighting settings of the femtosecond finger laser in bright orange.

Mona concentrated, electrical signals traveling from brain to GLIM to femto-finger, and the harmless guide laser sprang to life, appearing as a needle of green light through the artificial eye.

Mona pressed forward until her forehead touched the warm jelly, the ticker pulsing just beneath her. GLIM readings showed leakage rates into each of the arteries, dictating which needed to be cut and cauterized first. Mona searched the readings and found the one progressing most rapidly.

"Fujin's ass!"

The artery was dangerously close to two others. She risked nicking a second arterial pathway, depressurizing the channel and flooding it with power. Game over.

Worse, she could accidentally connect two charging arteries. Even if only for a millisecond, this would start a chain reaction of events that would lead to a full detonation before a curse could leave her lips. Game over.

Mona took another calming breath and slowly brought up the instrument in her left hand. It looked like tiny screwdriver, the thin shank narrowing to a two-pronged precision tip. Although it seemed as if a stiff breeze would bend it, the separator's advanced polymer makeup made it as hard to bend as a steel girder.

Leakage rates increasing, Mona carefully inserted the separator into the meeba flesh, her GLIM zooming in until the three arteries of interest filled the woman's vision. Her hand did not shake, nor her fingers tremble, as the instrument sank deeper, its forked tip approaching the vessels.

The separator found a small space within the jumble, and Mona spun it carefully, each prong finding a side of artery one—which had the highest leakage rate. Mona's left pinky slid down the handle, the separator still held motionless, and lightly touched a depression found there. At the tip, the two prongs began to grow as if they were living entities, reaching up and around to encircle the artery. After a beat, they connected, lassoing the vessel. Mona gently, ever so gently, pulled back on the separator, guiding the artery through meeba flesh and away from the other channels.

One of the GLIM's red readings turned yellow, then green, and Mona finally dared to inhale once more.

With artery one now a safe distance from the others, she locked her left hand and went to work with her right. She pushed her femto-finger into the jelly, the green guide laser leading the way. Mona paused when the guide laser perfectly intersected artery one, the GLIM analyzing distance and thickness.

Breath still held, Mona froze. The GLIM worked it calculations. Time seemed to stop. And then the calculations shot up on the screen.

Fire.

Electrical signals went from brain to GLIM to femto-finger, and two small bursts shot forth. The first cut cleanly through the artery, while the second cauterized both new openings.

The world didn't explode around her, and Mona finally exhaled.

"One down, my love," she said, studying the other leakage rates. "But this is going to take longer than usual. I hope the Keepers can give me the time I need."

"And if they can't?"

"Well, we'll still be free. It just won't be in this life."

"Rotters!"

After the initial clearing and a relatively quiet first ten minutes, activity began to pick up around the dead kameeba. Its ticker glowed like a miniature star, sending imperceptible pulses of energy deep into Mori Mangekyo.

Imperceptible to humans, at least. To rotters, it was like a dinner bell.

Waves of flesh beetles continued to crash and break against Maggot artillery. But then they were joined by other, more deadly scavengers.

Mickie Brass cleared the last flesh beetle on his side, a tatsumaki bullet cleanly taking head from thorax, and quickly looked around. He called out to the man on his right.

"Hinch! Can you and Milton hold the nine?"

The tattooed man snickered. "Mickie, if I can't hold out against a bunch of shit-eating bugs, then I might as well put on some lipstick and march myself down to Piccaro's Playpen. Put my ass to work since my trigger fingers don't." Hinch bellowed with laughter. "Maybe Darien can show me the way!"

"Not funny, mate," Mickie reprimanded. "Just hold the line. I got noise at the six."

"Something more than beets, I hope."

"Careful what you wish for, mate. Holler if you need support. I'm gonna float for a while."

Mickie jogged counter-clockwise around the kameeba, playfully slapping Salty Milton on the backside as he passed. The old man simply smiled, his wrinkled eyes remaining locked on the kaleidoscope forest at Karcass Five's eight. And although both arms were wrapped in blood-soaked gauze, Milton's Howa 500 did not waver.

Mickie was greeted with burst after burst of auto-mount and shoulder-turret gunfire as he rounded the head of the meeba.

"You rang, gypsy?! What are we…" The Space Cowboy's voice trailed off as his grey eyes studied the chaotic scene at the team's six. "Bloody hell, mate."

Ellis Sadler's dark mustache twitched as the Maggot fired into the mori, first with his shoulder turrets and then with his Howa 500 when the turrets paused to auto-reload. Just past Sadler, near the back of krawler two, Neela Patel stood wide-eyed, her finger frozen against the trigger of her weapon.

"Lass! Lass! Neela!" shouted Mickie, and the Lead Karver jumped, shaking her head as if waking from a deep dream.

"Sorry, Mickie," she called back.

"Nothing to be sorry for. Just shoot something."

Neela immediately complied, lighting up three flesh beetles in quick succession.

But as Mickie looked back out into Mori Mangekyo, he knew that it was no dream that Neela had fallen into. It was a nightmare.

The flesh beetles had been joined by other, more terrifying, rotters. Giant crystalline centipedes, six meters in length, wove their way through the lines of flesh beets, stopping every now and then to lift the front third of their flattened, shelled bodies into the air, bringing them eye-to-eye with the defending Maggots. Antennae twitched, legs waved menacingly in the cool air, and massive mandibles clicked together loudly. And just outside those bone-crackers sat pairs of poison-filled mouth-claws, so large that most bitten died from puncture wounds before the venom could even take hold.

They were the lucky ones.

Those who survived the bite could look forward to anaphylactic shock and pulses racing to the point that, in some documented cases, hearts literally exploded inside chests.

Unfortunately, the killipedes weren't the worst of the new arrivals.

Mickie narrowed his grey eyes. His grip tightened on his weapon. He sucked in through gold-capped teeth.

In the near distance, past the oncoming flesh beetles and killipedes, colossal creatures could be seen wrapping themselves around the subarashi trees. Translucent like the other rotters, they appeared more hideous hallucination than frightful reality.

Round, swollen bodies dominated by giant, teeth-filled maws were surrounded by eight thick, muscular tentacles, each one ending in a sharp, hooked claw. Splayed out, they were more than ten meters from tentacle end to opposite tip. And they were smart. Too damn smart.

"Bloody shokushu," he said. "Looks like this scav has invited everyone."

"I thought they went back underground," called out Neela between bursts, fear dripping from the woman's words. "One hasn't been seen in years!"

Mickie sent some spit to the rocky ground. "That ticker must be sending signals deep into Kalderra. We're not the only ones looking to score big on this one."

"What do we do, Mickie?" Neela asked in a panic. "I mean, what the *hell* do we do?!"

In response, Mickie fired a single shot from his Howa 500. The tatsumaki bullet made an audible whizzing sound before twisting itself into the head of a rising killipede, exploding the rotter's head and raining shell and brain bits onto the flanking flesh beets.

"Aim for the heads of the killipedes. Body shots will only slow them, lass. The buggers can't help but raise up to get their bearings, so feed 'em bullets when they do. Let the auto-mounts deal with the flesh beets. They're too stupid to alter their approaches."

"And shokushu?" Ellis cut in, the gypsy's mustache twitching so rapidly it seemed a living thing on the man's upper lip.

Mickie studied the mori.

Dozens of meters behind the encroaching flesh beetles and killipedes, the tentacled nightmares—Mickie counted three for now—silently wrapped themselves around the glowing trees. One leaped from a thick, colorful trunk, clearing twenty meters in the air before landing quietly on another subarashi, where it met with a companion stationed there. The two shokushu entwined tentacles for a moment before separating, one moving up the tree to disappear into the colorful canopy while the other slid down, coming to rest at the subarashi's base.

"Clever bastards," muttered Mickie before answering Sadler. "Worry about the beets and killipedes for now. And don't let the shokushu's lack of obvious eyes fool you. They see more than they let on."

"How do you know?" demanded Neela.

"Cause I can see them working things out, lass. I can see the bastards planning. We may lump them in with the rest of these rotters, but they're far from it."

"Meaning?!"

"Meaning they're gonna sit back and wait for their chance to strike. They're gonna let these stupid rotters take all the shrapnel and death, take down our ammo and numbers, before they make their move. And when they do..." Mickie's eyes searched the canopy.

"What?! What?!"

The Space Cowboy's gaze lowered. "They're gonna attack from above and below." Mickie shook free his dark thoughts. "But we'll worry about that when we get to it. For now, the shokushu seem content to keep their distance and watch us duke it out with the other rotters."

"So, what do we do?!"

"We give 'em a show, lass. We give 'em a show."

"How's this for show," said Sadler, strafing his Howa across a neat line of charging flesh beetles, staining the ground with brown innards.

"Beautiful, gypsy. Absolutely beautiful."

All three Maggots opened fire.

Mickie stomped up to Amos Bedford, careful to make his presence known lest he catch a bullet between the eyes.

"How they hanging, mate?"

"Hanging? Shit, Mickie, if they were sucked any higher up, they'd be ovaries."

"That bad?"

"Well, you missed the excitement. I was bulls-eyeing killipede heads when a damn beet slipped through the auto-mount fire. Bastard got me on the leg. Luckily, I was sliding forward at the time, so the mori roach couldn't clamp down. Otherwise, I'd be Long John Silver up in here."

"Who?"

"Who who?"

"Who's Long John Silver, Amos?"

Bedford shrugged, causing his shoulder-turrets to twitch. "Beats me, Mickie. Just something I heard once when I was a boy. Means you lost your damn leg."

"Let me take a look, mate."

Mickie dropped to his knees and pushed aside the flesh beetle carcass—one that had been very obviously stomped upon by a Maggot boot. The junker's hand pulled back as soon as he touched the right leg of Bedford's skin-suit. It was soaked through with blood.

"I need to cut your suit, mate."

"Do what you got to, Mickie. But it ain't nothing but—"

Mickie peeled back the sliced material.

"Fujin's ass, Mickie! You pouring acid in there?"

"I haven't touched it, mate. It looks bad."

"The bone still attached?"

"It is."

"Then I'm fine. Chicks dig scars. And the chicks that dig a Maggot like me *really* dig scars."

"Do they dig corpses, too, mate? Cause that's what you're gonna be if this isn't wrapped."

"Shit, they probably do, Mickie."

Mickie rummaged through his belt pouch. "Well, I don't, mate. Slows down the team. Hold still."

Bedford followed orders, sucking in as Mickie tightly wrapped his leg in lastogauze. When finished, the Space Cowboy flicked the freshly bandaged wound.

"Ouch! What was that for?!"

Mickie rose. "To wake you up. You lost a lot of blood, and I can't have you sleeping on the job."

"Shit, Mickie, I could kill rotters with both eyes closed and a girly on my lap."

"I believe you, mate. What else you seen back here?"

Bedford's tone got serious. "Shokushu."

"Where?"

"Half a click back. They ain't moving on us yet. It's like they're watching."

"That's cause they are, mate."

"That's what I was afraid of."

"Me, too, mate."

"How're the others holding up?"

Mickie looked to his right as he replied. "Neela and the gypsy needed some help, but they're ok now. Sheppard, Chance, and Maddox are keeping the bastards at bay. No shokushu at the three yet. What's Biggs been up to?"

Bedford laughed, sending his dreadlocks swaying side to side.

"No need to worry about that big, ugly bastard. Him and his giant gun are keeping the ten down all by his lonesome. I ain't heard any complaints."

Mickie smiled. "And you never will." The junker scanned the scene.

"Alright, mate, looks like you're in good shape. I'll check on Biggs on my way back to the nine."

"Ripper should have been done by now, Mickie."

"It's a whopper of a ticker, mate. My guess is it's a cluster fuck of one, too."

"Them shokushu ain't gonna just watch all scav."

"I know, mate."

A tense beat passed between the Maggots. Finally—

"I'll give you all I can, Mickie."

"I know, mate."

Mickie lifted his Howa 500 to his shoulder. A moment later, the head flew from a killipede twenty meters away. The junker made his way around the dead kameeba.

"Mickie!"

"Yeah."

"Thanks."

"Thank me by staying alive, Amos." And then he was gone.

Bedford belatedly grinned. "My man."

Mona breathed a sigh of relief, having completed another successful cut and cauterization. The woman's skin-suit was drenched in sweat, and her hands and arms now sported a whole new set of acid marks.

The Kisser had blocked out the increasing gunfire from outside, ignored the screams and calls for backup from her team. She was in the zone. Her dream was within reach.

Mona slowly moved to the next target when a voice from the tunnel entrance broke her concentration, making her jump.

"How we doing down there, lass?"

"Fujin's ass, Junker! I'd be doing a sight better if you'd leave me the heck alone and let me work!"

Even from afar, Mona heard Mickie mutter a curse. She smiled wickedly.

"Progress update, Mona?"

"I'm on my way to making you very rich, Junker."

The Space Cowboy took a beat. "Mona. It's getting messy out here, lass."

Mona immediately detected a shift in the man's tone. There was something hiding in Mickie's words that she'd never heard before—uncertainty. She turned to face her Lead Keeper, her GLIM focusing on his grey eyes.

"I got six more to do. I got this bastard down now, so I should be able to do it in another ten minutes." Mickie's face twisted. "Can you give me that, Junker?"

"I'll do my best."

And then he was gone. And another gun joined the fight.

"It sounds like it's getting pretty bad out there, Mona. Maybe it's time to go. There will be other kameeba, other scavs."

Mona shook her head and returned to her work. "No. Not like this one. This is the one, my love. This is the one I've been waiting all my life for. This is my ticket, and you are my prize. I won't give up on either. Now hand me that pen scalpel again. If I can make a little space, this next one's gonna be a cinch."

"Ok, Mona."

***

"Mickie! The bastards are making their move! Here they come!"

"Hold there," called out Mickie as he decimated three killipedes in one swipe with his Howa. Immediate threat neutralized, Mickie sidestepped toward Ricksin Hinch and looked to where the tattooed Maggot was staring intently.

"Yep. They're coming all right. Give 'em Susanoo's Wrath! Don't let them close the distance!"

Hinch spit before unloading his Howa 500 and both shoulder-turrets at the oncoming shokushu. But while the flesh beetles simply advanced straight ahead like unthinking creatures, and the killipedes crawled in odd but predictable wavelike patterns, the shokushu offered no such advantage.

The advanced rotters moved like ballerinas on their venom-tipped tentacles, cartwheeling to the left before spinning to the right, the brains of their bulbous central heads shifting color from blue to red to green to orange.

"I can't hit 'em!" cried out Hinch as his weapons swayed back and forth like a drunken Guntai after payday.

"Smart bastards," Mickie said to himself before addressing Hinch. "Just keep firing! Even a blind gava newt eventually finds a lucin cone!"

As Hinch unsuccessfully attacked the shokushu, Mickie picked up the slack elsewhere, assisting the auto-mounts in mowing down flesh beetles and removing the heads of any killipedes stupid enough to rise up.

After a minute of slaughter, Mickie took grim satisfaction in seeing that the numbers of lower-class rotters were dwindling, with fewer reinforcements coming to replenish the horde.

But as the beetle and killipede waves slowed, the real threat stepped forward.

"Now I got shokushu!" announced Salty Milton from the far left. Mickie rushed to the eight and slid to stop. Milton's destroyed arms shook with effort, and Mickie could not fathom how the injured man continued holding his weapon.

"Where?" asked Mickie.

"Right at the clearing line. They're all clinging to the backsides of those subarashi."

"How many, Milt?"

"Three that I could count. I'm sure there's more."

"Yeah, me too, mate. Forget about them for now. Keep clearing the other rotters. I don't think many more of them are coming at least."

"And the shokushu?"

"Oh, they'll come around those trunks shortly, no doubt. Probably right as we begin to run out of ammo."

"How would they know that, Mickie?"

"Cause these ain't monsters, mate. They're bloody smart, thinking, bastard monsters."

"Well, that doesn't cheer me up."

"Me neither, mate."

Mickie ran the circumference of the kameeba at a full sprint, his massive arms overloaded with weapons retrieved from krawler three. His message was the same to all the Maggots as he dropped the torch scythes at their feet.

"Cut the shokushu with this. Even at its highest setting, the bastards will have to be close. Watch out for fellow Maggots. And don't you dare touch a bloody subarashi with it."

"Aye, Mickie," came the reply from every Maggot manning the line.

As the Space Cowboy made his deliveries, auto-mount after auto-mount ground to a stop, bullet reserves totally depleted.

The shokushu drew nearer and nearer, continuing their beautiful but deadly dance.

When Mickie got back to his position at the nine, he was joined by Hinch.

"What's the plan, Mickie?"

"You keep firing that Howa. Don't worry if one gets through. I want it to. I'll be here to slice the bastard neatly in half with the torch scythe."

"Fujin's ass, Mickie! So, you want me to be bloody bait?!"

"Better bait than dinner, mate. You trust me?"

A short pause. "I do, Mickie."

"Good lad. I won't miss."

"The shokushu or my head?"

"Keep whining, mate, and I'll see if I can't go two-for-two."

A laugh erupted from the tattoo-covered face. "I guess better to meet my end at the hand of a Space Cowboy than the hook of a rotter."

Mickie slapped the man on the shoulder.

"Now you're talking like a real Maggot."

Peetso Maddox's once-tall hair laid slicked back against the Asian Maggot's head, heavy with sweat, his helmet having fallen off minutes before. He kicked at the jammed auto-mount with his right boot, and a grinding sound was emitted before the gun roared back to life, sending a line of flesh beetles backwards to land on their backs. Unable to flip themselves back over, the rotters desperately waved their legs in the air.

Maddox offered a silent prayer to Izanagi as this was the last working auto-mount on their side. With support returned, the man slung his nearly empty Howa 500 over his shoulder and retrieved his torch scythe from the ground. Making sure the setting was at its highest level—still not long enough to threaten the nearest subarashi—Maddox hit the activate button.

A deep hum emanated from the weapon and gentle smoke shot forward from the bottom of the handle. That smoke, too thin to significantly affect visibility, was necessary, making the length and curve of the laser scythe visible. From the vapors crawling in from his left and right, Maddox knew that his fellow Maggots had also progressed to closer, more frightening combat.

Removing his eyes from the scythe, Maddox saw that a shokushu had finally left the protection of the mori to enter the small clearing. Standing at full height on its eights tentacles, the massive mouth twisted into an evil grin.

"Come on then, you bastard," Maddox said to himself. "Peetso's got a surprise for you. Tip-toe your ugly ass over here and see what happens. Five meters. Get within five meters and you're mine."

The shokushu glided forward. Ten meters. Nine meters. Eight meters.

"That's it," the Maggot whispered. "That's it. I'm an easy target. An easy meal. Just a little farther."

At the line of upended flesh beetles seven meters away, the shokushu paused, its head flashing all the colors of the rainbow. Then the color shift stopped, the brain inside its clear shell dimming to a dull brown.

"What are you waiting for, you b—"

With a flick of its forward-most tentacle, the shokushu tossed a flesh beetle at the waiting Maggot.

Maddox's narrowed eyes went wide, and he swiped down at the living missile, attempting to intercept it from the air.

He missed.

The flesh beetle crashed into the man's left shoulder, its oversized mandibles snapping shut, ripping flesh and tearing tendon from bone. Maddox screamed out in pain and rage, dropping his torch scythe to rip free the attached rotter. With a loud grunt, the beetle came free, taking with it chunks of muscle.

"Bastard! Bastard! Bastard!" the man roared, stomping down with this boot until there was only a dark stain on the ground before him.

Maddox staggered but managed to hold himself upright. He gently touched his mangled shoulder, and his right hand returned covered in blood. As he stared disbelieving at the crimson liquid coating his fingers and palm, something moved just into focus of his failing eyes.

Peetso Maddox looked up through the break in the canopy and stared upon the too-violet, too-big moon.

"I hate this place. Amaterasu take me." Dropping his gaze, Maddox stared at the shokushu before him, its mouth open and vibrating, shaking the endless rows of sharp teeth within. "And Susanoo's Wrath take you rotter."

Maddox shot forth a thick loogie, landing it in the rotter's unhinged maw.

Peetso Maddox laughed hysterically. The shokushu attacked.

———

A scream penetrated the kameeba's thick body, clear and haunting over the ongoing noise of gunfire. Darien stared down the tunnel, the young man shaking.

"It's getting worse, Mona."

"I'm almost done, my love. Only two more to go."

"That sounds like two too many. I think—Oh, no! Mona, look!"

The Kisser took her GLIM from the ticker and peered up. Through the jellylike flesh, she could see that a form now sat above them, a giant mouth tearing at the clear meat.

"Fujin's ass!" she cursed. "Just what we need. A bloody shokushu got through."

"It's coming through, Mona!"

The GLIM fell back to the ticker, and Mona resumed her work.

"The rotter's eating, not trying to get to us. It's gonna enjoy its meal. I have time. I have to have time. Get ready to hand me the TRAP. It'll take both of us to lift the ticker out." Silence. "Darien!"

The young man's head swung back to the woman. "What?!"

"I said be ready."

"Ok, Mona."

———

Ricksin Hinch looked at his Howa 500 as if it had betrayed him.

"I'm out! Susanoo take me! I'm out!"

The timing could not have been worse. Three shokushu now stood at the edge of the clearing, their tentacles slapping at the ground, sending flesh beetles at the three Maggots stationed at the nine.

"Me too!" called out Salty Milton from Mickie's left.

The Space Cowboy took half a second to assess the situation. Then he acted.

"Drop 'em, lads!" Hinch and Milton immediately followed the Lead Keeper's orders. "Milt, catch!"

Mickie tossed his Howa to the veteran, who caught it with a grimace, blood dripping from his arms. The scarred man took a beat to compose himself then began firing, picking off two flesh beetle projectiles.

"Hinch! Pick up your torch scythe!"

The tattooed man shrugged free his empty shoulder-turrets and knelt down to retrieve his other weapon. As he did, a shokushu flicked a passing flesh beetle, sending the creature flying.

Its aim was true, and giant mandibles opened wide as the flesh beet closed the distance to Hinch's exposed, unprotected face.

The Keeper's eyes went wide, then slammed shut as the beetle exploded a meter from him, covering his face in gore.

Hinch wiped his eyes with the sleeve of his skin-suit, collected his torch scythe, stood, and looked over.

Mickie stood facing him, a tech-revolver in each hand. Metal compartments had opened on the outside of the Lead Keeper's thighs, right where Mickie had cut away the fabric of his skin-suit.

With a flourish, Mickie spun the gun in his right hand before returning it to its metal holster. The right thigh compartment closed.

Hinch laughed. "All Space Cowboys have that, Mickie?"

Gold teeth appeared once more. "Nah, mate. Just the exceedingly handsome ones."

Keeping the revolver in his left hand, Mickie bent down and took up his torch scythe with his right. Thin smoke billowed out, and the scythe came to life.

"I don't know about you, mate, but I'm tired of being the hunted. If death's coming anyway, let's meet him halfway. What say you?"

Hinch's torch scythe ignited.

"I say we show these bastards who the real scavengers are in this blasted mori."

"Good, lad. Milton!"

"Here, Mickie!"

"Keep clearing out those beets and killipedes. Shouldn't be many more. Hinch and I are going hunting."

"Give 'em hell, Mickie."

"It's all I got in my bag to offer, mate. Let's go, Hinch!"

With support from Salty Milton, Mickie and Ricksin Hinch waded into the clearing. The shokushu danced forward to meet them.

Mickie darted left, sending the shokushu there backpedaling, then cut right, throwing his torch scythe out in a vicious backhand. The shokushu to his right, leaping forward in an attempt to catch the Space Cowboy on his exposed flank, had no time to react. The scythe cut neatly through six of the rotter's eight tentacles, and the creature collapsed in heap. Its remaining legs desperately tore at the air between the two combatants, venom dripping from sharp tips.

"Not today, mate," said Mickie, raising his left hand and firing a single shot into the shokushu's flashing head.

Mickie spun back to his left just in time, bringing the torch scythe across his body just as a tentacle shot toward his chest like a spear. The venomous tip flew wide, falling harmlessly to the ground, while the stump of the tentacle struck the lead Keeper's chest, sending the man sliding backward and out of range of the other tentacles.

"That hurt, mate," said Mickie, sucking in air. The shokushu's head glowed red in response. "Come on then. I don't have all bloody night to—"

A tatsumaki bullet tore into the rotter's head, scrambling its brains. It fell to ground with an audible splat.

"Nice shot, mate! Appreciate the assist!"

"Bastard was focused on you, Mickie. Gave me a perfect shot," replied Milton as he stood in front of krawler one.

"Can't blame him for his good taste, mate."

Something caught Milton's eye. "Mickie look!"

The Space Cowboy pirouetted and found Hinch under attack. The man held his torch scythe in both hands, swinging it wildly back and forth as the shokushu slid in and out like a galactic champion boxer, tentacle tips just missing the Keeper's face, chest, and legs.

"Bastard, bastard, bastard," Hinch repeated, barely keeping the dancing, spinning attacker at bay.

Nerves fraying, Hinch stepped into a double-handed thrust. Unfortunately, just before scythe met glowing head, the shokushu splayed its legs out and dropped under the blow. It then rebounded like a ball, nailing Hinch's outstretched arms from below and sending the torch scythe flying off into the clearing.

Then it was atop him.

Back against the cool grey ground, four tentacles on each side pinning him down, Hinch looked on in horror as the shokushu's awful mouth opened above him and snapped down.

But then it was gone in a blur of movement.

Hinch's head turned to see Mickie straddling the shokushu, the Lead Keeper's right fist slamming down, over and over again, onto the bulbous head as tentacles writhed beneath.

Two more blows and the creature's legs fell limply to the ground. Mickie rose, flexed his right fist, and put a single bullet into the creature's head with his revolver.

"Benten's grin, Mickie, am I happy to see you!"

The Space Cowboy strode over to his fallen teammate, offering his blood-covered right hand.

"Sorry, mate. You two were too close to risk the torch scythe. Had to take a more barbarian approach."

"I don't care what kind of approach it was," said Hinch as he was helped to his feet. The man shook. "You saved my ass."

Mickie shrugged, his grey eyes already searching for more targets.

"Looks like we cleared this side, mate. Things might be looking—"

Above, something sprung from the kaleidoscope glow of the mori canopy. It soared through the air above the Maggots, slamming into the body of the dead kameeba to the left of the tunnel entrance. Tentacles moved in a blur as the shokushu scrambled on top of the carcass and began feeding. Only then did Mickie and Hinch notice that another shokushu was already there.

The pair of shokushu filled their mouths with meat.

"Well, that certainly complicates things, mate."

"Uhh, Mickie?"

"Yeah, mate?"

"Your arm."

Mickie looked down. A small cut could be seen atop the Space Cowboy's left forearm. It was the exact width of a shokushu claw tip.

"And the bloody good times keep bloody rolling, mate."

A third shokushu dropped heavily onto the dead kameeba and dove into the carcass's meat. The walls of the tunnel started to shake, and its roof began to sag.

"They're going to collapse the tunnel, Mona! We're going to be crushed!"

Mona ignored her young lover, focusing instead on the last artery. The power leakage had almost reached the first major branch. Her final cut would be dangerously close to the surging energy. And the danger was increasing every second.

Mona's GLIM zoomed in further, so much so that her field of vision no longer included the oncoming rush of power.

The kameeba shook again, causing the artery to vibrate away from its center line. But Mona remained motionless.

She waited until the dead meeba finished settling, held her breath, and sent the command to her femtofinger. A quick pulse just as the energy surge reached the target location.

The world did not explode.

Mona exhaled, staring in relief as the cauterized artery held. The ticker was contained. The ticker was free.

"We did it, love," said the Kisser as the tunnel shook and bulged inward. "Now bring over the TRAP, and let's get this bastard loaded. Love? Love?"

Mona turned to find Darien at the end of the tunnel, his panic-stricken face covered in sweat.

"It's too late, Mona! It's too late! She's gonna collapse!"

"We've got time, Darien. We've got—"

Darien scampered out of the tunnel, falling over himself in a desperate attempt to escape. And then he was gone.

"Fujin's ass!" spat Moan, pulling her shield gloves from her pouch and slipping them on. "I'll do it myself."

After sliding the TCx TRAP to her feet, the woman braced herself and thrust her protected hands into the kameeba meat. She grasped the massive ticker. It hummed with power, and its scorching heat could be felt through the shield gloves. Mona ignored the pain and pulled. The ticker refused to budge. She yanked hard. The ticker barely moved.

A shudder went through the kameeba as the shokushu above continued to devour meat.

"No," begged Mona as the translucent ceiling dipped lower, touching the top of her head. *Not like this. Please. Not like this. I'm too close. Too damn close.*

Mickie Brass brought his torch scythe down and across, slicing a killipede neatly in two.

As he did, movement at the edge of his periphery caught his attention. He spun back to see Darien Vance stumbling out of the kameeba tunnel. The young man's green eyes were wild with fear as he made his way toward krawler one.

"Darien! What's going on?! Where's Mona?!"

"It's gonna collapse, Mickie! They're eating through! Any second now!"

"Where's Mona, lad?!" the Space Cowboy repeated.

"The fool wouldn't leave! She's still in there! I'm not ready to die. Not for a ticker. Not for anything!"

Mickie pushed down the urge to cut the handsome man in half.

"Fujin's ass, boy! You don't leave your Kisser!"

"It's too late," Darien murmured. "Too late, too late."

The youthful Maggot began to climb into the krawler.

"Darien!" The young man jumped. "Get over here. Now!"

Darien looked around. At that moment, nothing in the clearing—flesh beetle, killipede, or even shokushu—looked as terrifying as Mickie Brass. The young man reluctantly made his way over.

Mickie plucked the DIGIrims from Darien's face and shoved the torch scythe into his soft hands.

"New orders, mate. Anything comes within five meters and you drop the scythe on them. It's already activated."

"But I've never used one of these before."

"See rotter. Swing at rotter. Kill rotter. Simple."

"But—"

"I'm not gonna tell you again, mate."

The young man nodded.

Mickie pushed Darien deeper into the clearing, where Ricksin Hinch had his hands full with a newly arrived shokushu. Meanwhile, bullets from Salty Milton continued to rip into the odd flesh beetle and killipede.

Commands delivered, Mickie donned the protective glasses and made for the kameeba carcass at a sprint, doing his best to ignore the three massive shokushu perched atop the dead creature, hoping that mouthfuls of meat kept them happy enough for the time being.

Mickie crashed into the tunnel, cursing himself for his carelessness as the walls dangerously shook.

"Need a hand, lass?"

Mona turned, both hands still wrapped around the ticker.

"Junker! Get over here! I need another pair of hands to free this thing! Take the extra shield gloves from my pouch."

Mickie raced down the increasingly narrow tunnel, found the gloves in the woman's waist pouch, and quickly put them on.

"Take the left side," the Kisser directed. "I'll grab the right. Pull on three."

"Wait, Mona! Let me get a grip on her, lass."

"You got it?!"

"Yeah, I got it. She's bloody hot."

Mona's GLIM met the man's grey eyes. Calls and screams filled the clearing. The kameeba vibrated, and popping sounds could heard. Small spritzes of acid hit the two Maggots' faces and arms.

"One. Two. Three!"

They yanked back simultaneously. The ticker moved—but only a bit.

"Keep pulling, Junker!"

"I am, lass!"

"It don't feel like it!"

Mickie bellowed, and Mona's GLIM went wide as the heavy ticker came free of the meeba meat. Both Maggots fell backwards, the energy-filled heart landing atop Mickie's chest. Smoke rose where the ticker began burning through the junker's skin-suit.

"A little help!"

Mona shuffled to her feet and moved to help Mickie. Together, they maneuvered the ticker over the decahedron-shaped TRAP.

As gently as possible with searing pain coursing through their hands, the Maggots released their grips, and the impossibly bright heart fell into the containment vessel. The swirling walls of the TRAP began to spin like tornados of stained glass as the lid slammed shut.

A reading in bright red appeared.

"Is it holding?" asked Mickie, his voice sounding strangely distant.

"It is. But barely." A massive chunk of meat fell from the tunnel ceiling. "No time to worry about that. We have to get out."

Mickie nodded and grabbed one end of the TRAP. Mona's GLIM noticed that the man's eyes seemed unfocused. She hoisted the other end and shuffled backward down the tunnel.

Mona was out, then the ticker, then Mickie. Just as the Space Cowboy cleared the exit, the tunnel collapsed, and the kameeba folded in on itself. The three shokushu found themselves buried in gelatinous flesh. They would be happy to eat themselves free.

"Maggots!" the Kisser cried out as she and Mickie staggered toward krawler one, the heavy ticker between them. "Clear out! Clear out! Clear —" Mona's voice caught as she glimpsed the shredded body of Salty Milton. The beloved veteran's arms and legs had been taken away, and his head was being consumed by a killipede. Mona swallowed the bile in her throat. "Clear out!"

Mona grunted, and Mickie almost tumbled forward as they lifted the TRAP into the krawler. The Kisser ripped the patch from her left eye and felt it narrow as she spotted something on the floor of the rover.

Darien was curled up in a ball, head in hands, incoherent ramblings pouring forth from his plump mouth.

"Darien!" One green eye appeared from between fingers. "Get in your seat. We're getting out of here, my love." Mona turned to Mickie. "Is it still holding?"

Mickie's head swayed back and forth. "I don't think it's gonna make it back, lass. Grab me that other TRAP you brought."

"Why?"

"Just trust me. And be quick about it."

Mona leapt from the krawler and was met by Ricksin Hinch. The tattooed man's left arm was tucked against his chest, the hand missing.

"Come with me to krawler three, Hinch. Make sure Patel and Saddler load up, and don't forget the meat barrels. Pass along word to Maddox, Chance, and Sheppard. They can take krawler two."

"Peetso's dead, Ripper."

"The other two then!"

Hinch looked like he had more to say. But the injured Maggot simply nodded curtly and made his way to the second rover, shouting out to his comrades as he did.

Mona followed him to the krawler, grabbed the extra TRAP cube, and returned to krawler one. Amos Bedford and Biggson Baft were waiting for her there. The massive Biggs was holding up the dreadlocked man, whose right thigh bore a deep cut.

"Get him on, Biggs, and take the wheel. Time to leave this madness behind."

"What about the meat, Ripper?" asked Bedford through gritted teeth. "That's a lot of yennies we're leaving behind."

Mona glanced into the clearing. New waves of rotters were entering from the mori, making a beeline for the fallen kameeba.

"We've earned enough today. And already sacrificed too much."

"Toro's not gonna like it."

"Toro can kiss my bloody ass. Now get your ass on the krawler."

"You got it, Ripper."

Bedford fell into the rover with a loud grunt. Biggs took the TRAP cube from Mona and handed it to a sleepy-eyed Mickie. Mona jumped in. After checking on Darien, she slid down to where the junker was working furiously despite his drunken movements.

"What are you doing, Junker?"

The Space Cowboy didn't respond. Instead, he pried open a hidden panel on the underside of the TRAP cube and removed some thick wire from one of the krawler's many compartments.

"Junker?"

Hands shaking, Mickie retrieved a knife from his grav-boot and used it to cut the wire into three, then six, then twelve pieces. Chin slowly falling to his chest, the junker continued to work, weaving the pieces together into a complicated braid which he surrounded in thick black tape. Mickie then put the tip of the knife to his mouth.

"Fujin's ass, Junker! What are you—"

Mickie grimaced as the blade cut into his gums, sending a blood-covered gold tooth to the krawler floor. Mona's scarred hands went to her mouth.

Mickie picked up the tooth, pried off the gold cap, and sliced it neatly in half with his knife. He examined the open panel of the TRAP cube and inspected a small, nearly invisible indentation in the TCx TRAP. The two bits of gold were returned to his mouth. He began to chew.

Behind them, more rotters filled the clearing and covered the kameeba. In thirty minutes, there would be nothing left of the creature.

Mona's GLIM went from kameeba to rotter to mori, zooming in as something moved between the magical trees.

Clear like all the organisms of Mori Mangekyo, the creature moved on two legs and had two arms hanging at its sides. It was humanoid. And it was staring right at Mona, diamond eyes searching her soul.

"Mona! Mona!"

The Kisser jumped, the interruption tearing her GLIM from the crystalline being.

"I need your help, lass."

Mickie's words were beginning to slur. He held a piece of gold, which he had fashioned into a kind of plug, to each end of the braided wire.

"What do you need?"

"Need to solder these here ends to this here wire. Use that magic finger of yours."

Removing her shield glove, Mona brought up her femtofinger. The tip folded back as her GLIM studied the space where gold met wire. One quick pulse. Then a second.

"How's that?"

"That should work," replied Mickie, although Mona doubted that he could see anything through his blurry vision.

Mickie moved one end of his improvised connector to the TRAP cube, pushing the gold plug into the small hole within the hidden panel. He took the opposite end and, after missing a few times, managed to force it into the TCx.

A loud buzzing sound cut through the noise of the feasting rotters, and Mona's hair stood on its end. The hum grew louder and louder, and she could feel both TRAPs vibrating at her feet.

And then they fell silent. Her hair fell. The red reading on the TCx had turned yellow.

"That should hold her," said Mickie in a whisper before passing out.

Krawler one lurched forward, falling in line with the other two rovers as they exited the clearing. Mona looked back to find a sea of rotters piled high atop the shrinking kameeba carcass.

Lightning streaked high above as two diamond eyes followed Mona Ripple as she and the remaining Karcass Five members tore through Mori Mangekyo—with greater profits and losses than they could have imagined just a few hours earlier.

CHAPTER 2

LOVESICK

"You should be dead, Junker."

Mickie Brass slowly opened his eyes to find himself in the sick bay of Camp Karcass. An IV hung next to his bed, replenishing his drained body with vital fluids. He smiled at the person standing to the side.

"I'm too stupid to die, lass."

"Why didn't you tell me that a shokushu caught you? I could have sent you back on a krawler. I could have—"

Mickie weakly raised a hand to stop the woman.

"Wouldn't have made any difference, Mona. Either die on my back on the way or help get the job done. No choice in that."

"But you didn't die. Why didn't you die?"

"Maybe lucky *and* stupid."

Mona sighed sadly, the woman appearing to have aged another two years in a few short hours.

"Luck is something none of us had, Junker."

"How many we lose?"

"Maddox and Milton. Hinch lost a hand. Bedford took a nasty bite, but we were able to save the leg. Chance isn't nearly as handsome as he used to be. But everyone else got by with cuts and bruises. Except Saddler."

"What about Saddler?"

"Not a scratch on him."

Mickie chuckled, and his head lowered. "Bloody gypsy."

"Yeah."

Mickie stayed quiet for a moment to honor the fallen. And then his grey eyes shot up.

"The TRAP?! Did she hold?"

"It did. Thanks to you. I don't know what kind of junker tinkering you did, but the added power of the TRAP cube gave the TCx just enough to get the ticker back to the power vault in the energy processing plant."

"Good payout?"

"Five times the highest ever recorded. At least. The yennies increase as certain tiers are hit. They had to make a new tier for this one."

"Then it was worth it."

Mona rubbed her face with a scarred hand. "Nothing was worth this, Junker." A beat. "Anyway, get some more rest. You look like shit but not so bad for a dead man. We'll celebrate and raise a toast to the dead when you're up and about."

"I can get up now, lass."

"Well, Bedford can't, so just cool your boots. Some more rest ain't gonna make you any uglier."

"Ok, Mona."

The woman began to say something but simply nodded in return. She made her way toward the exit.

"Mona."

She stopped without turning back.

"The juice was worth the squeeze, lass. Everyone here would gladly run it back. Even Peetso and Salty. And if it gets you the future you're after, no sacrifice was too great."

Mona swiped at something on her cheek.

"Go to sleep, Space Cowboy. We got drinking to do when you rise."

"Don't threaten me with a good time, lass."

"A good time," Mona mumbled. "Right."

The Karcass Five post-scav celebration was a mixed affair, the break room filled with sadness and pride, regret and hope. While the loss of two comrades and severe injuries of three others hurt, the promise of mountains of shitayen did much to dampen the pain.

As did the endless supply of booze.

Maggots passed around bottles of Yamazaki whiskey, sharing tales of Peetso Maddox and Salty Milton.

"I'm telling you right now," said Amos Bedford as he balanced on his one good leg. "There ain't a gal in the galaxy that could resist Peetso. Did I tell you about the time that we were sharing a room together at The Ruddy Lip? He was with this working girl from Ghostlight Go-Go—it was two-bed room obviously—"

"Oh, did that dancer steal your lover for the night?" cut in Neela Patel.

"It was a two-bedder, Neela!"

"Sure, Amos."

Bedford waved away the jab. "Anyway, Peetso puts 25,000 yennies on the table before he falls asleep, knowing that the girl will wake up before we do. And when we do finally get up, heads still full of smoke, what do we find?" He paused for dramatic effect. "50,000 yennies!"

The group roared in laughter.

"You tell that one before," complained Saddler.

"Cause it's worth repeating, ya damned gypsy!"

In another group, the chatter was much more subdued as they exchanged stories of the beloved Maggot veteran Salty Milton.

"It should've been me instead of him," stated Ricksin Hinch, the stump of his left arm tightly wrapped. "Biggs, remember when old Salty punched that shokushu right in its mouth? The one that had wrapped itself under the krawler?"

The silent Biggs nodded, a small smile perched on his face.

"What happened?" asked Marshall Chance, the young man's face wrapped in gauze, hiding jagged sutures that ran from forehead to nose to cheek.

Hinch continued. "The scav was over and we were hightailing it out of the mori. Lo and behold, a damn shokushu had been hiding under the krawler. It crept out from under the rover like a mazoku demon, rearing up right behind my seat. Bastard was bout to plunge a tentacle into my chest when old Salty stands up, looks the bastard in its ugly face, and drills it with a left hand. Salty's fist went into the bastard's mouth, maybe even connected with its stupid brain, and dropped it from the krawler. I'd never seen a shokushu before that day and hoped to never see one again. Salty's hand was a butchered mess; never quite worked the same after that. He never said a word about it. And I never properly thanked him." Hinch held up his stump. "I hope he took my hand with him up to Takamagahara. I hope it replaces the one he offered up for me."

"To Salty," said Betsy Sheppard.

"To Salty!" said the group, each tipping a bottle to their lips.

And so the evening went on, conversations drifting between the past and the future. As the group mingled, drinking their Japanese whiskey, Mickie Brass sat in the corner alone, greeting the odd passerby, including a few from other Karcass units who had stepped in briefly to offer congratulations and pay their respects. Mickie's black Akubra hat was back on his head, unlit cigar in his mouth. Unlike his fellow Maggots, Mickie drank from a bottle of Jack Daniels whiskey, exceedingly rare and expensive, especially this far from Chikyu.

The Space Cowboy sat back and reluctantly accepted words of gratitude and expressions of heartfelt delight in seeing his impossible recovery.

"Only this bastard," said a slurring Bedford, slapping Mickie on the shoulder. "Only this bastard could take a hit from a shokushu, shit out the venom, and still manage to rewire a TRAP cube. A bloody TRAP cube! No one even knows how they work!"

"They're simpler than they look, mate. And it wasn't a hit. Only a scratch."

"A scratch? From a shokushu? No such thing, Mickie." Bedford wavered as he stood. "You should be dead, my friend."

"Disappointed, mate?"

"Quite the contrary, Mickie. I love you, brother." Bedford spun to face the center of the break room, almost falling in the process. "To Mickie!"

"To Mickie!" the Maggots answered.

"I owe him my life!" declared Ricksin Hinch.

"We all do!" added Neela Patel.

Mickie, looking embarrassed, removed the chewed cigar from his mouth, highlighting a gap where a gold tooth had recently resided.

"Enough. Enough. You all owe me two things—jack and shit. We went in as a team. We left as a team. We lost some friends. We gained some wealth. Nothing much more to it. You want to thank someone? Thank Mona. She had the hard job."

"Thank me for what?" asked Mona as she finally joined the party, Darien in tow.

A momentary hush fell over the group before Mickie broke the silence.

"For the successful scav, lass. I saw the ticker you pulled out of that flesher. It was more complicated than a Syndicate contract. One wrong move and all of us would be roaming Takamagahara right now instead of celebrating swollen accounts. Rotter or no rotter." Mickie's eyes took in all the other Maggots. "Were it any other Kisser, there'd be a hole in Mori Mangekyo where a great Karcass unit once stood." Mickie raised his bottle of Jack Daniels. "To Mona!"

"To Ripper!" echoed the group, albeit with a little less enthusiasm than the toast to Mickie Brass.

As Darien moved off to fix himself a drink, Mona stood before her team. The woman shuffled uncomfortably from foot to foot, unsure what to do with the praise.

"It was a nasty one, to be sure. But I've got some good news. The official tally isn't in yet, but that ticker should be worth five times or more the greatest scav ever completed on Kalderra. For some of you, that means you can buy out your contracts and still start a new life with some real stake money. For some of you, that could mean an extended vacation—as much sex and drugs as you can handle."

"Here, here!" chimed in Amos Bedford.

"For others, maybe it's simply a light at the end of this dark tunnel that is Kalderra. In any case, our expected payout is enough to change the lives of everyone in this room."

"Not Peetso and Salty," muttered Hinch, although his words were clearly heard throughout the room. Mona ignored the man and continued.

"We mourn Peetso Maddox and Salty Milton. And we thank Mickie and Amos and Chance and Hinch for the injuries that they suffered in this scav." Mona paused to collect her thoughts. "We all know what we signed up for. We all know why some of us were assigned to this post. We all understand the dangers that we face every time we venture out into a mori. Kalderra is an unforgiving planet of risk. But that risk is balanced by potential reward. This past scav, we risked much. We lost more. But the rewards that those in this room will reap balances the scales… even if it doesn't feel like it right now."

Darien brought Mona a drink. She took it, and held it high.

"Here's to Karcass Five. The best bloody group of Maggots that has ever been assembled. You all played your role. You all did your jobs. You all gave me the time I needed to pull the greatest ticker from the greatest flesher this planet's ever known. To Karcass Five!"

"To Karcass Five!" the unit shouted back. All save one.

As bottles were being tipped and glasses were being raised to lips, a voice cut through the break room.

"But we didn't, did we, Ripper?"

All eyes swung to Ricksin Hinch, a deep scowl carved in his tattooed face.

Mona turned to the Maggot. Her tone shifted.

"What was that, Hinch?"

"We didn't, did we?"

"We didn't what?"

Hinch paused for a moment, his gaze scanning the rest of the unit.

"We didn't *all* play our roles, did we? We didn't *all* do our jobs."

Mona placed her drink on the nearest table. Mickie resumed chewing on his cigar.

"What are you trying to say, Hinch?" There was a dangerous edge to the woman's voice.

"You know what I'm saying, Ripper."

"Maybe I don't."

Hinch put down his bottle of Yamazaki.

"What I'm *saying*—and what all the others are *thinking* —is that not *all of us* did our bloody jobs. In fact, one person in this room not only didn't do *one* job, but *two* jobs!"

The other Maggots looked nervously to each other as Hinch went on.

"Darien, that... boy toy of yours not only bailed on you as Second Kisser, but he abandoned his Keeper post when Mickie had to cover for him. And you know what happened, Ripper? Salty died! Salty died because that little puke didn't have the stomach for the job or the requisite loyalty to his team!"

Darien sipped his drink as Mona took a threatening step forward. Mickie swigged from his bottle of Jack.

"What proof do have of this, Maggot?"

"I was there, Ripper! I saw it all! Salty was holding the seven and eight! He was doing his job! All he needed was protection from his blindside! And when he needed it most, when the rotters made a push, who wasn't there? Wanna venture a guess, Ripper?" An index finger shot at Darien. "Him! I watched him dive into the krawler to hide, leaving us all to pick up the slack! Leaving us all to lose lives and faces and hands!"

Other Maggots began to slide toward the walls of the break room as Hinch's tirade continued.

"So, Susanoo take me, but I won't partake in a toast to the team alongside the very worm who left us all to die!"

"Calm down, mate," urged Mickie from his seat. "What's done is done."

"Nothing's done, Mickie," Hinch shot back. "Not as long as that weasel walks among us." Hinch stepped into the middle of the room. "You and me, boy! You will answer for your cowardice!"

As Darien retreated to the back corner, his shoulders touching both walls, Mona met Hinch in the room's center.

"He will answer for nothing," she stated icily. "He is a Maggot. Just like you, Hinch. And he will be respected."

Hinch spat upon the floor.

"He's no Maggot. He's no man. And he doesn't deserve to leave here untouched."

"But he will, Hinch."

"Fujin's ass, he will, Ripper!"

A tense, frozen silence fell over the room, interrupted only by side glances and nervous sips of whiskey. After a beat, Mona simply nodded and removed the light jacket she was wearing, tossing it to the cowering Darien Vance.

"Fine then, Hinch. You feel the itch of misplaced vengeance? Let me help you scratch it."

Hinch's face twisted in confusion beneath his tattoos.

"What're you going on about, Ripper?"

"It's simple really. You blame Darien, who's completely innocent, by the way. Which means you blame me. So I invite you to exact your revenge on me. Or at least try to. I'm tired of your empty words hiding behind that tough veneer."

"Veneer is it?"

"I don't see you readying yourself."

"I can't strike a Kisser. Mickie might be able to get away with it, but I'd be arrested by the Guntai. You know that, Ripper."

Mona nodded as she replied. "I know that, Hinch. That's why I'm declaring it now, before all of Karcass Five…" Mona's GLIM took in all of her subordinates. "For the next thirty minutes, I am *not* this unit's Kisser. I am *not* a Maggot. I am no one." Back to Hinch. "Need anything else for your sack to drop?"

Hinch returned a wicked grin as he removed his black bomber jacket, using his teeth to slip out of his right sleeve.

"Nothing else, Ripper. And I won't need thirty minutes."

"Good. Neither will I."

All the Maggots, realizing the unthinkable was happening, shuffled back to the far walls of the break room. Bedford limped over to Mickie as the Space Cowboy drank once more from his bottle.

"You gotta stop this, Mickie."

Mickie patted the concerned man on his arm.

"I will if it gets too bad, mate. But this had to happen. There's bad air here that needs to be cleared. And not just coming from Ricksin."

"This is insanity, Mickie."

"This is Kalderra, mate."

The two combatants squared up.

"This is on you, Darien!" Hinch shouted. "This beating is for you, you little pissant!"

Mona circled the man as she spoke. "You gonna talk, Maggot, or you gonna—"

Hinch launched a straight right hand—the only hand he had—connecting flush with Mona's face. The woman staggered backward, eating another right to her ribs, and then took a glancing blow from Hinch's forearm that spun her in place.

"This is the for the team," said Hinch through gritted teeth as he kicked out, sending Mona to the floor.

And then Hinch was atop her, between her legs, pummeling the woman with elbows and fist. Beneath her attacker, Mona cupped her palms to her ears, letting her arms absorb the worst of the blows.

Hinch, enraged and head swimming with alcohol, released unintelligible words as he continued his assault, every fourth strike slipping through Mona's defenses to score bloody hits.

But after thirty seconds of this, Hinch's attack began to slow, his breathing deepening and growing more rapid. Mona smiled through crimson teeth. And then she countered.

After a lazy right cross from Hinch, Mona threw up her right leg, placing it over the man's left shoulder. Her right foot found the crook of her left knee, and she locked it. And squeezed. And squeezed.

Hinch's face, despite the many dark lines of his tattoos, immediately turned a deep red as his arm and neck were brought together by Mona's legs. He squirmed in protest to no avail as the blood flow to his brain was restricted and then completely cut off by the choke. His right hand grasped at air, and he formed a multitude of curses before finally succumbing and going limp.

Mona, her face bloody and her rage now spiked, pushed the Maggot to one side and mounted him. Visions of her beautiful Darien being maimed by ugly, jealous goons unknowing of true love blinded her judgement and vaporized her restraint. She struck the unconscious man once, then twice, then three times, opening nasty gashes on Hinch's cheek, nose, and eyebrow. Mona raised up for a fourth blow, but her wrist was caught by something that felt as unyielding as iron.

Mona looked up, her dull brown eye full of tears, to find Mickie Brass staring down at her.

"That's enough, Mona. He's had enough, lass."

Mona stumbled to her feet and shook free of Mickie's grip.

"Get your junker hands off me! I'm fine!" A deep breath. "I'm fine. I'm sorry you all had to see that. I hope it doesn't spoil the rest of your party. Let's go, Darien."

Mona looked to the corner where Darien was. But he was not there.

"I think he went back to your room, Ripper," offered Betsy Sheppard, the blonde woman's voice thick with sympathy.

Mona wiped blood from her face with a bloody hand.

"Good. Good. He didn't need to see that." Mona stumbled back a step. "You're all rich now! It won't solve all your problems, but it should handle a good bit of them. Now, if you'll excuse me… I need to powder my nose."

Mona fell against a table on her way to the exit and was caught by Mickie, who helped her to the break room door. She subtlety leaned against the Space Cowboy for support.

"Benten's grin, Junker, what did I do?" she hissed between loosened teeth.

"Had to be done, lass. You can't control a unit if you don't control a unit."

"No more, Mickie. No more. I'm done. This last scav's enough to buy out Darien's contract and start a new life together. I don't need to control any of these Maggots anymore."

"I know, lass."

Mona freed herself from Mickie.

"Do you? Because you don't sound so happy for me. In fact, no one sounds happy for me."

"We are, Mona."

"Whatever."

The Kisser was halfway out the break room door when she turned back to Mickie.

"Make sure he's ok, Junker. Whatever he needs."

"Nothing the auto-doc and a few hours of rest can't fix."

Mona leaned into Mickie.

"No. I mean his hand. I don't want one of those outdated grippers the Syndicate gives the wounded. I want him to have the best. The bloody best, Junker!"

"Ok, Mona."

"Just tell Toro what he needs. Tell him to pull the yennies from my account."

"That's not necessary, Mona."

"Yes, it is, Junker. Yes, it is." A pause. "I'm not stupid."

"No one said you were, Mona."

"They didn't have to." Another pause. "Take care of it for me?"

"Of course, Mona."

"Thanks, Junker."

Mona exited the break room, her hand running down the hallway wall for support.

"Any time, Mona Ripple," mumbled Mickie Brass before turning back to the still-stunned Maggots. "What? Never seen a little scrap amongst friends? What planets are you bastards from? I see whiskey undrank, stories untold, and a beaten comrade left on the floor. Can we fix these things?!"

The shoulders of every Karcass Five member loosened under the Space Cowboy's words. Bottles were scooped up, conversations began anew, and Ricksin Hinch was helped off the floor, his wounds cleaned with whiskey—much of which found its way into the man's mouth.

And the Maggot celebration went on, the dreams of future selves pushing the party well past Kuyomi's fall.

Darien was still asleep when Mona woke shortly after the rise of Anohoshi, Kalderra's blue sun. Her bruised knuckles ached, as did her heart, making a restful sleep almost impossible.

The woman slipped into her casual Maggot jumpsuit, lovingly replaced the blanket on Darien's sleeping form, and made for the exit. As she did, her eyes floated to the wastebasket placed by the door, and something made her pause.

She reached into the bin and slowly removed the object that caught her attention. The origami heart had come apart a bit, so she carefully refolded the edges, wiping away a bit of food that had stuck to the paper.

Mona glanced at the figure on her bed. A question formed on her lips, but she swallowed it down and left the room quietly.

Some questions are too frightening to ask.

Mona, her head swimming, had forgotten that the paper heart was still in her hand as she entered the break room. A familiar, annoying voice made her jump, ripping the woman from her dark thoughts.

"What're you doing up, lass? I thought you'd sleep through the day, for sure."

"Benten's grin, Junker! I should be asking that of you. Did you even sleep?"

Mickie laughed as he cleared empty bottles from the tables.

"I'm too wound up to sleep, lass. Betsy brought out some kofun powder a few hours ago. Don't know how any of those kids are sleeping right now."

"Fifteen bottles of whiskey probably helped, Junker."

"Well, not for me. Anyway, if I wasn't gonna rest, I thought I might as well get a jump on cleaning this place up. Was hoping to get it done before you got up."

"Mission not accomplished, Space Cowboy."

"Yeah, I see that. What about you?"

"Couldn't sleep either. I also thought about getting an early start on the cleaning. How's Hinch doing?"

Mickie tossed an armful of bottles into the recycling container.

"Ah, he'll be fine. Says he wants to apologize to you today."

"It should be me to apologize."

"Well, you both can. Shouldn't be a hard conversation. It's easy to say sorry when you're both at fault."

"Yeah, I guess it is."

"What you got there?"

Mona followed Mickie's eyes and gave a start, realizing he had spotted the paper heart in her hand.

"It's nothing," she said, quickly tossing the item into the nearest trash bin. "Just some garbage I picked up on the way. Here, I'll help you."

"Appreciate it. Apologies if I'm not my normal chatty self, lass. I might not be in my bed, but that don't mean I'm fully here, either, if you catch my drift."

"Not hearing your voice is the greatest gift you could give me right now, Junker."

"Fair enough, Mona." Mickie began to collect glasses from around the break room as Mona retrieved a broom from the corner. "Oh, one thing before I forget it. Toro stopped by after you and Darien retired. Said for you to call on him sometime today."

"Bad news?"

Mickie shook his head. "Don't think so. The tubby bastard seemed quite pleased. Even brought us a bottle of rare Hibiki 40 Year. The way he was prancing around, must be something good on the horizon."

"Like him fattening his accounts off our efforts?"

Mickie smiled, showing his gold teeth.

"You gotta get that tooth fixed, Junker. You're rough enough looking without that big gap staring at everyone."

"I will, Mona."

They cleaned in silence for a while. Mona was wiping down the sticky tables when a thought struck her.

"Betsy, huh? Didn't peg her for a kofun user. Bedford, sure. But not Betsy."

"Lass, I've worked all over the galaxy," said Mickie as he began washing the dishes piled in the sink. "And there's one unyielding truth I've learned. People will never cease to surprise you—in good ways and bad. Best way to mitigate that risk is to not make judgments based on drapery."

"Drapery?"

"Yeah, the drapery. The bullshit exterior we show to the world to hide our true selves. Look past that and you'll minimize your surprises. And your disappointments."

Mona didn't respond, but she did start wiping the tables faster. And they resumed cleaning in silence.

———

"Benten's grin, Ripper. What time is it?"

Toro's face was puffier than usual, and the bags under his froggy eyes seemed a darker hue than normal. The fat man stood in the opening of his Colonel's quarters, a kimono lazily thrown around his heavy frame.

"It's late afternoon, Toro. You told me to call on you today."

"On the intercom, Ripper. And not at this hour. You Maggots weren't the only ones celebrating, you know."

"I can see that. Well, I'm here now."

"And I, unfortunately, can see that. Come on in, I suppose."

"You sure it's safe, Toro?"

"Yeah, yeah," replied the man as he shuffled back into his room. "My company for last night is long gone. How's that for appreciation? She could have least stayed around to make sure I didn't die in my sleep." Toro flopped onto his couch and looked up at Mona through bleary eyes. "Why are you here, again?"

Mona pressed the button to slide the door closed behind her.

"You told the junker to tell me to call on you, Toro. I'm not here to catch a glimpse of that stubby chinchin of yours. Speaking of which, can you tie that kimono closed a bit more?"

Toro looked down, startled, and drew the flaps together.

"Sorry, Ripper. My head's empty."

"And your sack drained. Now, why did you want to see me? This place stinks of cheap ramen and cheaper women."

"She wasn't cheap, I assure you."

"Then you overpaid. Now, what is it?"

Toro made a calming hand gesture as he burped up the previous night's festivities.

"The scav was the biggest ever."

"I already know this, Toro. I'm the one who pulled the damn ticker out of the damn flesher."

Toro waved a fat hand.

"No, you don't understand. It was *really* big. Gonna be giant payday for all of us. And more importantly…"

Toro's head began to fall as his eyes slid closed.

"Toro!"

The Colonel's head snapped back up, causing his double chin to jiggle.

"What?"

"What's more important than *our* big payday?"

Toro offered a greasy smirk. "The Countess's big payday?"

"The Countess?"

"Yeah, this scav put her over her yearly quota—a full ninety days ahead of schedule. Apparently, this earned her some high praise from the Syndicate Board."

"Benten's grin, Toro, what does that have to do with me?"

"Nothing, I suppose. Except that the Countess wants to show her appreciation. She's having a yakai—a soiree since I know your Japanese is shit— three nights from now at Ghool Tower. To celebrate her good fortune. She's extending a special invitation to Karcass Five—to all the Maggots, in fact. So there. That's why I needed to see you. And now, if you'll excuse me, I have some—"

"I'm not going."

Toro cut his eyes at Mona.

"What's that?"

"I'm not going, Toro. I'm done. As soon as those shitayen hit my account, I'm out of here. I'm buying out Darien's contract, and we're getting off this pile of rock."

"That's fine and all, Ripper. But you *will* be attending."

"Says who?"

"Says your Colonel! I don't have your resignation in my hand yet, and you haven't filed the paperwork or even negotiated for Maggot Vance's buyout. As of right now, you're still a Maggot and still under my command."

"Why would the Crimson Lady care if I attended her party or not?"

"Because she invited you, Ripper."

"So?"

Toro tossed his plump hands in frustration.

"So, you don't turn down an invitation from Desma Ghool. Men and women of much higher stature than us have disappeared into Karudera IV for far lesser slights."

"So, I have no choice?"

"You do not."

"Fujin's ass! Then why even ask me?!"

"I didn't ask you, Ripper. I told you."

Mona calmed herself. "Fine. But don't expect me to be prancing around the palace all wide-eyed like a serving girl at her first formal dance."

"I don't even know what that means, Ripper. Just don't do anything to offend. That's all that I ask."

"You ask too much, Toro."

"I usually do."

"You want to tell the others or you want me to?"

"You tell them, Ripper. I'm gonna slip into a nice, hot bath."

"Don't cook yourself."

"Of course not. Not when I have a yakai to look forward to. I wonder if the Countess is going to give me a special honor. Perhaps she'll—"

Mona spun away, ignoring Toro's vocal delusions of grandeur. Her metal fingertip pressed the door button, and it silently slid open.

"Ripper!"

"What, Toro?"

"Three nights from now. Smile. Nod. Accept your congratulations with a bow. Then we can talk about getting you and your boy off Kalderra."

"The Maggots aren't gonna be excited to hear that they have to hobnob with the imperial elite."

Toro laughed. "Oh, I think you'll be surprised, Ripper. I think you'll be surprised."

"Benten's grin, Mona! A party at Ghool Tower?! How wonderfully delightful!"

Darien paced around the room before finding his way to their shared closet.

"What will I wear?" the young man asked as he desperately rifled through clothing. "I have nothing to wear. I mean, nothing for this sort of event. There's going to be dignitaries and trade heads and who knows who else. I have nothing to wear, nothing at all." His blonde head shot out of the closet. "What are you going to wear, Mona?"

"I haven't given it any thought."

Darien scowled before returning to the closet.

"No thought? That's insane. Benten's grin, Mona, this is our big shot!"

"Big shot?"

"Yeah. Who knows, I could meet an investor, a designer that wants to work with me, someone who'll understand my vision for fashion."

"I think it's just gonna be a bunch of politicians, Syndicate reps, and traders there, my love."

"But you don't know that!" the man exclaimed from between hangers. "You don't know that!"

Mona breathed in deeply to calm herself.

"Darien. My heart. It's just a formal gathering."

"Exactly. And my formal attire is all out of date. I mean, no one's wearing lapels anymore. Oh, what was I thinking with that ensemble! No, no, none of this will do."

Mona opened her mouth but slammed it shut a beat later. Instead, she rolled her eyes, causing her GLIM to glitch, and spoke into the air.

"K-nex, call Colonel Toro." The sound of ringing could be heard over the speaker system as Darien continued to shuffle through his meager collection of outfits. After almost a minute of ringing—

"Fujin's ass, Ripper! I was just about to slip into my bath."

"What are we supposed to wear to the this stupid soiree, Toro? Most of us only have our Maggot overalls, and I'm not sure how that will—"

"Oh yeah, I forgot to tell you. Apparently the Countess agrees that your fashion sense won't gel with her own. The Tower is sending over some outfits today for all the Maggots."

"She wants to dress us in uniforms?!"

Toro released a deep sigh, and Mona could almost see the fat man rubbing his temples.

"More like she doesn't want you to feel out of place among all the pomp. I think it's quite sweet actually."

"Sweet and Desma Ghool are two things I've never heard mentioned together."

"Well, there's a first time for everything, Ripper. Nothing brings out the sweet in these Syndicate types like a mountain of yennies."

"Whatever, Toro. One less thing for me to worry about, I suppose."

"There you go, finally looking on the bright side. Now, if you don't mind, Ripper, I'd like to get back to—"

Mona hung up with a blink.

"Did you hear that, my love? Good news."

Darien was now sitting on the edge of the bed, rubbing his chin absently.

"I suppose. New clothes from the Countess is certainly welcome. But how will they fit? I prefer a slimmer profile, you know. I wonder if I can make adjustments." Darien looked up at Mona. "Do you think the Countess would mind if I made some adjustments? Made it my own?"

Mona leaned down, cupped Darien's face in her hands, and placed a gentle kiss on his mouth.

"You do whatever you want, my love. If it makes you happy, you change it however you see fit. I don't give a flesher fart what the Countess thinks. Soon, we'll be off this rock and starting our new lives. No one can steal that from us."

Darien smiled, and his green eyes sparkled.

"Oh, how wonderful!" The young man jumped up walked to one of two chests in the room. "I have a sewing kit in here somewhere," he said as he opened several drawers at once. "Two days… that should be enough. Yes, I can do it. Oh, where is that bloody thing… Found it!" Darien gently placed the container on the top of the bureau. He turned back to Mona. "You'll tell me as soon as the clothes come in, won't you, Mona? I'll need to get started as soon as possible to create something truly my own."

"I promise, my love."

Darien danced in place, and Mona smiled at his joy.

"Oh, this is going to be greatest night ever, Mona! Just the best!"

"Until the night we leave this planet together, my love."

Darien was quiet for a moment, the young man's thoughts already on his outfit for the yakai. He noticed Mona staring at him.

"What was that? Oh, yes, of course, Mona. The best night until our escape. Of course, that will trump all others. Of course, it will."

Darien took Mona in his arms, kissing her neck as a moan escaped her lips. Her GLIM glitched with the rush, but her dull brown eye remained fixed on the sewing kit.

"I feel like a high-brow turd is this getup," complained Hinch as Karcass Five rode in one of the two imperial motorcoaches that had arrived to deliver the Maggots to Ghool Tower.

"You don't need that getup to look like a turd, Hinch," teased Neela Patel. "I, for one, feel like a VIP," said the woman as she ran her fingers down her silk furisode denoting a single woman. Simple and cream-colored like all the other supplied outfits, the kimono had long sleeves that Neela had neatly folded over her lap to avoid wrinkles. "But how did she know that I wasn't married?"

"Maggots ain't marriage material," shot back Hinch. "We're lucky to pay for a warm body next to us every now and then."

Neela shrugged, unable to argue the tattooed man's point.

"Still, quite presumptuous if you ask me."

Colby Chambers, Kisser of Karcass One, cut in from a few seats down. "They got files on all of us, kid. Probably know more about us than we do. They know you ain't married."

"If they knew all that," said Amos Bedford, "then they could gotten our sizes right." He pulled at his montsuki kimono. "This thing's swimming on me."

"It's supposed to be worn loose," responded Chambers, the Karcass leader looking dignified with his trimmed mustache and slicked back silver hair.

"Not this damned loose," complained Bedford. "Can't even make out my muscular frame through all these layers."

"Then she's done all of us a favor," joked Betsy Sheppard, the woman delighted by how well her cream furisode complemented her cropped blonde hair. "Ripper, don't you just love yours?"

Mona took note of the timer within her GLIM. *Four hours. This will all be over in four hours.*

"Ripper?"

Mona snapped back to reality. "I don't like the sleeves. Could catch on something if I try to throw a punch."

The group fell silent, except for Hinch, who chuckled loudly to himself.

"I still think it's too damn loose," repeated Bedford. "Chance! How's yours feel?"

The young man glanced down at his own montsuki.

"Fine, I guess. I've never worn any fancy clothes before."

Bedford scoffed. "Shit, yours looks loose, too. In fact, all the fellas look like they're wearing their daddies' clothes. Except for Biggs, but there ain't an outfit in the galaxy that would look big on that hill of a man." Bedford noticed Darien for the first time. "Darien! Man, why your montsuki fit so well? Looks like you were born in it."

Darien grinned. "I tailored it."

"Of course, he did," grumbled Hinch, not loud enough for Mona to hear.

Bedford's eyes narrowed as he studied Darien further.

"And why yours got all those little flourishes. Man, yours got red stitching and highlights?"

"Crimson, actually," answered Darien.

"Yeah, crimson highlights. Where're my highlights? I like to be high-lit."

"I added those, as well."

"You better hope the Countess doesn't take umbrage with your alterations," said the weasel-faced Vasily Pappas, Kisser of Karcass Two. Still upset about his unit being skipped over for the recent scav, it wasn't hard to guess how Pappas hoped Darien's changes would be received.

Darien smiled smugly. "It's said that the Countess is a woman of exceedingly good taste. I'm sure she won't mind."

Pappas snickered. "Good taste. Yeah, that's the skinny on Desma Ghool."

The conversation died down as the motorcoaches passed through a shimmering dome of light and entered Karudera City. While some of the Maggots may have visited the outskirts of Kalderra's lone metropolis once or twice, for most it was their first glimpse of the bustling capital.

Skyscrapers soaked in neon light sped by overhead as holographic images depicting news, fashion, pop culture, and anything else catered to the wealthy filled every inch of free space. Pairs of impossibly attractive women passed through the city on electric rickshaws as men in elaborate suits sauntered to and fro with ornate canes, oblivious to the horrors that resided across the planet.

Ellis Sadler whistled as he stared out through the windows, his dark gypsy eyes wide.

"This not Shonin Crossways," he said in awe, referencing Kalderra's other major settlement, a city more akin to Maggot sensibilities with its population of mid-level traders, blue collar workers, and military personnel.

"You can say that again, gypsy," commented Bedford, Karudera City's opulence growing as they delved deeper into the capital.

Minutes passed in stunned silence. And then—

"Benten's grin's. There she is."

At Sheppard's words, all the Maggots leaned against their windows to see the great spire looming ahead of them, a shadowed spike against Kuyomi, Kalderra's unusually large, violet moon.

"That's the home of the Crimson Lady," Sheppard went on. "It's certainly a palace fit for a queen."

"Or a bitch," said Mona Ripple.

Sheppard shrugged without removing her eyes from Ghool Tower. "Either way, it's magnificent."

"Agreed," said a wonderstruck Darien Vance.

The home of the Crimson Lady was simultaneously beautiful and terrifying. If any of the Maggots knew their ancient history, they may have referred to the tower as techno-gothic.

Mixed in with the pointed arches, flying buttresses, and ornate decorations were massive windows made of prism glass displaying moving scenes that changed every half minute. A depiction of the Morishitas' galactic conquest was followed by the image of a twenty-meter-tall

Desma Ghool, the woman smiling as cherry blossoms gently blew around her on an imaginary breeze.

Lights were embedded throughout the tower, creating a hazy glow the color of deep crimson. They dimmed and brightened, making the tower appear as a throbbing organ freshly ripped from a still-living body.

The effect was most likely a warning to anyone thinking of crossing the Syndicate or Desma Ghool. Or maybe it was simply created for wicked fun.

Dozens of surveillance drones hovered around the tower like wasps, each equipped with a high-resolution camera for eyes and highly lethal Shita-blaster for a stinger.

The imperial motorcoaches slowed to a stop before the extravagant entryway, where pointed arches outlined massive double-doors ten meters in height. Guntai stood at loose attention around the perimeter, looking typically smug in their black uniforms. Closer to the entrance to Ghool Tower, however, resided a different kind of soldier.

Taller and broader than the Guntai, the Chi o Mamoru Mono, better known as the ChoMM, looked like frightening statues. Unmoving and unblinking, their eyes peered from beneath somen masks to hide their identities. But unlike traditional somen masks, which were made of straw, these were printed using the most advanced carbon fiber—light, flexible, and nearly indestructible.

Although the ChoMM bodies remained frozen, the dark eyes beneath scanned left and right, all eventually settling upon the Maggots as they began to exit the coaches.

Gazes drifted upward as the Karcass units settled before Ghool Tower. One of the rose windows was projecting Desma Ghool riding a midnight stallion bareback through a field of golden flowers.

"Guess we gotta give her credit for one thing," said Bedford as he watched the scene unfold high above him. "At least she ain't even trying to pretend that she's one of us plebs. I respect the honesty if not the taste."

"Shut up, you fool," hissed Colonel Toro as he smoothed down his silks before wiping his sweaty brow with a handkerchief. Unlike most of the other Maggots, Toro's girth used up every centimeter of his montsuki's fabric. "All you Maggots—and I'm talking to you Kissers, as well. I need you to watch three things. Watch your manners. Watch your mouths. And watch your colleagues' manners and mouths."

"Colleagues? Is that what we are?" asked Hinch, the man's face looking as if he smelled something rotten.

Toro spun on the man. "You're what I tell you you are, Hinch. This is a very big night for me—for us—and I can't have anything go wrong. Ripper! Get your man in line!"

"Yep," replied Mona, although in truth she hadn't heard what Toro had said. She was too enamored with the young man standing next to her, his soft hand in hers.

Darien had never looked better. His montsuki hugged his lithe body, and his angelic blonde hair was brushed cleanly back except for one thick strand that dangled lazily in front of his handsome face.

Mona tightened her grip on Darien's hand, reminding herself that he was real, that the most beautiful man on Kalderra was hers.

She had never felt more proud.

A small, tinny voice removed Mona from her schoolgirl thoughts.

"Welcome, welcome! Welcome our most honored guests from our distinguished Karcass units," announced the little man.

Dressed in the traditional attire of imperial household officials known as a sokutai, the diminutive man immediately stunk of self-importance in his layers of black, red, and white. He took a moment to readjust his kanmuri, a black-lacquered, silk headdress with a long pennon.

"I am Grand Chamberlain Shinsuke," he said as his narrow eyes danced side to side beneath thick, gold-framed glasses. "The Countess is most excited for this evening, an opportunity for her to demonstrate her sincerest appreciation for the dangerous work that you do on behalf of the greater Imperium." Shinsuke swung his flat, ivory ritual baton toward the grand double-doors. "Please enter and enjoy the yakai. For this evening, as long as Kuyomi hangs heavy before the stars, Ghool Tower is yours. Eat, drink, dance, and be merry."

The Grand Chamberlain's words rang empty in Mona's ears, a show forced upon a great actor accustomed to more deserving audiences.

Toro stepped forward.

"We thank you, Grand Chamberlain, for such a—"

But Shinsuke had already begun moving toward the entryway, leaving Toro to cut his planned speech short and shuffle off after the little man.

The Maggots quietly chuckled.

As the group approached Ghool Tower, the massive doors suddenly vanished.

"Benten's grin," commented Mickie from behind Mona and Darien. "She's got front doors made of bloody wave matter. How much money are we actually making this sheila?"

Toro's big head snapped back from the front of the line, the Colonel's froggy eyes staring daggers at the Space Cowboy. Mickie simply held up his tattooed hands in mock apology.

The ChoMM guardians carefully studied the Maggots as the group passed between them. Black eyes took in every movement from beneath their frightening masks. Athletic bodies remained coiled beneath armored, blood-red skinsuits, and hands twitched on the handles of sheathed, nano-edged katanas.

Mickie Brass saw one of the ChoMM noting the star atop each of his hands.

"Not to worry, mate. I left that life behind. I'm just a lowly servant of the Syndicate now. I live to enrich the Imperium."

The ChoMM did not respond as Mickie passed him, even when the Space Cowboy mouthed a kiss before offering a toothy gold smile.

"I don't think he believed you, Mickie," commented Bedford as the men crossed the threshold into Ghool Tower.

"Well, mate, he wouldn't be very good at his job if he did."

When the last Maggot had entered the home of the Crimson Lady, the entranceway shimmered momentarily, leaving two solid doors of impossible strength behind.

Looking around, Mona was almost floored by her surroundings, senses assaulted by an onslaught of sights, smells, and sounds, all of which she found offensive. She turned to Darien to make a snarky remark but stopped short.

Darien looked around in wonder, his green eyes almost as large as his smile.

"Can you believe this place, Mona?! It's like a dream."

"More like a nightmare," the woman shot back.

Darien flinched as if he'd been wounded.

"I'm here with you. How can it be a nightmare?"

Mona cursed herself for her careless words and placed an arm around Darien's slim waist.

"It can't be, my love. You're right. I'm just not used to such extravagance."

"You see extravagance, Mona. I see the spoils of success."

"Maybe you're right, my love." She squeezed, bringing Darien closer to her. "But you know, of all the treasures that I see here, I don't see any as irreplaceable as the man now in my arms. And that makes me the most successful woman on Kalderra."

Darien leaned over and kissed Mona Ripple as the couple moved forward through Ghool Tower.

Mickie Brass silently marched on behind them.

The Grand Ballroom was an obscene show of status and wealth. Serving drones silently floated around the massive space, most holding trays piled high with exotic meats, fruits, cheeses, and other delicacies from across the galaxy. Others carefully balanced crystal glassware containing champagne delivered straight from Chikyu. In each corner of the room, long tables were staffed by robot bartenders, expert mixologists capable of crafting any concoction known to man.

To the left of the entrance, a large stage had been erected, housing a menagerie of eclectic musicians playing instruments both familiar and alien. The sounds filling the room were simultaneously haunting and hypnotic, lending weight to the unusual scene laid bare before the Maggots.

Syndicate members stood around smugly in tight groups, each wearing expensive suits of dark purple, nano-carbon fabric. As they sipped from their champagne glasses or brought thick cigars to their lips, the kamon, or crest, of the Morishita Clan—a bonsai tree encircled by an octagon of bamboo—could be clearly seen tattooed on each left hand, the glowing ink acting as a warning beacon to all who would approach. Their eyes shone a digital blue deep within the irises, proof that every face, conversation, and movement was being recorded.

Elsewhere, Gashira from the Merchant Web flitted from one conversation to the next, putting their honeyed tongues to good use. As they moved around the Grand Ballroom like flower-seeking bees, their multi-hued cape coats, all made of the finest silks, billowed behind them. The Gashira's bright colors were meant to attract and caution, the unvoiced promise of either great wealth or greater trouble.

Among these titans swam courtesans of every shape, size, and color, each more striking than the next. Young men in tight breeches and crop tops laughed loudly at jokes while the women, draped in thin dresses highlighting every curve, coyly giggled at whispered remarks, their manicured fingers covering painted lips.

On the edges, powerful women dressed sharply in houmongi kimonos studied the scene like raptors watching a dying animal from the sky.

"I guess it's not so formal an occasion for these bitches," whispered Neela Patel to Betsy Sheppard, drawing another dirty look from Colonel Toro as the Maggots stood at the entrance like hesitant party crashers.

The Grand Chamberlain returned to the group and gestured to the center of the ballroom with his ivory baton.

"Please, please, come in and make yourselves at home. After all, this yakai was put together in part to honor you. Now is not the time to be shy. You're amongst friends." The little man's face did not appear as welcoming as his words despite his best efforts.

The Maggots pressed forward, officially entering the party, Colonel Toro boldly leading the way.

Bedford drifted down to walk with Mickie.

"*In part* to honor us? I thought we were the whole bloody point."

Mickie snickered.

"This lot only honors themselves, mate. Look around you. Look at who's here. There's more at play this evening. And we ain't even pawns in this game."

Bedford frowned as he limped on. "Well, that doesn't make me feel very festive."

Mickie clapped his friend on the shoulder. "Sorry, mate. Don't pay attention to me. We're far enough under this lot's radar that we don't exist. Get a drink. Get a dozen. Get a girl on your arm. Have fun. We're no threat. And even this collection of human waste can be civil if you don't have anything they want. Which we don't."

"No offense, Mickie, but I'm gonna hang out with the gypsy for a while."

"I don't blame you, mate."

The Maggots formed into small groups at the Grand Ballroom's edges, some grabbing food and champagne from serving drones while others headed for the nearest bar.

Darien, his green eyes wide and his mouth frozen in a toothy smile, plucked two glasses of champagne from a passing drone, offering one to Mona.

"Look at this, Mona. Beautiful people wearing beautiful clothes surrounded by beautiful music." He turned to her. "Now, *this* is the life I want. For us."

Mona downed her champagne in single gulp. "And we'll have it, my love. As soon as the scav reward comes in, we can have anything you want."

"Oh, Mona, I love you so much. You make me so happy."

"I hope so. Because I can't imagine life without you."

The young man kissed her on the forehead. "No need to. I'm not going anywhere."

The yakai went on for an hour, the Maggots filling their bellies with food and booze. Every now and then, a Syndicate member or Gashira would wander over, offering measured congratulations before returning to those of their station. Courtesans joined the Karcass units, their heavily perfumed bodies sliding easily beneath arms or around shoulders, pleasing none more than Toro. Soon, almost every Maggot was attached to a beautiful companion.

Mickie shook off a hand at his waist, much to the chagrin of a striking young girl who couldn't have been older than fifteen.

"Do I not please you, sir?" she asked in a soft voice. "Would you rather a young man join you? I can—"

"You can run to the bar and get me a whisky, lass," said Mickie. "That would bring me great pleasure. Do they have Jack Daniels here?"

"We have everything, sir. Including much more expensive brands. Perhaps I could interest you in—"

"Just the Jack, lass. And make it a triple. And thank you. You're doing a bang-up job."

The teenager bowed seductively. "Perhaps we can talk more after you've had your… Jack."

When the girl floated away, Mona approached, leaving Darien to further gawk at the festivities.

"Jeez, Junker. You can't even sweet talk a girl paid to be sweet-talked to."

"She's a child. And I'm in no mood."

"Toro doesn't seem to mind."

Mickie and Mona turned as one to see Toro surrounded by three young women. One of them fed him a long, shrimp-like creature as the other two ran slim fingers over his considerable girth.

"Toro doesn't have a mind. Just a groin."

"In any case, Junker, everyone else is trying to have fun. You know fun, don't you? It's what people have when they're about to be rich."

"You don't appear to be having fun, Mona."

Mona shrugged. "I don't need to have fun tonight, Space Cowboy. I have a lifetime of that ahead of me. I doubt you do, so you'd better make the most of this evening."

"Ok, Mona."

"Ah, your girl's back with your drink. May it soothe that junker soul of yours. Now, if you'll excuse me, I have a date to attend to. He's the most gorgeous man here, in case you missed it."

Mona left, falling back into Darien's arms a moment later.

"I didn't miss it," Mickie muttered.

"Miss what, sir?" asked the teen courtesan as she handed Mickie his drink. "Miss me? Already?" Silence. "Sir?"

Mickie downed his whiskey in one gulp.

Just as the yakai was rounding into full swing with lightened heads and loosened hands, a massive gong reverberated throughout the Grand Ballroom. The band immediately went silent, followed by the dissipation of conversation.

All eyes swung to the back of the ballroom, where Grand Chamberlain Shinsuke stood before a massive spiral staircase dominating the space.

"Ladies and gentlemen, it is my greatest honor to present the hostess of this evening's wondrous festivities—the Countess of Kalderra, Desma Ghool!"

On cue, the band launched into an updated version of Gagaku, the traditional court music of old Japan. Slow, stately, and regal, the strings, flutes, and drums filled the ballroom silence as a figure rounded into sight on the ornate spiral staircase.

Breaths were held as the tall figure floated down like a phantom, escaping the shadows and coming into full view. A collective gasp, drowned out by the music, was felt and shared across the room.

Wearing a junihitoe kimono, Desma Ghool paused halfway down the stairwell, pausing to admire the galactic players that she had brought together. All twelve layers of her outfit were the same shade of crimson, and she stared out from beneath a red hannya mask, complete with twin horns, oversized eyes, and fanged mouth.

Standing above some of the most powerful figures in the galaxy, Desma Ghool struck every bit the figure of a demon queen.

Satisfied that all gazes were upon her, the Countess resumed her fluid descent. Arriving at the bottom, she paused once more, her terrifying stare sweeping back and forth to take in all those in attendance as assistants rushed from the shadows to place a gilded stool next to Ghool. The Grand Chamberlain stepped onto the stool, bringing the small man even with the large woman, and carefully removed the hannya mask.

Desma Ghool greeted her audience with a ruby-encrusted smile, and all broke into exuberant applause. The Countess had crimson eyes that matched her red lipstick and butterfly eyebrows. Her alabaster skin, while flawless, looked to be pulled impossibly tight, adding to the Crimson Lady's dramatic and intimidating visage.

Marshall Chance, once-handsome face still bandaged, leaned in closely to Mickie as not to be overheard.

"I think I liked the mask better."

"She's still wearing a mask, mate," replied Mickie, and the young man simply chuckled in response.

One crimson glance toward the band, and the music faded away along with all other noise in the ballroom.

"Welcome one and all," Desma Ghool declared in a commanding voice that rolled across the cavernous space. "Tonight, I have brought you all here to Kalderra, under the violet gaze of Kuyomi, to celebrate the most profitable period in this planet's history. Later, I'll share another announcement that will permanently alter Kalderra's place in the galaxy." The Countess smiled wryly. "But for now... celebrate! Touch what looks soft! Taste what looks delectable! And give yourself over to your most primal of desires! Ghool Tower is yours!"

"Here, here!" cried out a voice.

"To the Countess!" called another, and a great cheer went up for the Crimson Lady.

Desma Ghool held out her hands, showcasing long, red-lacquered nails as the band redoubled its efforts, playing an upbeat tune that quickly transformed the center of the Grand Ballroom into a dance floor, with courtesans pulling even the stodgiest of drunken elite in with their youthful gyrations.

The alcohol flowed once more, and the Maggots settled into loose revelry away from those of high society, content with their food, drinks, and courtesan attention.

Toro, Sheppard, Bedford, and Hinch pawed at beautiful women. Biggson Baft and Ellis Sadler ate enough to feed an army. Patel giggled as a young man nibbled on her ear. Marshall Chance, even with his face half covered, playfully fought off two especially young female courtesans. Mickie Brass stood alone pouring glass after glass of whiskey down his throat. But Mona Ripple was truly in heaven.

Held tightly in Darien's arms, the couple swayed to the music, their hips locked together, stopping only long enough to feed the other an exotic fruit or slip in another glass of champagne. Soon, Mona was again lost in her lover's green eyes. They were the only two souls in the world, surrounded by an ocean of people who didn't matter. This would mark the beginning of their new life together, one that would—

"And here they are! My Maggots! Now, why would my guests of honor seclude themselves?"

As one, the Maggots turned to find the Countess, regal and terrifying, standing at the edge of their celebration. Courtesans were shrugged off as the Karcass units quickly fell into a makeshift line. Colonel Toro, mustering what little confidence he had, stepped forward to greet their host. The rotund man bowed so low that Mona was sure he would fall over. But Toro surprised her, managing to pull up with a wide grin splitting his fat face.

"My Countess! I am Kenji Toro, Colonel of the Karcass regiment. We could not be more grateful for your generous invitation to this yakai... at your home, no less! We are truly honored. I have no words for—"

"Of course I know of you, Colonel. I wouldn't be much of a countess if I didn't know the name of the man overseeing Kalderra's most lucrative export, now would I?"

Toro looked as if he had swallowed a bug.

"Certainly you would, my Countess. I did not mean to infer that you did not. I was merely—"

Desma Ghool waved a long-fingered hand.

"Calm down, Toro. I'm merely having some fun." Ghool's crimson eyes scanned the Maggots. "Now, I'm delighted to have all of the Karcass units in my home, but I'm especially eager to meet those who managed to pull off this most recent scav. They are, after all, one of the reasons for the evening's festivities."

Toro motioned the male Kissers, including Colby Chambers and Vasily Pappas, back. Pappas looked ready to throttle the Colonel.

"Five step forward," announced Toro, bringing the group forward a step. The fat man pointed to the lined up Maggots with a flourish. "My Countess, I present to you Karcass Five, my most elite unit."

"My, my," said Ghool as she approached. "Some of them are a little worse for wear, are they not?"

Toro cleared his throat before answering. "It was a most difficult scav, my Countess. The largest and most challenging in the history of Kalderra."

Ghool continued to float forward.

"Well, that's why their compensation's going to be so great."

"We lost two good men, my Countess."

Ghool's demeanor went unchanged.

"And a lot of good meeba meat from what I understand, Colonel." Toro wobbled in place. "But I'm sure tough decisions had to be made. I mourn your losses, Colonel. But good for the survivors, no doubt. Less to share."

"Of course, my Countess," Toro responded meekly.

The Crimson Lady floated to the far end of the line, where Ellis Sadler stood.

"Thank you for your hard work," said Ghool. "You've made your Countess proud."

The mustached man bowed awkwardly. "I put on show for dough."

Ghool's too-tight face twisted. "Come again?"

"He's a gypsy, my Countess," Toro cut in. "Words aren't his strong suit."

"But good at kill bugs," Sadler added with a smile.

Ghool offered a smile that didn't touch her eyes. "How charming."

She moved past Baft, Sheppard, Patel, and Bedford, offering words to each, before stopping at Marshall Chance.

"Ahh, a young one here."

"Yes, ma'am. I mean, Countess."

"My dear boy, it looks like you had a number done on your face."

"Yes, Countess. A flesh beetle got me good."

Ghool studied Chance's face, making the young man shift his weight from one foot to the other.

"A pity. It looks like those rotters ruined a once-beautiful face. Well, I thank you for your sacrifice, in any case."

"Thank you, Countess."

Ghool moved on to Mickie Brass, who stood like a statue, his hands held behind his back.

"And look at this specimen. Now *this* is what I thought all Maggots looked like —rugged, no nonsense. The type of man unafraid of battle." She noticed his many scars. "The type of man accustomed to battle." Ghool's ruby teeth appeared. "Yes, I can see why some of my courtesans have their lips puckered for this one. Not my cup of tea, but please enjoy yourself this evening."

"Countess," Mickie replied tersely with a nod.

After a quick word with Neela Patel and Ricksin Hinch—and an insensitive joke about *lending a hand*—Ghool reached Mona Ripple. As she did, Toro spoke up.

"And this is Ripper, my Countess. She is the Kisser of Karcass Five, responsible for the extraction of the ticker."

"A woman leading men? Now, that is something I know a fair bit about. Kisser? I must admit that's not a term I'm familiar with."

Toro answered for Mona. "It is said that anyone who enters the kameeba and touches the ticker is kissing death, my Countess. There is little room for error."

"Kissing death?" Ghool rolled the words around in her mouth. "I quite like that." To Mona, "I see we have even more in common… Ripper. I, too, have kissed death on many an occasion. Of course, I've kissed many other things as well." Toro forced out a laugh. "I see I owe you a debt of gratitude, Kisser Ripper. Your efforts have put me over my yearly quota well ahead of schedule."

"Just doing my job, Countess," Mona said flatly.

"Yes, yes, everyone is doing their job. But not everyone's job entails dancing with death every time they do it."

Mona straightened.

"Death dances around all of us, Countess. We have no choice but to dance with it lest we be danced upon."

Crimson eyes narrowed.

"My, oh my, what a fatalist view. You know, I used to be a fatalist. But then I learned that power gives you choice. I hope you're able to discover that yourself one day."

Mona bowed.

"As do I, Countess."

Ghool continued to examine Mona.

"Ripper? I like it. It announces the power hiding within such a drab exterior. In fact—"

The Crimson Lady's jaw fell open as her eyes slid from Mona to Darien Vance standing beside her. A wicked grin formed on her tight face as the Kisser before her was quickly forgotten.

"Benten's grin, who is this delicious-looking young man?" asked Ghool as she slid over.

Darien shrunk under her crimson stare.

"Darien Vance, my Countess. It is a most wonderful pleasure to meet you."

"No, no. The wonderful pleasure is all mine. Is that the montsuki that we had sent over?"

Darien grimaced as if a knife had been placed at this throat. He forced out the words.

"It is, my Countess. But I did some... alterations." The Countess continued to study his montsuki. "I didn't mean any offense," he stammered. "I just wanted to get the fit right."

"Is that all you did?"

Darien's green eyes shot over to Mona, a drowning man grasping for help. Mona took his hand in hers. Ghool noted it.

"No, Countess. I also added some stitching. I didn't mean to offend. Really. Had I known—"

A sharp nail found the young man's lips, silencing him.

"I think it's brilliant. Why shouldn't a beautiful man wear an equally beautiful montsuki?" Ghool ran her fingers over the silk. "And you did this all yourself? Silk is exceeding difficult to work with."

Darien straightened, finding strength in the Countess's kind words.

"I did, my Countess. Fashion is my true passion. I hope to be a famous designer someday."

Mona's hand tightened on Darien's as Ghool closed the distance between her and the young man.

"Well, with *that* face and *those* eyes and the talent to match, I can see you going very far, Darien Vance. With the right backing, of course."

"That is my dream, my Countess."

The Crimson Lady's tight face shifted. Mona could make out strange folds of skin at the woman's hair and jawline.

"Dreams? Yes, I remember those. Careful with dreams, Darien Vance. They are a katana with two edges."

"Of course, my Countess."

Ghool's eyes drifted from Darien's face to his chest, down his right arm to where he held Mona Ripple's hand in his.

"And you have a woman, I see."

"He does," answered Mona, hoping to sound confident despite a swelling feeling of nausea.

Ghool looked from Mona to Darien, a viper considering two mice.

"An odd pair if I ever saw one," said Ghool. "But… I suppose the heart wants what the heart wants, does it not?"

"The heart wants what completes it. And it doesn't let go once found."

Ghool's red eyes met Mona's challenging stare. The two women locked eyes, and a complete conversation took place over several silent beats. Maggots shared uneasy glances as Toro nervously smoothed his kimono over his large belly.

Finally, Desma Ghool broke the spell, gliding backward.

"Well," she declared, "I want to again thank all of the Maggots, but especially Karcass Five, for a job well done. You have made your Countess proud." Another heavy beat passed. "Now, all this talk about dancing with death has made me hungry for a dance myself." She held out a long hand, the jewels surrounding her wrist catching the light. "Darien Vance, could I trouble you for a dance?"

"He's spoken for," Mona blurted out before she could wrangle the words. Toro looked ready to pass out.

Ghool offered a wicked smile.

"My dear, I'm not asking him for a kidney. I have plenty of servants from whom I could procure one. I'm simply asking for a dance. I'm sure he'll save many more for you."

Mona could feel her palms releasing sweat.

"It's not that, Countess. It's just—"

"Just what?" Ghool's smile had vanished.

Darien stepped forward, his hand sliding from Mona's. He took Ghool's hand.

"I'm honored, my Countess."

Ghool's ruby-encrusted teeth reappeared.

"See, that wasn't so hard, now was it? Don't worry, Kisser Ripper. I'll get him back to you in one piece."

Desma Ghool glided toward the center of the Grand Ballroom, Darien in tow.

"Darien!" Mona called out, and the young man looked back, worry marring his perfect face.

Toro quickly stepped to Mona. She could feel his alcohol-stained breath on her ear.

"Fujin's ass, Ripper!" he angrily whispered. "Are you trying to get us all killed?! Over a bloody dance?! I've seen some stupid stuff in my life, but this is—"

"If you value your tongue, Toro, you'll stop speaking to me."

Sensing no lie in the woman's words, Toro did just that.

The Maggots, relieved to be free of the notorious countess, reached for the nearest serving drones. Mickie Brass approached Mona and handed her a glass of whiskey.

"Here, lass. Looks like you could use one."

Mona accepted and downed the drink.

"The gall of that bitch."

"Quiet, lass. Soon this will all be over."

The center of the room cleared as Desma Ghool entered the makeshift dance floor with her chosen partner. The music fell, drawing all eyes to the two figures standing alone.

The Countess waited a few moments, ensuring all attention was on her, before motioning to the band.

A hypnotic flute melody began to play, layered over booming drums, crisp snares, and rapid hi-hats. Heads began to bob to the entrancing beat.

Desma Ghool spun, and Darien Vance matched her. In short order, they were twirling across the emptied floor, Ghool gliding as Darien showcased complex footwork. The Countess's back twisted and bent. Darien's hips seemed to move independent of the rest of his body. Ghool placed her hands around his neck. Darien's hands found the Countess's waist.

"Look at 'em go," commented Neela Patel, mesmerized by the beautiful show of skill.

Hinch snickered. "Of course he can dance like a princess."

Mona shot a look the tattooed man's way, and Hinch's hands went up in mock surrender.

"Sorry, Ripper."

Mickie leaned closer. "You ok, lass?"

"I'm fine, Junker!" she snapped back.

As the other Maggots returned to their chit-chat, drinks, and courtesans, Mona stood like a statue, watching Desma Ghool and Darien Vance.

Ghool said something in the young man's ear, and he returned a laugh and a smile.

A bloody smile! And what could be so bloody funny?!

As the song slowed, the two dancers drew closer, foreheads almost touching. Ghool placed her chin on Darien's shoulder. Another turn, and the Countess was facing Mona, staring at her over the shoulder of the Kisser's one true love. That wicked red smile grew larger, threatening to split the Crimson Lady's tight face in two.

I'm gonna kill that bitch. I'm gonna grab the nearest bottle, break it over Toro's fat head, and ram the end into that bitch's—

Mona's raging internal monologue was cut short by roaring applause as the dance ended. Ghool bowed in false appreciation before motioning to Darien, who bowed even deeper. The Countess placed a kiss on the young man's cheek and said something that made him blush before melting away into the sea of onlookers. The ballroom's center refilled with new dancers.

Mona sprung toward Darien as soon as the man returned, burying him in a desperate embrace.

"Are you ok, my love? Oh, how terrifying for you."

"Mona, you're crushing me," he said with a gasp, and she released him.

"Are you ok?" she repeated.

"I think so. It was pretty scary, but I think I did alright. She's actually quite a good dancer."

"Well, it's over. The bitch had her fun, and now you're mine again. Let's find a quiet corner and ride out the rest of this horrible spectacle."

"We can't do that, Mona."

"And why is that?" she demanded, more harshly than intended.

Darien grinned, his green eyes sparkling.

"Because I promised to save you a dance."

Mona melted.

"Oh, Darien, my love."

Late into the yakai, the music trailed off, and a hush fell over the attendees as Desma Ghool once more commanded the center of the Grand Ballroom. This time, however, it was not to dance. It was to deliver a speech.

"My distinguished guests," the Countess began, her voice booming across the room, now amplified by a hidden microphone and unseen speakers. "I hope you have enjoyed this evening. And don't worry; I'm not kicking you out. I simply want to make a couple of announcements before brains become too fogged with drink.

"The first is what brings us here this evening. The second will change the trajectory of Kalderra forever."

A low murmur broke out amongst the Syndicate members and Gashira. Ghool continued.

"First, I want to take this opportunity to celebrate our Maggots, especially Karcass Five, making this the most profitable year in Kalderra's relatively young history. With energy prices soaring as the Morishita Syndicate continues its galactic conquest, our yearly exports have shattered records, surpassing a lofty goal well ahead of schedule. The Sindo-Emperor himself, may he live for a thousand years, called to offer his personal congratulations. I've never been so honored.

"So, thank you, all Karcass units here tonight. I hope you've had your fill of fun. It's but a small token of our appreciation. A much larger token will be hitting your accounts shortly. To the Maggots!"

Attendees applauded politely, but only a few bothered to turn toward the Karcass units as they did.

At the back edge of the audience, Mona Ripple gripped Darien Vance so tightly that she feared leaving bruises on the young man's soft skin. She trembled as she stood, waiting for the Countess's red eyes to find Darien in the crowd. Waiting for that demon grin to be aimed at her once more.

But the Countess seemed focused on the more important yakai participants, her stare reserved for those wearing suits and capes.

"Here comes the real news, lass," Mickie whispered to Mona from behind. She didn't respond.

I couldn't care less what this bitch has to say. This planet can fall into its blue sun next week. I'll be living a new life by then. Away from all this madness.

"The second announcement," Desma Ghool went on, "is one that I'd never thought I'd have the privilege to make. As you all know, Kalderra was colonized, in large part, to harvest the subarashi trees found in Karudera III and Karudera V. Absolutely singular in their beauty, the subarashi would have made Kalderra the galactic epicenter of the lumber trade."

The yellow-caped Gashira began to chatter quietly.

"Of course, things did not go as planned. Lurking beneath the surface of the planet was a native group of extraterrestrials now known as the Kodama. With their bizarre, symbiotic relationship with the subarashi, they were able to control the trees of Mori Mangekyo and Mori Hotaru and thwart our best attempts to harvest the invaluable resource. For a long time, it appeared as if Kalderra would be nothing more than a backwater trading post. A dream held prisoner by the sleeping mind."

The Countess paused for dramatic effect.

"But as we always do under the supreme guidance of the Syndicate, we invoked *kishikaisei* and managed to turn foul water into wine. We discovered the kameeba and, more importantly, the possibility that they contained. We risked it all to make use of their bodies and hearts—"

"What did that bitch ever risk?" Mona asked Darien. But if the young man heard her, he made no effort to respond.

"And much to our surprise, the Kodama allowed us. Maybe they saw our scavs as doing them a favor, keeping their mori clean. Or maybe they simply didn't care as long as their subarashi went unharmed. Regardless, a new economy was born. One that breathed life into this rocky planet, transforming it from lowly trading stop to galactic player!"

Another burst of applause.

"And look at what we've done! Karudera City is now a beacon of wealth and taste. Shonin Crossways is a key hub for trade across the Scutum-Crux . Our exports of energy and minerals are consistently among the highest of any Tier-3 planet. We. Have. Made. It."

More applause.

"And yet, we were panning for gold in a stream filled with diamonds forbidden to collect... until now." The air in the Grand Ballroom grew thick. "For a hundred years, we've thought the Kodama to be stupid, simplistic creatures. Dumb animals gifted with the uncanny ability to command the subarashi. Troglodytes who controlled lightning as if ripped straight from the loin of Susanoo. Beings too witless to know that they held all the cards in the most critical of games.

"But we were wrong."

Across the audience, heads leaned toward each other as whispered words were exchanged.

"For several weeks now, the Kodama have been in contact with Morishita Galactic. Some say they have even spoken directly with the Sindo-

Emperor. How, you may ask? I do not know. Some things are even above my pay grade. But conversations have occurred. Negotiations have taken place. And a bargain has been struck."

"Bargain? A bargain for what, Countess?" asked a tall Gashira loudly.

"What else? A bargain to begin harvesting the subarashi."

Excited conversation exploded throughout the Grand Ballroom. Syndicate members congratulated each other as Gashira entered into tense negotiations, already dividing what none had in hand.

Desma Ghool raised a hand, ushering a return to silence.

"Now, before I'm accosted by endless questions, you need to know that this is all I have to say for right now. Some secrets are not for me. Most others are not for you. But I can tell you this. Plans are already in motion, and things are poised to move quickly. Tonight we celebrate not only Kalderra's past and present but also our limitless future. To the future of Kalderra!"

The attendees began to stamp their feet in unison, storm troopers priming themselves for attack.

"Yes!" declared the Countess, her red eyes wild. "Yes! Drink more! Eat more! Touch more! For soon, we begin anew!"

The band struck up another song, drowning the room in raucous music that reflected its rabid energy.

Toro looked concerned as others celebrated around him.

"What does this mean for us? For me?"

"Relax, mate," responded Mickie. "There's still a lot of money in scavs. This lot's not one to give up five to make twenty. They want all twenty-five. No matter what it costs in lives."

"I, for one, couldn't care less," said Mona as she pulled Darien farther along the Grand Ballroom's wall toward the exit. "We're outta here as soon as the yennies hit our accounts. Best of luck dodging the kikkorii's harvesters, forwarders, cranes, and loaders on future scavs. I won't be giving it a second thought."

Hinch stepped forward.

"Yeah, well, that's stuff we can bloody worry about tomorrow. I think this yakai's shot. All the big wigs are now maneuvering, and the courtesans have either coupled up or are drifting upstairs. What do you say we take this party to Shonin Crossways? There's a pair of twins at Bottom's End that can clean corrosion off a metal pipe with their mouths, if you catch my drift."

"Metal pipe?" Neela Patel responded. "What can they do with a trim nail like yours, Hinch?"

"Why, Neela? Care to watch? I'm sure it can be arranged. But I'm not cheap. Colonel, you think they'd mind dropping us off at the Crossways instead of Camp Karcass." No reply. "Colonel?!"

Toro jumped, torn from his ongoing concerns.

"What?! Yes, I don't think they care. We've stayed long enough to pay our respects. And these courtesans are lovely, but they don't have the same… *je ne sais quoi* that the ladies at Okaasan's Milk do."

"Is that French for *low standards*, Colonel?" joked Betsy Sheppard.

Toro frowned.

"It's French for get your asses in the coaches. Let's move."

"Gladly," said Mona, relief finally beginning to overtake anxiety. She squeezed Darien's hand as they made for the Grand Ballroom's large, open doors. "Ready to start our new lives, my love?"

"I was born ready, Mona."

Just as the Maggots reached the exit, Grand Chamberlain Shinsuke appeared, accompanied by two ChoMM guards.

"Our distinguished guests," said the small man. "I take it you enjoyed the yakai?"

Toro rushed to the front of the group.

"It was a wonderful evening, Grand Chamberlain. Please pass along our deepest gratitudes to the Countess. I dared not bother her after such a monumental announcement, or I would have expressed my appreciation in person."

"Yes, I'm sure the Countess will be distraught that she didn't get to speak with you again, Colonel. In any case, the imperial motorcoaches have been brought around and are ready to depart."

"Grand Chamberlain, would it be possible for us to get dropped off at Shonin Crossways?"

"Do I look like a coach driver, Colonel?"

"No, no, of course not, Grand Chamberlain. My apologies. I'll ask the appropriate person."

"Good. Then I bid you a good night, Colonel. And to all you Maggots."

The group pushed forward but were stopped by a wave from Shinsuke's ivory baton.

"Oh, I almost forgot. Just one last thing." Mona's heart jumped as the Grand Chamberlain's gold glasses snapped to Darien at her side. "Young man, the Countess was quite struck by your skill with needle and thread. She was hoping that you could stay behind for a conversation once all of her imperial duties have concluded. She would love to hear your thoughts about fashion. As you can probably tell, the Countess shares your passion."

"No!"

All eyes turned to Mona Ripple.

"What?" asked Shinsuke, unused to hearing that word.

Mona scrambled for a response, her mind spinning like a vortex as her heart pounded in her chest.

"No, I just mean… we have plans to leave Kalderra soon. Lot's of preparations to make… Lot's of—"

The Grand Chamberlain smirked.

"My dear woman. It's just a conversation about fashion. Not one I imagine you have much to add to. Don't fret. We'll get him back to you shortly. And in tip-top shape."

"But our plans!"

"I'm sure the young man's absence for an evening will not throw a wrench in these undoubtedly vital plans of yours." Back to Darien. "Young man, you may come with me."

Darien looked to Mona, fear etched on his perfect face. "Mona?"

"Impossible!" Mona blurted out, and the Grand Chamberlain's smile disappeared. "Darien's coming home with me. I'm not leaving without him."

The Maggots glanced at each other uneasily.

Shinsuke stepped forward.

"My dear woman. Your part in this evening's tale is at an end. Young… Darien still has a role to play."

"It's ok, Mona," Darien said meekly. "I don't want any trouble. I'll go with him."

"Over my dead body."

Shinsuke's eye's narrowed behind his gold-rimmed glasses.

"That can be arranged, dear woman."

Mickie Brass studied the scene as the words were exchanged. ChoMM hands had made their way to katanas, and several Guntai had taken position in the hallway, each holding an automatic laz repeater.

Toro slid next to Mickie, his desperate whisper interrupting the Space Cowboy's analysis of the situation.

"Fujin's ass, Mickie! She's gonna get us all killed… again! I'm gonna need you to drag her out of here, if necessary."

"That's gonna be tough, mate."

"That's an *order*, soldier! And don't call me mate!"

Mickie's grey eyes bounced from ChoMM to Guntai. The man's muscles tensed beneath his kimono. His mouth twitched within his thick beard.

Toro decided on another tactic.

"Look, Mickie, if you don't want to see Ripper's head taken clean off her neck—and that's what'll happen if things keep on like this—I suggest you help me get her out of here. And now!"

"Fine," said Mickie, danger coloring the word.

Toro sprang into action.

"Of course, that won't be necessary, Grand Chamberlain. The young man would be honored to chat more with the Countess."

"The hell he would!" shouted Mona, and the ChoMM began to pull their blades.

"Mickie, get her out of here!" commanded Toro, and the Space Cowboy grabbed Mona from behind by the waist, easily lifting her into the air.

"I'm sorry, lass, but you have to live to fight another day," he said as he carried the woman forward, past the Grand Chamberlain and the deadly ChoMM.

"Put me down, Junker!" screamed Mona, thrashing in the powerful man's arms. An elbow cracked Mickie's head. "Darien! Darien! Let go, you bastard!"

Shinsuke giggled as Mona was taken into the hallway and looked back at Darien.

"Young man, you must have much more to offer than your fashion sense to bring out such emotion. The Countess was right to want to see you. Take him!"

The ChoMM grabbed Darien by the arms, dragging him back into the Grand Ballroom. The young man hopelessly looked back over his shoulder.

"Mona!"

"Darien!" called out Mona, punching Mickie's arms with all her might.

"I'm sorry, lass," Mickie repeated, spinning to back his way toward the front doors so no one ahead of them would suffer Mona's wrath.

As he did, Mona faced the Grand Ballroom once more. She cried out for her love, who disappeared amidst a sea of amused onlookers.

And then she saw her, standing at the foot of the spiral staircase, wearing a wicked red smile that touched two wicked red eyes. Desma Ghool tossed Mona a wink.

"You bitch! I'll rip your face off, bitch! Darien! Darien! Darien!"

Mickie stumbled as he passed through the entranceway, sending him and Mona to the marbled ground, the imperial motorcoaches waiting a few meters ahead. Amos Bedford quickly limped forward, with Ellis Saddler and Marshall Chance springing to meet him. Along with Mickie, the four managed to force Mona into the second coach, each gaining bruises, black eyes, and scratches for their efforts.

The other Maggots, dumbstruck by the night's rapid descent into chaos, staggered to the motorcoaches.

Hinch looked to Toro.

"Does this means Shonin Crossways is off the table, Colonel?"

Toro smoothed down his montsuki in an attempt to regain his poise.

"Nonsense. There are two motorcoaches. We'll just take the first."

CHAPTER 3

LOVELORN

Mona pounded on Colonel Toro's office door. She could sense the large man shuffling inside.

"I know you're in there, Toro! Open the bloody door, or I swear I'll break it down!"

Although virtually soundproof, Mona could sense the man's deep sigh from within the room. The door slid open, and Mona stormed in.

"Where is he, Toro?! Where's Darien?!"

Toro looked up at his top Kisser from behind his desk. Never a beauty, Mona looked truly haggard, with one bloodshot eye and a GLIM set above two dark, puffy circles.

"Benten's grin, Ripper. You look terrible. Have you slept yet?"

"Hard to sleep when your life's been taken away. Now, where is he?"

"I'm sure he's fine, Ripper."

"That's not what I asked, Toro." There was a dangerous tone in the woman's voice, the promise of violence on her thin lips.

"As far as I know, Ripper, he's still where we left him. I'm sure—"

"Two days!" Mona roared. "Two bloody days, Toro! Who knows what that demon is doing to him! If he's still alive!"

Toro nervously shuffled some papers on his desk, eyes bulging like he swallowed an insect.

Mona's eyes narrowed.

"You're not telling me something."

"That's ridiculous, Ripper."

"You're not telling me something because it's something I don't want to hear."

"Nonsense."

A tense silence fell over the room.

"Very well, Toro. I'm going up there. Try to stop me and I'll remove that fat head of yours."

Toro swallowed hard; there was no doubting the woman's sincerity.

Mona spun on a heel to leave, speaking as she did.

"And if he's dead or harmed in any way, Toro, I'm gonna carve that bitch's heart out. And anyone else's who gets in my way."

When Mona reached the door, Toro finally spoke, the man out of options.

"He's not dead, Ripper. And he's not harmed." Mona turned back, and Toro swallowed once more, harder, under her raptor gaze. "But he's not coming back."

"The heck he isn't."

"Ripper. Please. Sit down for a moment."

"I'm fine standing."

"You're making me uncomfortable."

"Good."

Toro let out a heavy sigh. "Very well then. Tell me, Ripper, what do you know about Desma Ghool?"

"I know she's a man-stealing, imperial bitch."

"You're speaking out of rage, but that doesn't mean you're incorrect."

Mona's GLIM zoomed in on Toro's face. Any suspicion of dishonesty and she would cut the man open.

"Go on, Toro. And choose your words carefully."

"Of course. As you could tell, Desma Ghool appreciates the finer things in life. Clothes. Food. Drink. Jewels." A pause. "And beautiful men. She has a… collection of them that she keeps at Ghool Tower. She calls them her paramours. She has made Darien one of them."

"We'll see about that," Mona said flatly, turning to leave.

"Ripper!" She paused. "It's not without recompense. Have you checked your account?"

"Why would I?"

"Shitayen from the scav have been distributed. The largest payout in history. And there's a bonus for you. A rather generous one."

Mona's body tightened. She looked back at Toro over her shoulder. Her voice became deadly calm.

"She thinks she can *buy* him from me?"

"She doesn't think she *can buy* him from you, Ripper." Despite the Colonel's selfish nature, there was real sympathy in his words. "She's *bought* him."

"I see."

Toro rose as he continued.

"Look, Ripper, I know it's a blow. But look on the bright side. You're a wealthy woman now. With a lot of good years ahead of you. There will be other lovers, Ripper. Take it from me; there's always other lovers."

"Is that what you think he was, Toro? A lover?"

"What else is there?"

"And that's why you'll always be alone, Toro."

Mona made for the exit.

"Ripper, it's done! Don't do anything foolish!"

"I'm a lot of things, Toro," Mona stated flatly as she passed through the open doorway. "But a fool isn't one of them."

"Fujin's ass, Mona! You're a bloody fool!"

"I'm not the one who's gonna be bloody, Junker," said Mona as she continued to stuff Howa 500 magazines into the pockets of her tactical outfit.

By the time Mickie Brass had reached the armory, Mona had already set aside several automatic weapons, strapped an assortment of pistols to her sides and legs, and loaded numerous magazines.

When the Space Cowboy had asked what she doing in the armory—in the middle of the night—her simple, too-calm response had put the man back on his heels.

"I'm going to get Darien back."

The woman moved like an automaton—efficient, emotionless, dead inside.

"I can't let you do this, lass."

She was upon him in an instant, laz-pistol pressed firmly under his chiseled jaw.

"I don't like you, Junker. But that doesn't mean I want to kill you. Try to stop me, and I'll do just that."

"Easy, Mona. It was a poor choice of words. What I meant was, give me a chance to talk you out of this."

The pistol remained tucked under Mickie's chin.

"There's no talking to do, Junker."

"Then your mind's made up?"

"It is."

"You're going to die, Mona."

"Someone's going to die. If it's me, so be it."

Mickie closed his grey eyes, and the man seemed to struggle internally. Finally—

"So be it, lass."

"Can I take this pistol off you, Junker? Or do I need to permanently end this conversation now?"

"You can put it down, Mona."

"Don't make me regret it, Junker."

"Ok, Mona."

The woman slowly removed the weapon and stepped back. She then returned to her work—calm, composed… as if nothing had just happened.

"So, what's your plan, lass?"

"I told you the conversation was over."

"*That* conversation is over. *This* one has just begun. Now, what's your plan?"

Mona spoke while sorting through the racks of weaponry.

"I'm gonna drive up to Ghool Tower. I'm gonna shoot anyone who gets in my way. I'm gonna find Desma Ghool and run a knife across her throat. Then I'm gonna rescue Darien and get off this shit planet."

"And then you'll live happily ever after, I suppose."

Mona stopped for a moment and shot Mickie a look.

"That's right."

"Well, I must say, that's a brilliantly laid out plan, Mona."

"The simple ones usually are."

Mona resumed her search of the armory.

"Can I tell you what's really going to happen, lass?"

"No," she replied, refusing to look up.

"Well, I'm going to anyway. You're going to drive up to Ghool Tower. The Guntai are going to stop you as you approach. You'll try to plow through them, but they'll remotely turn off your vehicle. I assume you were gonna use one of the ones stationed here at Camp Karcass? You know, one of the ones supplied by the Imperium?" No response. "Yeah, so they'll easily shut that thing down. And then there'll be a shootout. You versus a squad of Guntai. You'll take out one, hell, maybe two, three, or four because you're a nasty, dangerous woman. But eventually, you'll get hit."

"Yeah, yeah. I'll get hit, and I'll die. You said that already."

"You better hope that you die, Mona. Because if you don't, they're gonna capture you. Do you know what they do to assassins, Mona?"

"I ain't no assassin."

"Yes, you are. Do you know what they do to assassins?" A silent beat. "*Ishikozume.*"

"Sounds fun."

"It's anything but, Mona. First, they'll bury you waist-high so you can't move. Then, they'll take turns throwing stones at your head and body. Everyone from the Tower will come to watch. To participate. Hell, some may even fly in from across the galaxy to enjoy the show. It will be painful. It will be slow. And the last image you process will be that of Desma Ghool cackling loudly as your life slips away."

Mona had frozen.

"How do you know this, Junker?"

"I just do."

The air within the armory thickened as the silence grew heavy.

"He isn't worth it, Mona. You're so much more than this."

"He is, Junker. And I'm not."

Mickie's broad shoulders sank.

"So there's nothing I can say to stop you?"

"Nothing."

"Very well…" His voice trailed off. "Then I'll have to help you, lass."

Mona straightened.

"What?"

"I said, I'll have to help you."

"And why would you do that?"

"Because you're gonna pay me, Mona. Handsomely."

"And what, pray tell, do you have to offer?"

"Your plan's trash, Mona. One of the worst I've ever heard. I'll come up with a better one. One that actually has a chance to work."

"And what makes you think you can do that?"

Now it was Mickie's turn to straighten, bringing himself to his full, impressive height.

"Because I'm a Space Cowboy. And stealing shit is what I do bloody best."

Later that morning, Mickie Brass entered the quarters that Mona Ripple once shared with Darien Vance.

"Took you long enough, Junker."

"I was hoping you'd get some sleep, lass."

"Well, you should be used to disappointment by now."

Mickie handed her a list, which she immediately began to read.

"Benten's grin, Junker. This is a long list."

"I've spent the night thinking it through. Getting into Ghool Tower won't be easy. Even if things go according to plan, they won't go according to plan. We'll need to be prepared for anything."

Mona continued to scan the list.

"Most of this stuff can't even be had, Junker."

"It can, Mona. And it won't be cheap."

"I don't care about money. The money was just a means to an end. A way to get Darien and I off this rock. Together. Now that he's been taken— with no fight put up by Toro—I consider his Maggot contract null and void. The money I'd set aside for him can now be used."

"For him. Again."

"You trying to say something, Junker?"

"Not at all, Mona."

"Good, then don't worry about *my* money. You'll get your bloody bounty."

"Ok, Mona."

The woman sighed and placed the list on the bed next to her.

"So, what's the plan?"

"We're not gonna blast our way in, Mona. We're not even gonna sneak in. We're gonna walk right past everyone, maybe even earn a few welcoming nods as we do. We'll locate the package and walk out the way we came."

"Darien."

"What's that?"

"He's not a bloody package. He's a man. A prisoner. And his name is Darien."

"I know that, Mona."

"Then act like you do."

Mickie almost snapped back but took a calming breath instead.

"We'll find Darien and escort him out. With any luck, no one will even know that we were there."

"Until they do."

Mickie shrugged.

"By then, we'll both be off-planet."

"You going somewhere, Junker?"

"Well, I'm not sticking around here to suffer Desma Ghool's wrath. With what you're paying me, I can buy out my contract. And they're not gonna chase after an old Space Cowboy like me. I ain't worth the trouble."

Mona snatched up the list once more.

"So that's why we need all this stuff?"

"It is."

"You still haven't told me where you hope to procure all these items. These *highly illegal* items."

Mickie smirked. "The only place you can on Kalderra. The Laughing God."

Mona's eyes went wide. "The Laughing God?! That's your idea?! They won't let either of us in there!"

"They will."

"Idiot junker! We work for the Syndicate! Oh sure, maybe not directly, but don't fool yourself about who pays for our scavs. And the criminals who run the Laughing God know that. We'll be turned away at the door. Or shot! Most likely shot."

"You let me worry about that," said Mickie as he made his way back to the door. "Pack up, Mona. Take whatever you don't want to leave behind. Once we go, we won't be returning here. Ever."

"The only thing I need is being kept in Ghool Tower, Junker."

"Then we can leave this evening."

"I'm ready now."

"Well I'm not. And neither is the Laughing God. It's a city of night. It only wakes up when Kuyomi does. Plus, *I do* have things that I care about brining."

"What could you possibly care about bringing, Junker?"

"My lucky cigar. And my hat."

"Ugh, that bloody hat."

"Get some rest, Mona. You're going to need it."

"Don't tell me what to do, Junker."

"Ok, Mona."

At nightfall, Mickie and Mona left Camp Karcass, taking two of the small but stout monocycles typically reserved for short trips. They were simple and, more importantly, without tracking modules connected to the K-nex network.

Under the bright, violet light of Kuyomi, they sped through Kalderra, traveling south on the Maggot Trails. Armored Guntai vehicles and trader vans flashed past, paying no mind to the two travelers.

As they approached the mountain range bordering the eastern edge of Mori Hotaru, instead keeping to the Maggot Trail, which wound around the rocky border and into Karudera V's forest, Mickie broke off, heading directly for the sharp peaks. Mona followed.

As the mountains rose up to meet the pair, Mona could see no path through. She called out to Mickie, her voice muffled by the handkerchief covering her nose and mouth. The man brought his monocycle to a stop.

"You trying to kill us, Junker?! There's no way to get across this mess."

Mickie lowered the bandana protecting his face. "There is. You just have to know the way."

"What good is a city of villains if most of the villains can't get to it?"

"Well, this is the back entrance. The back, secret entrance."

"You mean there's a front entrance?!"

Mickie wiped some planet dust from his forehead.

"Yeah, it's much more accessible."

"More accessible?! Then why in heck are we going in this way?!"

Mickie laughed before answering. "The Laughing God is not unknown to the Syndicate, Mona. They just can't do anything about it. Or don't want to. Yet. Anyway, they have satellite surveillance on the main entrance to observe comings and goings. We probably wouldn't raise any alarms, but better safe than sorry."

Mona thought for a moment. "Well, if we die before even reaching Ghool Tower, I'm gonna kill you, Junker."

"Fair enough. Now, can we be on our way?"

"I don't know. Can we?"

Mickie laughed again, lifting his bandana back into place. "Follow closely. And watch your wheel. It can get a bit dodgy in places. Don't want you splattered against Kalderra before those yennies hit my account."

"I hate you, Junker."

"But you need to trust me. Now let's move."

The monocycles weaved up and down thin, almost invisible pathways. They rounded sharp bends hundreds of meters above the ground and sped across narrow metal bridges spanning deep chasms.

Like the majority of Kalderra, nothing stirred. There was only lifeless desolation, mirroring the emptiness Mona Ripple felt within.

After nearly an hour, the monocycles dropped from a high passage onto a flat expanse that ended in another massive set of peaks. Mickie halted his vehicle and motioned Mona to do the same.

"We're here."

"Here? Benten's grin, Junker, I don't see anything but more bloody mountains."

"Because that's all you're supposed to see. Lower your face mask so they can see you and approach slowly."

"Who's *they*? There's no one here."

"They're here. And they'll shoot first and ask questions later if we spook them. This goes without saying, but our bodies would never be found out here."

"If it goes without saying, then why bloody say it?!"

"Just for emphasis."

"Get on with it, Junker."

Mickie and Mona slowly made their way across the flat terrain, a shadowy peak growing to meet them. As they drew closer, a voice cut in from the side.

"Stop or you'll be shot!"

Mickie and Mona complied, turning off their monocycles.

"What's your business here?!" the voice called out.

"You just said it," replied Mickie. "Business is our business."

"How do you know of this entrance, and why are you using it?"

"I know many things, mate. For example, I know you lot appreciate discretion. As do we."

A silence followed, then low whispering. And then—

"Get off your vehicles, and take two steps forward. Make any sudden moves and you'll be eliminated."

"Fair enough, mate."

The two Maggots stepped off their monocycles, advanced two paces, and stood patiently.

From the darkness of the mountains, six armed individuals emerged. Four of them had guns pointed squarely at the unexpected visitors.

A gruff voice emanated from the tough-looking man leading the group.

"Well, you ain't Guntai. And you don't have the look of traders. So who the hell are you?"

"We're Maggots," Mona blurted, and Mickie rolled his eyes.

"Then begone. Maggots ain't welcome here. Go back to sucking on the imperial tit."

"She meant *ex-Maggots*, mate."

The head guard snickered. "Once an imperial stooge, always an imperial stooge. Now be gone! This is the last time I'll tell you."

"We can't do that, mate."

Fingers went to triggers as the guard leader angrily stomped toward the Maggots.

"You can, and you will, ya bastard! And in five seconds, I'm gonna have my men open so many holes in your chest that—"

The man's words caught in his throat as Mickie moved to adjust the bandana around his neck. Violet rays of Kuyomi struck Mickie's hands, highlighting the large star tattoo found on each.

The guard's eyes took in the markings, then rose. He noted the thick salt-and-pepper beard, the grey eyes, the black Akubra hat. His jaw slackened.

"Mickie? Mickie Brass?"

"The one and only, mate."

"Fujin's ass! We almost shot you!"

"*Almost,* I can handle. No harm done."

"What, what are you doing here?" the man stammered, and Mona looked to Mickie, surprise and curiosity painted on her face.

"I told you, mate. Business."

"Of course, of course." The guard then remembered those behind him. "Put those bloody things down!" he yelled over his shoulder before returning to Mickie. "Well, you're always welcome, Mickie. Obviously. But I can't say the same about your friend here."

"She's with me, mate," Mickie stated flatly, as if nothing more needed to be said.

Despite the evening's lessened light, Mona saw the guard's face blanch.

"Of course, Mickie. But we've got protocols to follow. Set from high above."

"Such as?"

"We're gonna have to at least scan her."

Mickie motioned toward Mona. "By all means, mate."

The head guard nodded, apparently relieved, before addressing his waiting team.

"Opi!"

"Here, boss," said a young man.

"Gimme a quick scan of this woman." He eyed Mickie. "And be respectful about it."

"You got it, boss."

The young guard stepped forward, removing a handheld device from his belt.

"Please stand still, ma'am. And apologies for the closeness. There's really no other way to do it."

"Do what you have to, boy," said Mona.

Opi knelt down, running his scanner across Mona's shoes, legs, and waist. The young man hesitated before moving up.

"There ain't nothing magical up here, boy," Mona teased. "Get on with it."

Opi did as he was told, tracing Mona's arms and chest with the device. It remained silent.

The young guard, thankful that his task was almost complete, lifted the scanner higher, examining the neck and—

Beep!

"Uh, boss?"

"What is it, Opi?"

"I got something. I think it's the eye."

"Fujin's ass!" Mickie cursed from the side. "She's got a GLIM." He turned to Mona. "Sorry, lass. I had so much to think through, I totally forgot that your GLIM is connected to K-nex."

"So, what does that mean?" asked Mona.

"It means you can't come in," said the head guard.

"No, it doesn't," corrected Mickie, and the guard shifted uncomfortably. "It means you can't come in with that GLIM attached. What's your name, guardian?"

"Gates," the rough-looking man answered.

"Fitting. Listen, Gates, just let us in. We'll beeline it for the nearest tech-med and have this thing out and scrambled before you know it. Before *anyone* knows it."

Gates looked as if he was suffering from a rectal exam.

"If it were up to me, that'd be fine, Mickie. But, you see… we have—"

"Protocols," finished Mickie.

Gates nodded vigorously. "Yes! Set from high above!"

"Yeah, you mentioned that, mate." Mickie mulled over the problem for a beat before continuing. "Ok, I tell you what, Gates. Send in one of your fellas there, and bring us out a tech-med. They can do the procedure out here."

"And how long will that take?" asked Mona, the woman's annoyance growing by the second.

"Could take a while, miss," replied Gates. "Yuki!"

"Yeah, boss," answered the lone female guard.

"You think Doc Foon is around?"

"He's around, boss. But it's high Kuyomi. Doc's probably full of opium smoke by now."

"What about Mendoza?"

"He's probably with Doc Foon, boss."

"Cheener?"

"Left this morning to see his boyfriend who stays in the Crossways."

This went on for some time. And then—

"Benten's grin! Sounds like you all run a tight ship," said Mona. "I'll take care of the bloody thing myself."

The group, Mickie included, watched in shock as Mona removed a long, thin knife from her belt and brought it to her face.

"Are you mad, lass?!" exclaimed Mickie.

But Mona did not slow.

The Kisser ran the blade into the lower part of her right eye, let out a pained grunt, and flicked her wrist. The GLIM popped out, and blood rivered down Mona's right cheek. It swung freely before her face, a cybernetic cord connecting artificial eye to very real optic nerve.

Some of the guards looked away in disgust. Others stared open-mouthed as Mona grasped the cord with her left hand and neatly cut it. Vision on her right side blinked out, wobbling her legs.

After regaining her balance, Mona tossed the dead GLIM into the rocky darkness and returned her knife to its sheath. She then removed her handkerchief, wiped the blood from her face, and pushed the dangling nerves back into her now-empty eye socket. Quickly folding the handkerchief several times, she tied it around her head to cover the gaping hole that once held her GLIM.

"There now," said Mona to the gawking onlookers. "You can get out of our way."

"Bloody hell, Mona," was the only commentary Mickie could offer. "Gates. Gates!"

The head guard shook himself from his disbelieving stare.

"Yes! Yes, of course. Open the postern!"

The guard named Yuki ran back into the shadows. A few seconds later, the grating of rock on rock could be heard as a large slab slid into the ground, revealing a tunnel carved through the mountain.

"Welcome to the Laughing God," Gates announced. "I'd tell you to be careful, but I don't think we have to worry about that."

"It's been a real pleasure," Mona said snidely as she returned to her monocycle. Mickie moved to follow, but Gates grabbed him by the arm.

"Who is that woman, Mickie?" the man whispered.

"A gal on a mission, mate. I wouldn't get in her way."

"I wouldn't dream of it."

"Good lad."

The two Maggots, now seated on their monocycles, fired up their vehicles. Mona turned to Mickie, her makeshift eyepatch soaked through with blood.

"How do I look, Junker?"

"Pretty cool, lass. Pretty cool."

"So straight ahead?"

Mickie nodded. "That's right. I assume you're comfortable with tight tunnels?"

"How's this for comfortable?"

Mona twisted the throttle, and her monocycle took off. In seconds, the woman had disappeared into the blackness.

"And *that*, mates, is how you make a bloody entrance!"

Bright neon light assaulted Mona's lone pupil as she exited the mountain tunnel. After quickly parking their vehicles, Mona turned to face the planet's illicit city.

She found a kaleidoscope of color—red, orange, purple, green, and blue neon signs, oddly dressed characters parading to and from establishments, glowing graffiti on walls and doors and stone walkways.

Above, a thick, shimmering light hung over the city, reminiscent of the one covering Karudera City and Ghool Tower.

Loud, forbidden music blared from many buildings, and the air was heavy with a potpourri of aromas, compliments of the dozens of food carts running along the sides of unusual metal roads.

Men and women and everything in between danced drunkenly between buildings without hindrance. Were this Shonin Crossways or—even worse—Karudera City, Guntai would be flexing their muscle on every corner, demanding to see papers and discreetly requesting bribes—if you were deemed below a certain class.

Mona breathed in deeply, the mix of smells bringing her back to another place at another age. It was both nostalgic and unsettling. But much more of the latter than the former.

Mona shook off the painful memories.

"What is this place, Junker?"

"The Laughing God, Mona. The pimple on the face of Kalderra. The Syndicate knows it's here, can see it every day. But there's little they can do to facilitate its disappearance, and they know picking at it will only make things worse."

Mona motioned upward. "And that?"

"Oh, just a state-of-the-art protective shield. Keeps them from sending missiles down from orbit and also prevents satellite surveillance."

"I can't believe Morishita Galactic would allow this place to exist, Junker."

Mickie shrugged. "Well, it's not all bad for them. Sometimes even the Syndicate wants things done off the books. Plus, I'm sure they get thrown plenty of bones from the Laughing God. I mean, this is a city of degenerates, sure. But it's not like anyone has ridiculous notions of overthrowing the Syndicate or anything. Most here just want to make a few yennies, have a few laughs, and shag anything that moves."

"If anyone tries to shag me, I'm gonna carve them up."

Mickie laughed. "I'm sure you will, lass. I'm sure you will."

Mona looked around, doing her best to conceal her awe of the city.

"Well, where to, Junker? This is your city, apparently. Not mine."

Mickie noted the woman's blood-soaked kerchief.

"It think the first thing we need to do, lass, is get that eye taken care of. There's gotta be—"

"No. You heard them out there," she said, pointing to the mountain at their backs. "Everyone's either drunk, or high, or drunk and high, or shagging some guy in the Crossways. I still got one good eye. And that's all I need to see Desma Ghool's throat before I cut it."

Mickie placed a calloused hand on Mona's shoulder. "Need I remind you that this is a clandestine operation, lass. If a suicide mission is what you're after, we'll need to reconsider our arrangement."

"Get your hand off me, Junker. And calm down. I'm just talking here. Just trying to say there's more pressing matters to attend to than my eye… or lack of one."

Mickie removed his hand. "Fair enough, Mona. Then the second stop will become our first. And with any luck, our only stop."

"Lead the way, Junker."

The pair winded through the Laughing God, past the large central square, denoted by a massive, spinning, red neon sign depicting a fat, Buddha-like character with an open mouth. The neon flashed between different tube segments, animating the design. The neon man twirled high overhead, cackling at a joke that only he heard.

"A little on the nose, isn't?" commented Mona as they passed under the red light, their boots echoing off the strange, metal ground.

"This isn't the place for subtlety, lass. It's neither understood nor appreciated."

"Not very Japanese of them."

"That's the point."

Turning left at the city center, Mona and Mickie walked toward a gang of men and women loitering outside an obvious sutorippu—or flesh club. They all wore the same padded leather jacker, cut short, with animal fur collars—none of which seemed to come from a similar beast. Theirs numbers were such that they were completely blocking the walkway. Eyes were wild and fierce but intelligent, and Mona feared that a brawl was imminent.

Instead, the group neatly parted as the pair approached, some offering nods to Mickie as he passed through. Mona glanced at a woman's hand as she sipped a beer and noted three small stars on the top of her left hand.

Mona turned to Mickie once they were out of ear shot.

"Space Cowboys?"

"Yeah, there's a few of them always circling the city."

"Friends of yours?"

Mickie shook his head. "Nah, lass. I left all that behind. Old Mickie rides solo these days."

Mona almost continued her questioning but instead decided to leave things alone. Answers to such questions would get her no closer to rescuing Darien, so they pushed on in silence.

Several minutes later, Mickie cut down a small alleyway to their left, and Mona followed.

The twisting passageway grew darker as the pair left the neon-lit streets behind. Left, then right, then right again, and Mona found herself at an illuminated dead end.

A brick wall stood before them, a nondescript metal door in its center. Several meters above the ground, a purple neon sign hummed in the muted space. It read, *Theodore Feenk's Findings and Sellings*. Each *i* was dotted with a small star.

Mickie stepped forward and loudly banged on the metal door. Nothing. He struck it three more times with the edge of his fist. Silence.

"Congrats, Junker. No one's home."

Mickie waved Mona away. "He's home, all right. Teddy's always home." He pounded on the metal door twice again. "Teddy, ya bastard! Open the bloody door!"

A beat passed. And then—

A sharp, metallic voice cut through the alley from a hidden intercom. "We're closed for the night! And the day! And the next evening and day! So be gone!"

Mickie looked up at the neon sign and pushed back his Akubra.

"Even for an old friend, mate?"

There was no further response from the intercom, but the metal door released an audible *click*, and Mickie pushed through, motioning Mona to follow.

To say that Mona Ripple was not impressed as she entered Theodore Feenk's Findings and Sellings would be an understatement. Dusty shelves held only a few fairly common items, most of which looked broken or well on their way to obscurity. A third of the fluorescent bulbs overhead were out while another third blinked rapidly on the edge of outage. The air was stale and musty, soaked through with memories of old farts.

And Mona's mind began to whirl.

"Junker, I'm really starting to question our business relationship."

Mickie made a calming gesture. "Chill out, lass. The ugliest fruits produce the sweetest juice."

"I've never heard that."

"That's because I just made it up. Teddy! Unplug and get your old bones out here!"

An old, rusty door behind an even more decrepit counter slid open, and a small, disheveled man stepped through.

Pudgy and black-skinned, with random bald spots peppering his cropped hair, Teddy's eyes were enveloped by a shiny visor, the metal band fused directly to his flesh.

"Mickie Brass," declared the man as he found the counter and collapsed into a dirty hydraulic salon chair. "Apologies for the lackluster welcome, my friend. But if you knew how many inquiries I've fielded lately about the new VaVoom sex droid then you'd understand my hesitance to answer the door. I mean, it cleans itself. Big whoop. Is that such a game-changing feature?"

"Hi, Teddy. I suppose for those who don't like to clean up after themselves, it is."

Teddy shook his head. "Savages! The lot of them!" The visor swung to Mona Ripple.

"Ahh, I see you've brought a friend. It's about time, Mickie. I've always said—"

"This is Mona," Mickie interrupted. "I'm helping her with something. And to do that, I need your help with many somethings."

Teddy's visor moved from Mickie to Mona and back again.

"Ok, ok, Mickie. No time for small talk for an old friend, I see. Always so busy with plans within plans within plans. Definitely no room in your busy schedule to ascertain how old Teddy's doing or—"

"How are you doing, Teddy?"

"About as well as Daniel in the lions' den, Mickie! Oh, that's from the Bible, if you didn't know. You know, *The Bible*! Humanity's moral compass before the Morishitas forced all this Shinto nonsense on us!"

Mona cut in. "Daniel made it out of the lions' den. God saved him. So you can't be doing that bad."

Lights on Teddy's visor came to life as he stared at the woman. "And how do you know that?"

"I read the bloody thing."

"What thing?"

"The bloody Bible!"

Teddy faced Mickie. "I don't care for her, Mickie. She's disagreeable."

"Her name's Mona, mate. And she's on a mission. One that will need a lot of items. A lot of items that will cost a truckload of shitayen, if you catch my drift."

Teddy reached up to adjust his visor, even if the metal band refused to move.

"What good is shitayen to me, Mickie? Might as well pay me in thoughts and prayers."

"Your Bible holds thoughts and prayers in the highest regard, Teddy," shot back Mona. "Seems to me it would be your most trusted currency."

"I don't care for this woman," Teddy said sourly to Mickie.

"You may have mentioned that, mate. But you didn't let me finish. Mona's got a mission needing lots of things that cost lots of money. And she'll be paying in tamari."

Teddy's head cocked to the side. "In that case, she's already starting to grow on me a bit, despite her rough edges."

"Excuse me," said Mona, her patience wearing thin. "Sorry to break up your little brain trust, but what are we talking about? I have yennies, and I'll be paying in yennies. I don't know what…"

"Tamari," filled in Mickie.

"Exactly! I don't even know what that is, Junker!"

Teddy smiled beneath his flashing visor, and Mona's lone brown eye caught what appeared to be a series of diamond-encrusted teeth.

Mickie's response stole Mona's attention back before she could question Teddy's exceedingly expensive mouth.

"Mona, you're going to need to transfer all your money to the Dark Tide."

Mona's face twisted in confusion. "The Dark Tide?! That's just a marketplace for organs and assassins and miscreants!"

Teddy giggled.

"It is that, Mona. But it's also much, much more. The Dark Tide is the galactic economy that flows beneath the feet of the Syndicate, far from their taxes and regulations and oversight and greed. It's a decentralized network, and within it is the Dark Pool, the bank of the people. You want to do business in places where you shouldn't? You're gonna need a Dark Pool account. And you're gonna have to pay in tamari."

"I don't like it, Junker."

"You don't have to, Mona. Take a moment and think on it. What do you think is going to happen at the end of this? The Imperial Sosakan—you know, the special investigators—may not be geniuses, but they're far from stupid. Even if everything goes according to plan, it won't be hard for them to put two and two together. A missing paramour. A missing Maggot partnered with said paramour. A missing Maggot who caused a major scene regarding said paramour only a few evenings prior."

"Stop talking like a bastard, Junker."

"My point is, Mona, they're gonna know that you sit at the heart of this thing. And the first thing they're gonna do is freeze your accounts. Freeze them and then confiscate them." Mickie paused as Mona thought things through. "Starting a new life is hard. Starting a new life with nothing is damn near impossible. Love is grand, but it won't pay the bills."

A tense silence followed, broken finally by Teddy Feenk.

"If I may, Miss… Mona. The Dark Pool has been reliably stable for almost five years now. And tamari have been tied to shitayen, resulting in a nearly one-to-one exchange rate. You'll lose nothing and gain something immeasurable."

"And what would that be, Blinders?"

Teddy offered another diamond smile. "Freedom. True freedom."

Mona's hand went to her blood-caked head wrap, as if thinking was causing her great pain.

"Very well. If this is the way, then this is the way. I'd toss every yenny into Homusubi's Breath if it meant getting Darien back."

"Who's that?" asked Teddy.

"Don't worry about it, Blinders. Just tell me how I can get my money into the Dark Pool."

Teddy scooted his seat closer to the counter as he spoke. "Oh, I can do better than that, Miss Mona. I can transfer it for you."

Mona looked around at her dingy surroundings. "And what makes you think you can do that?"

Teddy looked taken aback. "Because I created the Dark Pool. Didn't Mickie tell you?"

Mona shot her companion with a look. "No, he doesn't tell me much at all, to be honest."

Teddy pushed forward over the counter and spoke conspiratorially. "Well, don't take it personal, Miss Mona. Mickie Brass is a mystery to most. Himself included." He leaned back. "Now! Let's free your money from the shackles of the Syndicate!"

The numbers continued to scroll up on Teddy Feenk's dark ream, a thin touchscreen tablet connected directly to the Dark Tide. When they finally settled, Teddy's forehead scrunched, as if the man was raising an eyebrow beneath his digital visor.

"Not bad, Miss Mona. Looks like you're a fairly wealthy woman. You sure you don't want to stop while you're ahead? Take the money and run?"

"I'm here for services, Blinders. Not advice."

Teddy chuckled. "Then no more will be given."

Mona turned to Mickie. "I assume you have a Dark Pool account, Junker?"

"I do."

"Give it to Teddy. We can transfer your fee now."

Mickie shook his head. "Not now, lass. Payment upon completion. And there's a good chance that the only completion will be that of my life."

"Are you trying to upset me, Junker?"

"Just trying to lower expectations, Mona. Underpromise and overdeliver and all that."

"Fine. Then let's move on to important matters. Our list, Teddy."

Teddy placed the dark ream on the counter and accepted Mickie's list, raising it toward his visor to study it further.

"My, my, you're cooking up a little scheme, aren't you? If you're trying to do what I think you're trying to do—"

"We are, mate."

"This is a risky move, Mickie."

"I know, mate. Can you help us or not?"

Teddy continued to examine the list. "Yes, yes, some of this stuff I have. Some will be harder to come by."

Mona looked around the dirty room once more.

"Have where, Blinders? Are they under the dust balls or hiding behind the broken transmitters?"

Teddy's visor blinked rapidly.

"This is a world of illusion, Miss Mona. And only things that aren't as they appear survive."

"Benten's grin, Blinders. What's that supposed to mean?"

Teddy motioned to the rusty door at his back as he answered. "It means the back's a lot fancier than the front. You, in particular, should understand that."

"What's that bloody mean?!"

"Careful, Teddy," warned Mickie. "Mona's not above throttling the impaired."

Teddy held up a hand in surrender. "Just trying to dance a little here. You'd begrudge an old man a dance, would you?"

"The list, mate."

"Yes, yes. Like I said, I have some of this. But for the rest I'll need to get with Urek."

"He's back?"

"He is. With quite a few new connections and resources, I might add. Last I heard, he was shacking up with a lady Guntai. Not a looker by any means, but the intel he's getting is top-notch."

"He's playing a dangerous game, Teddy."

"Those are the only ones worth playing, Mickie. Someone told me that one time." Teddy's finger went to his chin contemplatively. "Now, who was that…"

Mickie cleared his throat. "How long, Teddy?"

"You're in luck. Urek doesn't even get up until Kuyomi's at her height. He should be fresh enough to work on this through the night and into the morning."

"Costs?" Mona asked.

"Substantial, Miss Mona."

"Do I have enough… tamari?"

"Oh, yes. Plenty."

"Good. Take what you need."

Teddy waved the woman away. "We'll put you on credit. Mickie's vouched for you, so that's good enough for me."

"Then we're done here for now, Blinders?"

"We are, Miss Mona."

"Good. Because I need some fresh air. There's more mold than oxygen in this room."

Mona spun to leave.

"Uhh, Miss Mona?"

"What?" she said, turning back.

"No offense, but that bloody kerchief around your head will offer a frightful first impression. How bad's the injury?"

"Not bad at all, Blinders."

Mickie jumped in. "Not quite an injury, Teddy. Crazy sheila ripped out her own GLIM."

Teddy's forehead rose again. "Impressive. Then I would suggest visiting a med-tech."

"They're all drunk or shagging," stated Mona.

Teddy smiled as he considered the woman's words. "Oh yes, I suppose they are. Well, you can't go out looking like that. Here." Teddy reached below the counter and began shuffling through items. "Ahh, there it is!"

Teddy placed a strange piece of black fabric on the counter, a small wire escaping its largest section.

"What's that?"

"A GLIM-patch, Miss Mona. Well, it's actually not called that, but it's a fitting name given your situation."

"What does it do?"

"It should suffice until you get a med-tech to install a new GLIM, hopefully one not connected to K-nex or any other Syndicate-based network. May I recommend the GLIMveil? Very powerful. And very hush hush."

"I can't install this bloody thing."

"But I can."

"You can't see, Blinders!"

Teddy leaned back in mock offense. "I see like a hawk, I'll have you know!"

"You're not a bloody med-tech! You're a bloody merchant! Of stupid findings and sellings!"

Teddy grunted as he dropped from his chair and made his way around the counter, a plastic container in his hand. He spoke as he slowly walked.

"Miss Mona, you may not have noticed, but I'm quite familiar with ocular issues, particularly those of the digital variety. As long as you didn't muck up your human wiring, I should be able to install the patch."

"Should?! Mickie?"

"Let him try, lass. We're gonna need everything for this mission. And that includes four good eyes."

Teddy reached Mona. "Ok, take off that garish wrap. Let's see what I'm working with."

Mona carefully removed the kerchief, grimacing as the dried blood pulled at her skin. The gaping hole stared back at Teddy.

"Kneel down, will you? You're a big woman."

"You're a tiny man."

"Even more reason."

Mona reluctantly knelt before Teddy, and the merchant carefully studied the opening.

"Well, despite you doing the work like an absolute butcher, you managed not to harm the natural ocular nerve. Even better, the HMI node appears intact." Teddy removed several sharp metal tools from his container. "Now, I'm going to need you to remain very still. Mickie, hand me the GLIM-patch."

"If you blind me, Blinders, I'm going to kill you."

"You're already blind, Miss Mona."

"Permanently blind."

"Fair enough, Miss Mona."

After five minutes of tense silence, Teddy stepped back and admired his work.

"There! Now, how's that for an installation?"

"I still can't bloody see anything!"

"Oh, sorry! Forgot to turn the blasted thing on." Teddy reached forward and pressed a small button on the lower part of the patch. "There! Now, how's *that* for an installation!"

Mona lost her balance as the GLIM-patch booted up and roared to bright life. Mickie caught her by the shoulder and gently placed her upright once more. A few seconds later—

"Yes! Yes! It's working. I can see!"

"Of course, you can. I'm Teddy Feenk."

Mona rose to her feet. "How does it look?"

"You look like a real Space Cowboy, Miss Mona."

"That's the last thing I want to look like, Blinders."

"Ok, then. You look like a dangerous woman about to embark on critical mission of love."

"Who told you that?"

"I have ears, Miss Mona. And they don't need digital enhancement."

"Very well then. I still need to get out of this room. Junker, you coming?"

"I am, lass."

Mickie joined Mona and made for the exit, but Teddy held him back by the arm.

"Stay for a bit, Mickie. I have some things to show you in the back."

"We don't have time for this, Teddy."

"Make time, Mickie. You're *really* gonna want to see what I have."

"Very well. Mona, enjoy the city for a while. I'll find you in a bit."

"How're you gonna find me in a city this size, Junker?"

"It's what I do, lass."

"I thought taking things that didn't belong to you is what you do."

"I do both."

Mona's one eye rolled. "Fine. Enjoy your little date."

Mona went to leave but paused at the door.

"Thank you, Teddy. I do feel better having two working eyes. Put it on my tab."

"Of course, Miss Mona."

She left.

"Strange, Mickie. That woman really grew on me in the hour I've known her. Despite the rough edges. I can't imagine how I'd feel with more time together."

"You had something to show me, Teddy?"

"Of course, of course. It's back in my lab. And it's extraordinary."

"Don't forget about my list, Teddy."

Teddy made his way back to the counter.

"I didn't, Mickie. This must be added to it."

"And obviously, mate, there's no tab."

"Of course not, Mickie."

Mona Ripple roamed the streets of the Laughing God, bathed in the light of neon signs and the aromas of cooking meat. Massive vents lined many of the metal streets, every now and then releasing jets of warm, surprisingly fresh-smelling air. Strangely clothed figures passed her on the walkways, outfits representing planets and cities from across the galaxy. Each shot Mona with a wary glance, their eyes inevitably going to the woman's GLIM-patch. Small, wheeled robots and bipedal androids cut across streets and down alleys, their lives an endless series of errands.

Above, the giant purple moon known as Kuyomi sat heavy, turning night into near-day as its rays passed through the shimmering dome covering the outcast city.

Storefronts glowed brightly, attracting customers like moths to a flame. In their windows sat objects both rare and common, priceless and unfamiliar. Kalderra, if nothing else, was a key trading post in the Scutum-

Crux Arm of the Milky Way, a critical refueling station along several important merchant routes. It was only natural that cities like Shonin Crossways would appear. And shadowy counterbalances like the Laughing God would rise.

Mona turned right and continued on, seeing skins of white and black, brown and blue, sickly green and indigo. Some bore eyes that glowed in the purple light, others had metal gadgetry fused to their heads, chests, arms, or legs. Most had weapons overtly swinging from belts. But whether open or concealed, all were armed. Inhabitants and visitors alike measured each other, nods serving as greetings and warnings.

It was Shonin Crossways, but not. The bustle of commerce was the same. The vibe couldn't have been more different. The Laughing God was a serious place but without the undercurrent of constant oversight. The Guntai were nowhere to be found, and the Syndicate troops were not missed. Absent were the random ID checks, the indiscriminate seizures of property, the constant bribes and extortions. Where Shonin Crossways was rotten beneath a veneer of prosperity, the Laughing God ripened under a cloak of secrecy.

Another right and Mona was assaulted by color and the sounds of revelry. Music and laughter filled the square she had entered, drunken groups plunging into massive buildings while others poured out of bars vibrating with music, surrounded by opium smoke.

A tall Japanese woman in an overcoat stood on the corner, long cigarette in one gloved hand, a dark ream in the other. Mona slid next to her, careful to keep both hands in clear view.

"What is this place?" Mona asked.

The woman did not look up from her dark ream as she responded.

"First time in the Laughing God?"

"Is it that obvious?"

"From your question, it is. This is Yorokobi Square. Anything you want, it's here. Anything you don't want, it's here, too."

Mona's eye and GLIM-patch scanned the scene.

"There's so much."

The woman shrugged. "No Guntai."

"Where should I go?"

"Do I look like a tour guide to you?"

"Come on. Help a sister out."

The woman sighed, obviously annoyed.

"Try The Corkscrew. But get a drink first. Some find it disquieting."

"Then why would I go?"

"Because it's beautiful."

"What's beautiful?"

"Go and you'll see."

With that, the woman dropped her cigarette to the ground and stamped it out with a metal foot, bringing the conversation to an end. She spun toward Mona, revealing a robot body beneath the folds of cloth, and sped away from Yorokobi Square, the whirr of rotors and hiss of pistons trailing off as she disappeared into the distance, metal feet clanging against metal road.

After drinks at Goya's Tavern and The Open Palm—luckily they accepted paper shitayen—Mona found her way to The Corkscrew and entered.

Loud, pounding music filled the massive establishment. Coliseum seating surrounded a flat central area where party-goers danced around a raised, empty stage. Servant bots swerved around feet and up ramps on wheeled legs, delivering drinks, pills, and everything else to tweak one's mind.

Mona found herself on the edge of the dance floor. A servant bot screeched to a stop before her.

"Welcome, esteemed Miss. Stand or sit?"

"What's that, Rattles?" asked Mona.

"Stand or sit, esteemed Miss?"

"Why would I sit?"

"The show, esteemed Miss. The show's about to begin. Stand or sit?"

"What show?"

"The show, esteemed Miss."

"I've been walking for while, Rattles. I guess I'll sit."

"A most prudent choice, esteemed Miss. This way."

The little robot spun off, heading for the nearest ramp leading up into the seats. Mona followed.

It stopped five rows up, where two seats were empty at the end.

"How's this, esteemed Miss?"

"Fine, Rattles," said Mona as she collapsed into her chair. Looking around, she noticed that the seats were filling up quickly, excited conversation audible over the loud music.

"Drink, esteemed Miss?"

"Whiskey."

"What kind, esteemed Miss?"

"I don't care, Rattles. The wet kind."

The servant bot remained frozen for a moment, attempting to process Mona's answer. Then it raced off down the ramp.

A swarthy merchant dressed in purple robes two seats down noticed Mona and leaned toward the woman. A nose ring in one nostril was connected to an earring by a long, gold chain, and bright green eyes shone under thick eyebrows. Although ugly, those eyes reminded Mona of Darien, and a sharp pain tore at the woman's stomach.

"This is my fifth time seeing them. You?"

"First time."

The merchant slammed ringed hands together. "Oh, what a treat you're in for! You'll be telling your grandkids about this, no doubt!"

"No doubt," said Mona flatly.

The man leaned further over the empty seat.

"The show has an intoxicating effect, you know. It titillates. Should you feel yourself… swelling, just let me know. Happy to help you out."

The merchant put two fingers together and wiggled them grossly in the air.

"Good to know. I think my drink's here."

The merchant offered a toothy grin before settling back in his seat. "Well, you know where to find me."

The servant bot returned, a metal cup in its little metal hand.

"You're wet whiskey, esteemed Miss."

Mona accepted the drink.

"I only have paper yennies, Rattles."

"Just slide it into the bill validator, esteemed Miss."

Mona slid a shitayen note into a slot imbedded in the front of the servant bot. Small rollers sucked the money into the robot.

"One moment for your change, esteemed Miss."

"Keep it, Rattles."

"Truly an esteemed Miss. Enjoy the show!"

As the servant bot wheeled up the ramp, the lights of The Corkscrew began to dim, and the music faded.

"It's starting!" exclaimed the pervert merchant.

Mona sipped her whiskey as a hush fell over the audience. The lights of The Corkscrew went dark except for those highlighting the stage. Trancelike music filled the great room, waves of sound cascading over the enthralled watchers.

From high above, six pale discs, fleshy and spiraled, descended from clear cables. They gently touched the stage and fell flat in two neat rows as the cables returned to the darkness above the lights.

A lull in the music, and then—

The discs quickly unraveled as the music returned, six pale, naked figures twisting into full, slender heights. The crowd roared.

"Benten's grin, what am I seeing?!" demanded Mona.

"The Rubber Dancers of Jommuss XII!" stated the merchant over the applause.

The dancers onstage moved like water, their lithe bodies moving along impossible angles, bending at impossible degrees. Three twisted their bodies around like wrung rags while the other three bent backward into perfect circles. The human circles began spinning like coins, so quickly that they appeared as ghostly orbs.

"But how?" called out Mona to the merchant.

The merchant shrugged, white teeth bright within his dark face. "Something about the atmosphere on Jommuss XII! Softened their bones! Rubberized 'em! Another Morishita colony with unanticipated effects! Most died within the first few generations! But those that didn't?! Oh, what a treat!"

The merchant went on, but Mona had tuned him out, focusing instead on the Rubber Dancers. Moving in step with the hypnotic music, bodies intertwined and separated. Chests and hips faced one way while heads faced another. The group came together, creating 3D polygons with their bodies.

The music pushed the performers on, driving them into more bizarre stunts and increasingly sexual poses.

The crowd roared. Mona's head spun. Time lost all meaning within light and sound and twisting flesh…

And then it was over, the Rubber Dancers of Jommuss XII merging into a perfect ball of pale meat that rolled off the stage, onto a roped-off path on the dance floor, and into the back of The Corkscrew, where it (they) vanished behind a midnight curtain.

Mona was ripped from her stupor by the subsequent standing ovation.

"I told you!" the merchant gleefully shouted to Mona. "Swelling!"

Feeling suddenly trapped amidst the throng of celebrants, Mona dropped her empty metal cup and descended the ramp, aggressively pushing aside anyone not mindful enough to move from her path.

"Hope you enjoyed the show, esteemed Miss," cheerfully voiced a servant bot at the entrance. "See you next time!"

"Don't count on it, Rattles."

Mona took a deep breath as Kuyomi came into view once more. She bummed a cigarette from a silent man with a metal nose and three small stars on his right hand and moved off to be alone, her mind trying to reconcile what her eye and GLIM-patch had seen.

Her cigarette had burned halfway down when a familiar voice caught her attention.

"Nothing gets me juiced up like the Rubber Dancers," said the smiling, purple-draped merchant. "I can see they had a similar effect on you. I have a room at the Slippery Eel; it's just around the corner. Perhaps we can help each other… unwind."

"I'd rather rip that shit out of your face."

The smiled vanished.

"Now, now. You're not pretty enough to talk like that."

"But pretty enough to follow me out?"

The merchant shrugged. "Something about the eyepatch attracts me. Tell me. Is there a dead eye behind it. Or just a hole. Oh, I hope it's a hole. Imagine the fun that could be had."

"It's a hole. Similar to one I'm about to carve in your chest if you keep talking."

The merchant's face twisted. "You dare threaten me?! You mangy little slit! Do you know who—"

Mona flicked her cigarette at the merchant's face, and he cursed loudly as it crashed into his upper cheek, sending embers into his eyes.

"You bitch!" he roared, reaching for something hidden in his robes.

Mona braced for a fight.

"There you are, lass!" came the booming voice of Mickie Brass as he approached from behind. "I see you've made a friend."

"He's no friend, Junker."

Mickie moved to stand between Mona and the merchant.

"Not a friend, eh? Then why are you here, mate? Is there a problem?"

The merchant's green eyes went wide, and his hand came out from under his robes, empty and open.

"No problem, Mickie. No problem at all. I simply misread a situation."

"I doubt you can read at all, mate."

"No, of course, you're right. No reading at all. I'll be on my way, Mickie."

"See you around, mate. Or maybe it's best that I didn't."

The merchant turned to leave so quickly that he stumbled over his robes in his haste, clutching his burned eye as he rushed away.

"I didn't need your help, Junker."

"I know, Mona. But better to save your knuckles. We may need them unbruised and in full working order soon."

"How did you find me?"

"Wasn't hard. You see the show in The Corkscrew?"

"I did."

"What did you think?"

"Shock and awe, Junker. And horror. And beauty."

Mickie rubbed his beard. "Yeah, that about sums it up. How're you liking the city?"

"It's fine… for a city. At least it's not filled with the stink of Guntai. Did Teddy get our stuff?"

"Some of it. He's meeting with Urek now. Probably be late morning before everything is squared away. Which means we have some time to kill, lass. Can I squire you around the Laughing God? Take you to some of my favorite places?"

Mona thought for a moment.

"I have a better idea, Junker. Follow me."

"Where to?"

"Back to the monocycles."

"Benten's grin, why?"

"I've seen your refuge—at least, as much of it as I care to. Now I wanna show you mine."

Mickie adjusted his Akubra. "Mona, we don't have time to—"

"It's close."

"Impossible."

"You'll see."

"I don't know…"

"What's the matter, Junker? Scared?"

"Of you, Mona? Always."

"Then shut up and start walking. I don't want to miss it."

"Miss what?"

"You'll see, Space Cowboy. You'll see."

The Maggots sped down the streets of the Laughing God on their monocycles, heading west. When Mickie finally recognized where Mona was leading them, he motioned for her to stop.

Ahead, a massive gate had appeared, manned by several Laughing God guards.

"Mona, no."

"Junker, yes."

"Why?"

"Because I want to show you something."

"Not in there!"

"Yes. In there."

"This is foolish, Mona."

The Kisser adjusted her GLIM-patch.

"Fine. Stay here. But I'm going. Two days from now, I'll either be dead or off-planet, so this is my last chance to see them."

"See who, Mona?!"

"Guess you'll never know, Junker."

Mona hit the throttle and lurched forward.

"Stubborn sheila," cursed Mickie under his breath before rushing to catch up.

Guards' hands went to guns until one noticed the thick beard, the black Akubra.

"Let 'em through!" she announced to the other sentries, and the massive gate slid open, just enough to allow the two cyclists through.

And then Mickie and Mona were out of the Laughing God, heading down a path carved into the stone, a steep slope descending into Mori Hotaru.

The deep purple shroud of Kuyomi was torn off in an explosion of color as the pair entered the forest, the subarashi canopy glowing brightly above.

Lightning crackled between trees as Mona weaved her way through crystalline giants, west then north.

The woman rode with confidence, as if she were traversing well-paved roads and not a dangerous, unmarked mori. Her brown eye and GLIM-patch scanned up as much as the route ahead, soaking in the majesty of Mori Hotaru, an indescribable beauty on the face of an otherwise dead planet.

Odd creatures, and even a few rotters, could be spotted on the periphery as they raced through the forest maze. None seemed to pay them any mind.

Eventually, the Maggots arrived at a seeming dead end, a place where a line of subarashi had managed to grow in close proximity of each other, their thick roots breaking free of the grey, rocky terrain to intertwine, blocking any further advance on the monocycles.

Mona parked her vehicle along the root barrier, slid off the monocycle, and strapped on her pack.

"We're walking from here, Junker."

Mickie's grey eyes broke left, then right, searching the mori for any sign of danger.

"There's no boogie men out here, Junker."

"How do you know?"

"I'm still here, ain't I? Now let's go."

Mickie hesitated before complying, parking his monocycle next to Mona's and lifting his own pack from the rear basket. He motioned Mona ahead.

The woman climbed over the first set of subarashi roots and slid under the next.

"Try not to break an ankle, Space Cowboy. A one-legged junker is useless to me."

It took five minutes for the pair to squeeze through the clear barrier. Mickie stopped often, marveling at the veins of blue and pink within the wood, sad that such rare beauty might soon be in the hands of the Morishitas.

"I'm through," Mickie heard Mona announce from ahead, and the man plowed forward, pushing his considerable size between one last set of roots, which seemed to slide away ever so slightly, granting him passage.

"Well, Junker, this is it."

Mickie took a moment to take in the scene.

The Maggots were standing on the southern edge of a small clearing surrounded on all sides by connected subarashi. Although the ground was of the same grey rock as the rest of the planet, the clearing's center held something special.

There, not twenty meters from the Maggots, grew a giant tree, ten meters in height and leafless. It stood, dark and skeletal, against a backdrop of color, as if pulled from the realm of shadow to balance the scales of Mori Hotaru.

Mickie spoke breathlessly. "I didn't know anything else grew on Kalderra."

"As far as I know, this is the only one. I call it Bonsai Tomo."

"Bonsai trees don't grow that large, Mona."

"This one does."

Mickie continued to study the striking curves, thick trunk, and empty branches.

"Is it dead?"

Mona paused for a beat before answering. "Not quite."

"What does that mean?"

"Here, let's put our packs down and rest for a while. We've had a long day, Junker."

"That we have, Mona. That we have."

Bedrolls were laid out on the hard clearing floor a short distance from Bonsai Tomo, a heat orb placed between them to offer a bit of warmth in the cool mori. Mona and Mickie took out several skewers of meat they had purchased in the Laughing God and ate silently. When they had finished—

"How did you find this place, Mona?"

The woman shrugged, returning the wooden skewers to her bag.

"Most Maggots visit Shonin Crossways during downtime. I've never cared for cities, Junker. Too many bad memories. So, I just ride through the forests, the only beautiful places on this rock."

"You weren't afraid to venture out alone?"

"I'm a Kisser, Junker. I made peace with death a long time ago." When Mickie didn't speak, Mona continued. "Anyway, I stumbled upon this place a few years ago, somewhere I could be alone with my thoughts. It was the most beautiful thing I'd ever seen. Until I met Darien, of course. I haven't been back in quite a while. It's nice to see it again, one last time." More silence. "Well, what do you think? I know it's not the Laughing God but—"

"It's better than any city, Mona. Reminds me of my childhood."

"You were a child once, Junker? I refuse to believe that."

Mickie laughed. "It's true. I grew up on a forest planet, surrounded by trees. They weren't subarashi, obviously, but to me they were just as magical."

"Tell me about it. What was it like growing up?"

Mickie placed his hands close to the heat orb, a thin smile forming on his lips.

"It was pretty great, actually. We were a forest folk, so our little town was a canopy village, built in the highest limbs. Benten's grin, Mona, you should have seen the view from my little bedroom."

"What did your family do?"

Mickie removed his hands from the heat orb and lay back on his bedroll.

"Same thing everyone did, I suppose. We were ijiru, or tinkers. Just outside the forest, there was a large trading city, so merchants would bring us anything that needed fixing—engines, circuit boards… you name it. My dad was the best, could take anything you gave him and make it work, always better than before."

"So that's where you get it from, Junker."

"It is. He had me wiring, soldering, and fabricating as soon as I could walk. If I could hold a tool, he had me master it. We worked outside whenever we could. The air was sweet with pollen, and woodland creatures would eat right out of your hand. At night, my little sister would sing from our balcony, filling the treetops with the loveliest of melodies. Everyone loved her; she was truly a daughter of the village."

"What's her name, Junker?"

"Lissa. Lissa was her name."

Mona caught the word—was—and a lump appeared in her throat. She decided to change direction.

"Did everyone talk like you, Junker?"

"Like what, lass?"

"Like an idiot."

Mickie laughed, crossing his legs as he did. "Nah, that was all my doing."

"I don't understand."

Mickie rolled on his side to face Mona.

"Well, since our customers were the trading community, lots of stuff found its way to us. Lots of stuff banned by the Syndicate. I didn't care about any of it. Except for old music and movies. One movie, in particular, really grabbed me as a young boy. It was about a man on old Chikyu who lived off the land, had a strong moral code, and hunted large reptilian beasts. I thought he was the coolest man I'd ever seen..." Mickie trailed off. Mona remained silent, and he eventually continued. "Anyway, when everything went to shit and I had to escape the planet, I needed a new identity, a new father figure. So I started to talk like the guy, dress like the guy. Benten's grin, I even borrowed his bloody name. I was still a boy, alone and scared. That new identity, so different from the one I lost, was the shield I needed to push on." Mickie chuckled. "It was supposed to be a bloody part-time thing, Mona. But I guess you play a character long enough and the lines between real and fake thin and blur. And then they disappear altogether." Mickie tipped his Akubra to Mona. "And *that's* why I talk like a bloody idiot, lass."

"What was your village called, Junker?"

Mickie stared off into the subarashi trees. "It was called Kyywin. In the Goldthrush Forest. On planet Nodiss Thune."

Mona's heart sank.

I remember it. I was a girl, but I still remember it. Locked in that hotel room in Tokyo, he had the news on. A wildfire had swept through the southern part of Goldthrush Forest, a place long-desired by the Morishitas for its bright yellow trees and the beautiful lumber they could produce. The bastard commented on the story—"Fools. Everyone has to learn the hard way what happens when you say no to the Morishitas." Then he climbed on top of me. And I watched a video clip of the forest burning as he..."

"Oh, Junker. I'm so sorry."

Mickie's head cocked to the side. "You know the story?"

"I do."

"Most don't. The Syndicate buried it."

"Is that how you got those scars?"

"Some of them. I tried to pull my mum and dad out of the fire. It was already too late for Lissa. But I was too small. Too weak. And I vowed to never be that helpless again."

Mona ran her hands down her legs, unsure of what else to do with them.

"Well, Junker, there's a lot of things people can call you. Small or weak ain't one of them."

Another heavy silence, broken only by the quiet hum of the heat orb. Kuyomi was starting to vanish beneath the tree line when—

A massive butterfly, a meter wide with glowing blue wings, broke into the clearing from the forest beyond.

"Junker! It's starting!"

"What's starting?"

"Shut up and watch!"

The butterfly circled the clearing twice, its luminescent wings leaving a trail of color in its wake, before settling on one of Bonsai Tomo's bare branches.

Seconds later, a second butterfly tore through the subarashi. Then a third and fourth. And then more. So many more.

A cyclone of red, orange, yellow, green, and blue filled the clearing, stirring the air and causing Mona and Mickie's hair to waver in the cool breeze. Trails of color twisted together and crossed, confounding the eye and filling hearts with wonder.

One by one, they settled onto Bonsai Tomo, filling in every space where a leaf should normally reside. After several minutes, Bonsai Tomo was transformed, its once-bare limbs now filled with moving light and kaleidoscope life.

Mona looked over and found that Mickie's jaw had fallen. She smiled.

"Well, Junker? What do you think?"

"It's wonderful, Mona. It… it reminds me of…. Never mind."

"I understand."

"How long will they stay like this?"

"Not long. I think they just come here to say hello to each other. Always at this same time. I guess all creatures, whether human or insect, feel the pull of community. The need for family. A place to call home."

Mona and Mickie lay back on their rolls, enjoying the magical scene in silence.

"Thank you for showing me this, Mona. I'll never forget what I've seen here tonight."

"Sure beats The Corkscrew, eh?"

"It does, lass. It certainly does."

The pair resumed their silent viewing. Eventually, an orange-winged butterfly peeled off Bonsai Tomo, painting a bright line across the clearing as it returned to Mori Hotaru. Soon, the clearing was full of the magical insects once more as they flew in every direction, leaving home with a quiet promise to return soon.

As always, Mona was sad to see them go but found joy in the understanding that they would always find each other again.

That is, until the bloody Morishitas start lumber production. Will the Syndicate destroy this place of wonder? Will they capture the butterflies and sell them off to rich ladies across the galaxy? Will lives of freedom be exchanged for cages?

The low sounds of snoring snatched Mona from her dark musings. She turned to find Mickie Brass asleep, face hidden under his ridiculous Akubra.

Suddenly realizing her mouth was dry, Mona rose and moved to kneel before Mickie's pack, where both skins of water were stored. Working quietly as not to wake the man, Mona carefully undid the pack and searched for the water. She found it in short order and drank deeply from the nano fiber bag.

As she did, her eye and GLIM-patch fell on the closed front pocket of the pack. She drank more before returning the water skin to where she discovered it. Mona then started to stand but paused, her hand going to the front pocket. She slowly unzipped the pocket and pushed it open to see inside.

Mickie's chewed up cigar sat on top. Having no interest in touching the saliva-soaked cancer stick, she nudged it out of the way. Beneath was an assortment of papers. She slipped out the first, which was covered in random numbers. A second contained strange glyphs. A third was a hand-drawn map of Kalderra, with dots and notations strewn throughout.

Benten's grin, his handwriting is awful. How can anyone read this?

Mona was ready to close the pocket when she noticed something red tucked away in the bottom. She reached in to retrieve it. And froze.

Between the metal tip of her index finger and thumb was a flattened origami heart.

Mickie stirred on his bed roll, and Mona quickly dropped the heart back in place and closed the pack. She then returned to her bed roll and lay down, her mind spinning. She tried to sleep but found nothing but questions.

And Bonsai Tomo stared down at the Maggot named Mona Ripple, begging her to see past the facade of bare branches. Begging her to remember it at its fullest, truest self.

CHAPTER 4

LOVELESS

"This isn't what I had in mind, Teddy."

"I know, Mickie. This is better."

"It's more complicated, Teddy."

"It's more timely, Mickie. Urek couldn't believe the luck when I told him about your plans."

Mickie sighed deeply as Mona entered the room and joined the men. "Ok, walk me through it."

Teddy's visor flashed in an assortment of color.

"So, I told you that Urek has been seeing a lady Guntai."

"You mentioned it."

"Well, turns out, she's stationed at Ghool Tower. And she likes to talk. A lot. Especially when she has a head full of sake. Which Urek has been feeding her more often than not. Anyway, amidst her general complaining, she let it slip that she'll be working double shifts for the next week or so. Urek carefully dug a little deeper and found out that the bloody Sindo-Emperor will be visiting Kalderra. Is already en route, matter of fact. Something about an inspection or announcement or whatever else could get that moldy old creature to travel halfway across the galaxy.

Obviously, they're trying to keep it on the hush, but massive preparations still have to be made, including a tripling of security."

"Benten's grin, what kind of Guntai spouts imperial secrets to a drinking buddy?" asked Mona.

"The female kind," responded Teddy. "Urek has a… way with women. Makes him an invaluable ally."

Mona rolled her brown eye. "Fine. I'll take your word for it. But wouldn't increased security and heightened attention work against us? I don't see how this is good news."

"If this was all the info we had, it's not. But an opportunity has been created. Fell right into our bloody laps."

"And that being?" prodded Mona.

Teddy smiled beneath his visor. "The Countess's vanity."

"Go on."

"You may have heard—or better yet, noticed—that Desma Ghool is quite particular about her appearance. The best hair and makeup."

"She still looks like a monster," interrupted Mona.

Teddy went on. "The best jewelry. And most importantly to us, the best clothing. Once a month, she has a shipment of the finest fashion flown in from Tokyo. Costs a bloody fortune. But for this affair—a meeting with Sakuramachi Morishita himself—well, this won't suffice. To make the best possible impression on the Sindo-Emperor, Ghool is bringing in a Wasai no Takumi—a master tailor from the craftsman guild—to outfit her for the occasion."

"I don't see how this helps us, Blinders."

"That brings us back to our loose-lipped Guntai. The Takumi's arrival has thrown a wrench in the security planning. Ghool has demanded that he be treated like imperial royalty; she even has a special entrance for him to use, one that circumvents the usual checkpoints and protocols."

"So the Takumi has already landed on Kalderra?" asked Mickie.

"He has. With one female assistant—his Deshi. His container of clothing was already scanned, processed, and sealed upon arrival at the Spaceport.

Meaning they won't go through it again at Ghool Tower. The Countess wants the Takumi to have a clean, unencumbered trip into her home so as not to offend. Apparently, these Takumi are a touchy bunch."

"They sound like pricks," added Mona.

Teddy shrugged. "There's more imperial princes and princesses than there are Wasai no Takumi. They're in high demand, and they know it."

"Where is the Takumi now, mate?"

"I did some digging. He and his assistant are being shown all the hospitality that Kalderra has to offer. At Luxx Manor in Karudera City."

"Luxx Manor?"

"That's right, Mickie. Shivantae Tong's place."

Mona shook her head. "I'm sorry, but what does this have to do with us?"

"Don't you see, lass? They want us to pose as this Takumi and his assistant. There's just one little problem."

Teddy's visor swung to Mickie. "And what's that?"

"I'm not bloody Japanese, mate!"

Teddy grinned. "And neither is this Takumi. The guild doesn't care about gender or skin color or where you're from. The guild only cares about skill. And this guy… this *white guy* is among the most talented."

"All white guys don't look alike, Teddy."

Teddy waved Mickie away. "Close enough. Plus, only members of the elite are allowed to look a Takumi in the eye. I doubt any of the security detail could pick this man out a of lineup."

"And the assistant?"

"Assistants are basically proteges. They remain completely covered, including their faces, until they reach the rank of Takumi. Only then are they allowed to be seen… to receive the praises they so desperately seek. Mona can easily hide under the outfit."

"Well I can't hide, mate!"

Teddy let out an exasperated breath. "Benten's grin, have some faith, Mickie. I spent all morning hacking my way into K-nex. I swapped out the scanned image of the Takumi from the Spaceport and replaced it with your ugly mug. How about a little pat on the back? That wasn't easy!"

"And how is the switch supposed to happen?"

"Shivantae will make sure that it's you two who come down from the suite and not the Takumi and his assistant. Do you doubt her ability to do so?"

Mickie laughed. "When it comes to that woman, I doubt nothing."

Teddy slammed his hand down on the table. "Then it's settled. You've got a clear path into Ghool Tower. I've already penetrated their outdated security system and burned passkeys for you both. Should grant you access to any room in the Tower. Once you're in, the rest is up to you."

"And when do we go?"

"Tomorrow morning would be best. Given that the Guntai will all be working non-stop once the Sindo-Emperor arrives, the Tower will be operating with a fairly skeleton crew for next couple of days. It's your best chance."

"I don't like it, mate."

"Me neither, Mickie! But your plan would have certainly ended in a shootout, mucking up years of planning!"

"What planning?" asked Mona.

Teddy grimaced. "Nothing, Miss Mona. I'm just an old man babbling. An old man nervous for his friends."

"We ain't friends, Blinders. This is a business transaction."

"Of course, of course."

"All right, mate. This does seem like a slightly better plan. The downside is the same, but the upside might reduce the body count. We'll head to Karudera City, get with Shivantae, and work out the rest of the particulars, like securing passage on a smuggling vessel."

"I already took care of that, Mickie. Get the package back to the Crossways, and Urek will get Miss Mona and her beau off-planet."

"Thank you, my friend. It seems like you've taken care of everything. As usual."

"Uh, just one more thing, Mickie."

"What's that?"

"Very few people know what the Takumi looks like. But they know what he *should* look like. And it ain't like you."

"I don't follow, mate."

"It means you're gonna have to clean up, Junker."

"I don't like the sound of that, lass."

"I have the perfect woman for the job," said Teddy. "Go see Lisbeth at Curtain Call. We won't be able to recognize you when she's done."

Mona cackled. "I'm liking this plan more and more, Junker."

The trio listened until the sounds of two bodies dropping to the floor could be heard in the room beyond.

Shivantae Tong placed her slender finger against a small pad, and the secret entrance to Luxx Manor's suite slid open.

"Best hurry," said Shivantae as she stomped into the hotel's best set of rooms in her high heels and color-shifting power suit. Mona Ripple and Mickie Brass followed the tall woman.

"Why?" asked Mona beneath her uchikatsugi, a Japanese veil required for all Takumi assistants. "Will they be waking up soon?"

"Don't be silly," snapped Shivantae. "They'll stay out until I decide to bring them back. If I decide to do so at all. I don't care for their elitist ways."

"Could have fooled me," shot back Mona, motioning to the surrounding opulence.

Shivantae's thin lips curled in a tight smile. "The best place to hide is in clear sight, my dear. You'll learn that soon enough." The grand hotelier quickly turned to Mickie, her tight bun of hair locked in place. "I called Ghool Tower on their behalf—it seemed like something that arrogant

Takumi would demand—and requested a pickup. There was some resistance given that it came several hours ahead of schedule, but I handled the fat mouthed Guntai on the other end of the line. Anyway, the Countess's personal transport is on its way. Will probably be here any minute. I've already had the Takumi's container brought around back for pickup."

"Fujin's ass! This bastard doesn't look anything like me!" exclaimed Mickey as he shuffled over to study the incapacitated Takumi.

Shivantae waved her hand dismissively. "He's larger than average. White. Dark hair. Close enough."

"No one's gonna buy this, Shiv."

"Have you looked in the mirror, Mickie?"

"I know what I bloody look like!"

Shivantae looked to Mona, and the women shared a look of amusement.

"He doesn't even have a bloody beard, Shiv!"

"Look," said Shivantae as she moved around the suite, "no one at the Luxx looked at this bastard. And even if they did, *my people* know better than to open their mouths when they're paid to keep them shut." The woman bent down and plucked something from the large crystal table dominating the center of the room. "If it makes you feel better, put this on. Looks like the bastard was planning on wearing it."

Shivantae handed Mickie the massive kasa hat. Made of bamboo, the traditional piece was folded down on both sides and protruded far out in the front, creating a shadow over the wearer's face. It was painted vermillion, with gold leaf applied liberally in unique designs across the surface.

Mickie sighed upon examining the item. "Of course the bastard would be wearing *this* absurd thing."

Shivantae and Mona each stifled a laugh before the hotelier moved to the elevator doors.

"Ok, this is you. The suite elevator doesn't make any stops and will take you directly to the back VIP exit. The imperial transport will probably be waiting. Don't talk. You don't need to. Remember, you're above all of these peasants. Think like that. Act like that. No one will give you any trouble. Passes and key cards?"

Mickie slapped his kimono, referencing the imperial pass at his neck and freshly burned key cards in his pockets. "Check."

"Weapons?"

Mickie nodded. "Tucked away. As tight as we could get them. But if we're patted down or scanned, we'll be made. And then—"

"You're the Takumi!" Shiv shouted. "And *this* is your loyal Deshi! You have been personally invited by the Crimson Lady to honor the arrival of the Sindo-Emperor! Remind them of that, and watch them dive from your path."

"I think I like you, Shivantae," said Mona. "At least, as much as I can like someone who lives in a place like this."

"And I respect those willing to put themselves on the line for something greater than themselves," responded Shiv.

Whether the woman was offering compliment or offense, Mona Ripple couldn't tell.

The gilded elevator doors opened, and Shivantae motioned the Maggots in. Mona entered, but the hotelier grabbed Mickie by the arm, stopping the large man.

"Are you sure about this?" Shiv hissed. "This is foolish, Mickie. Now more than ever. We're so close."

Mickie gently removed the woman's hand.

"Do you trust me, Shiv?"

"Always, Mickie."

"Then wish me luck, lass."

"Best of luck, Mickie."

The Space Cowboy joined the Kisser in the elevator, leaving Shivantae Tong to watch them from the suite.

"Mona Ripple," said Shiv, "if Mickie Brass dies on this mission, you'd best die alongside him."

"We all come out or none of us come out," replied Mona. "I promise you. Thank you, Shivantae Tong."

The elevator doors slid shut.

"You're welcome, Mona Ripple. But you'd better be worth it."

"I guess some girls do have a taste for junker—eh, Junker?"

"We're old friends, Mona. Nothing more."

"None of my business, Junker."

Mickie stared down at the gaudy kasa hat in his gloved hand. "I can't believe I have to wear this bloody thing."

Mona's brown eye and GLIM-patch naturally went to the kasa before slowly winding upward.

Mickie Brass, the unkempt junker with the unrefined personality to match, had been reborn by Lisbeth, proprietor of Curtain Call. The man's black kuromontsuki kimono was perfectly fitted to his large, athletic form. And although close inspection would reveal the sub-par stitching and inexpensive thread, no Guntai would be able to tell the difference between Lisbeth's handiwork and that of a true Takumi.

But Lisbeth's real magic trick had nothing to do with the wardrobe.

Mickie's beard had been conditioned, trimmed, and combed to a fine point. His once-random tangle of salt and pepper hairs now flowed seamlessly together, as if dyed that way to follow the hottest trend. The beard now ran down his cheek in clean lines that looked carved by a laser.

The Space Cowboy's hair, once a disheveled mess, was now professionally clipped. Long hair on top was brushed back and held in place by expensive wax that shimmered in the light. Shorter, silvering hair on each side was tucked cleanly behind an ear.

Some dark liner, applied despite Mickie's many protests, made the man's grey eyes pop against a weathered face, one that appeared much less leathery thanks to several coats of skin cream.

Mickie finally noticed Mona staring at him.

"What?"

Mona quickly turned to watch the elevator floor numbers descend.

"Nothing."

"I know I look ridiculous. I *feel* ridiculous."

Mona began to say something but stopped herself. Instead—

"No, you clean up well, Junker. Real classy."

"Really?"

"Yeah. I mean, you're no Darien, but no one is. Now throw that kasa on to hide that new face of yours. We're almost there."

Mickie did as he was told, placing the oversized kasa on his head. He turned to Mona for approval.

"Ok, *now* you look ridiculous. You'll fit right in at the Tower. Let's go, Space Cowboy."

The shiny imperial transport was waiting for the Maggots as they exited Luxx Manor. Mickie marched forward with all the pomp a man like him could muster, the first rays of Kalderra's blue sun cutting across the planet to leave the false Takumi's face drenched in shadow.

Mona played her part as the Deshi, careful to meekly glide forward, always two steps behind her master. Her apprentice's white kimono flowed around her as she appraised the scene from beneath her veil.

Four Guntai, dressed in typical all-black and donning high-tech samurai helmets known as kabutex that covered head, face, and neck, stood at rapt attention.

When none spoke, Mickie took control.

"Where is my container for the Countess?"

Mona's ear twitched at the junker's voice, which had traded its strange, backwoods twang for a somewhat believable posh accent.

"Already placed inside the vehicle, honored Takumi," replied one Guntai, following the words with a deep bow.

"It better be well-secured. Do you think the Countess likes wrinkles in her clothing? Have you ever tried to iron Lotus Silk, Guntai?"

The once-confident soldier shifted from one foot to the next.

"I'll check it again, honored Takumi. Personally. As I do, please feel free to enter the transport when you are ready. I serve at your command." Another deep bow.

Mona noticed that all of the Guntai had their helmets pointed downward at small angles, as if trying to make it obvious that they were following orders by not looking the Takumi in his eye.

Benten's grin, this might be easier than I bloody thought. I could be in Darien's arms before midday.

Mickie didn't bother speaking again, electing to simply stomp past the bowing Guntai to enter the luxury vehicle. The Space Cowboy smoothly slid into soft leather that automatically conformed to his shape and took a long drink of sake from a glass placed on a seat-side table. Only after getting fully comfortable did Mickie motion Mona—his Deshi—to join him.

You're a real bastard, Junker. I'm sure you're really enjoying making me feel like a servant. Just remember who's paying who here.

After the Guntai had double-checked the Takumi's container—probably three or four times—the transport was off, cutting through an empty Karudera City that had yet to wake.

Mona and Mickie did not speak during the tense trip, a safety precaution in case the imperial transport was bugged. Familiar landmarks sped by, ones Mona had taken note of just a few evenings past.

The night my love was stolen.

After several minutes, the eyesore that was Ghool Tower came into view, rising above the Maggots like a giant boot prepared to drop.

Several checkpoints were passed through without the transport even slowing. Mickie shot Mona a hopeful glance.

Instead of pulling up to the front of Ghool Tower, where a half-dozen ChoMM guardians waited, the imperial transport was guided to the right by waving Guntai, taking the Maggots around the fortress in a counter-clockwise direction.

Rounding the northernmost side of the imposing structure, Ghool Tower climbed out of sight on Mickie and Mona's left while the vast emptiness of Karudera IV dominated the scene to the right.

Mona heard Mickie mumble lowly as the transport slowed, then stopped.

"Checkpoint."

"Be the Takumi," she responded quietly.

The transport door slid open to reveal two-dozen Guntai stationed in neat rows, leaving a clear path from vehicle to back entrance. All bowed as the Takumi exited the transport, his faithful Deshi trailing.

A Guntai bearing the red bands of a sergeant stepped forward.

"We are honored to be in your presence, honored Takumi. If you would allow me to please scan you, I'll get you quickly inside with all the comforts that you deserve."

Mickie did not bother answering the soldier; he simply offered a barely perceptible nod. Mona's heart pounded in her chest.

The Guntai sergeant raised a small hand scanner to Mickie's face, careful to only look at the reading.

It will take but a second to grab my weapon. I can shoot three before they even reach for theirs. If Mickie acts quickly, he can maybe take out five more. We'll have to duck behind the—

A confirming *beep* and green light snatched Mona Ripple from her suicidal planning.

"Thank you, honored Takumi," said the bowing sergeant. "Once your Deshi is validated, we'll be done here."

Fujin's ass! Blinders didn't saying anything about me being scanned! As soon as I'm dead, I'm gonna kill that little—

"My Deshi is not to be scanned," declared Mickie, and Mona marveled at the evenness of the man's voice under such pressure.

"But, honored Takumi, all must be scanned before entering. It's literally the *least* of security protocols that must be followed."

Mickie seemed to grow larger beneath his kimono.

"The Deshi has not earned the right for her face to been seen. She is not a person; she is an extra set of hands for her Takumi. To validate me is to validate her, for she is an extension of her Takumi."

Mona could sense the sergeant's anxiousness swelling behind his face guard.

"But… honored Takumi," he stammered, "it is but a quick scan. I'll have everyone turn away if that helps."

"It does not!" bellowed Mickie. "And I tire of speaking with you. Please tell the Countess that I am most sorry that I was unable to outfit her for the Sindo-Emperor's arrival. Tell her—"

The sergeant fell into one of the deepest bows Mona Ripple had ever seen.

"Of course, your scan is more than acceptable for your Deshi, honored Takumi. Consider yourself free to enter."

Mona, finally able to release the breath she'd been holding, saw that the massive container of clothing had already been removed from the transport and carefully placed on a flutter pallet that gently hovered a half-meter above the ground.

Mickie waited until the container floated past, guided by four Guntai, before moving to follow, Mona following the requisite two steps away.

Large double doors, significantly less ornate than Ghool Tower's front entrance, slid open. Mickie and Mona advanced, four more Guntai behind as a rear guard.

And just like that, the Maggots had infiltrated Ghool Tower. Mona Ripple smiled brightly under her Deshi veil.

I'm here, my love. Can you feel me? I'm coming to save you. We'll be together soon. Forever.

Mickie and Mona were taken to the 25th floor of Ghool Tower and ushered into a massive, lavish room filled with mirrors, stands, couches, refreshments, and a variety of sewing devices both modern and traditional. At its far end sat a single elevator door, highly decorated in gold with two large red gemstones embedded in the metal—unblinking crimson eyes staring into the space within.

Four of the Guntai lowered the flutter pallet and slid the container free. As several worked to adequately position the invaluable wardrobe cube, another pressed an invisible button on the flutter pallet, causing it to retract and fold until it was no more than a small square that could be held in one hand. After placing the flutter square on the nearest crystal table, a Guntai approached Mickie and bowed before speaking.

"Honored Takumi, would you like assistance in removing items from the shipping container?"

"I have a Deshi for that. Just remove the lock seal and be gone. I have many preparations to make before the Countess comes down."

"The Countess has been made aware of your arrival, honored Takumi. Despite the accelerated schedule, she is eager to see what you have brought."

"Please let the Countess know that there is no need for haste. We arrived early only to have everything perfect for the Crimson Lady. And there is much that needs to be prepared."

"It will be done, honored Takumi. I will have someone stationed outside should you need anything at all. The Countess has ordered that no request of yours go unfilled."

"I request to be left alone. And not to be disturbed until the Countess is fully ready to be fitted."

"Of course, honored Takumi."

In short order, the container was unsealed and placed neatly to the side of the large chamber. The Guntai wasted no time in filing out of the grand fitting room, eager to be far away from the Takumi and his Deshi.

As soon as they were alone, Mona turned to Mickie.

"Benten's grin, Junker! I couldn't even detect that stupid accent of yours. And good thinking on the face scanner excuse. Although, honestly, we should have anticipated that. Ok, when do we move?"

Mona's speech was hurried, hopeful excitement making her sound more schoolgirl than Maggot Kisser.

Mickie ignored her and looked around, fully taking things in now that he was no longer in character.

"First things first, lass. See if you can pull up the Tower floor plans in your GLIM-patch."

Having been given a crash course in GLIM-patch operation by Teddy Feenk, Mona ran the metal tip of her index finger along the side of the strange material, tapped twice, and then added her middle digit. When she closed her left eye, the superimposed layout of Ghool Tower was displayed before Mona in clear blue lines.

"Got it, Junker."

Mickie nodded toward the ornate elevator. "Does that one go where we need it?"

Mona studied the plans for a moment, virtually traversing floors.

"Yep. That's the Red Lyft." She continued her examination. "Goes all the way from the Countess Quarters down to the imperial garage. Only Desma Ghool and a few trusted servants have regular access."

"And us, lass."

Mona smiled wickedly. "And us."

Mickie made for the Red Lyft, stopping to collect the contracted flutter square on the way.

"What do you need that for?"

The Space Cowboy tucked the object away beneath his kimono.

"Emergencies, lass. Emergencies. Now, you ready?"

Mona inhaled deeply to steady herself. She could almost smell Darien a few floors above, terror-stricken and desperately awaiting rescue.

"I am. Time to take back what's rightfully mine."

Mona joined Mickie at the Red Lyft. They held their collective breath as Mickie retrieved the burned key card from a deep pocket and touched it to the elevator's scanner. A quiet hum emanated from behind the bejeweled doors as the cabin began to quickly descend.

Seconds later, the elevator entrance slid open, releasing an overpowering smell of perfume into the grand fitting room.

Mickie and Mona let out relieved sighs.

"I think I owe Blinders an apology. And maybe a few extra tamari."

"Teddy is already well-compensated, lass."

Mona made to enter the Red Lyft but was stopped by a hand on her arm.

"Up and down, Mona. Quietly. We get your boy. We get back in the lift. We go down to the garage. We commandeer a vehicle. We take the trails northeast through Karudera IV. With any luck, we'll be in the Crossways before anyone knows what's happened."

"I know the bloody plan, Junker."

"Just making sure, Mona."

Mona shook her arm free. "Then consider yourself sure."

The Maggots entered the Red Lyft, and Mickie pressed the uppermost button. The pair stared ahead as the doors slid shut.

"But if I see that bitch, Junker, I'm gonna carve her heart out."

"Benten's grin, Mona! That's the opposite of *quietly*."

"Not if I cut her throat first."

Mickie shook his head. "Bloody sheilas."

The Red Lyft opened onto the imperial quarters of the Crimson Lady. The Maggots stepped out into a cathedral-ceilinged parlor, complete with stocked bars on each side and plush sofas upholstered in the finest of fabrics. Cleaning bots criss-crossed a white marble floor veined in gold and red. None of the automatons took note of the strange pair who had entered their domain.

"Alright, lass," whispered Mickie, "which way to the paramours' rooms?"

"Give me a moment," replied Mona in a low voice as she ran through the floor plans with her GLIM-patch. A beat passed. "The Countess's private quarters are through those large double doors straight ahead. To the left of her chambers is some kind of recreation room. Who knows what kind of twisted business goes on back there? It looks like there's a whole mess of rooms that branch out to the right, just down that hall. That must be where the paramours are kept."

The bitch likes to keep her toys within reach for easy play. Well, there's one toy that's coming home with me.

Mickie nodded, his grey eyes studying the gilded double doors across the parlor. He offered a silent prayer to Izanagi that they wouldn't open.

"Let's move fast, lass."

Mickie and Mona moved quickly through the parlor and turned right, entering the hallway found there. After a short walk, the corridor opened onto a large, circular room, this one outfitted much like the main parlor. White doors could be seen along the walls, seven in total, each embossed with a large heart made of hundreds of rubies.

Mickie's eyes traced the circumference of the mini-parlor.

"He could be in any of them, lass. Do we just start opening doors?"

"Just wait," said Mona, her GLIM-patch zooming in on the floor plans.

All of the paramour rooms appeared identical... except one. The room at the far end, opposite the hallway, was different from the others—larger, with a massive window overlooking Karudera IV.

Examining that door more closely, Mona could see rows of diamonds outlining the ruby heart.

The favored room for the favored paramour. And my Darien would definitely be favored by that bitch.

"There. The room at our twelve. Darien's in there."

"How can you be sure, lass?"

"Because I know it, Junker."

Because I can feel him there. Our hearts are intertwined by tendrils of love that care nothing of distance.

"Then let's get him and get out of here."

Mona nodded and made her way across the room, growing increasingly dizzy with each step, anticipation threatening to overcome balance.

They reached the door and noted a small scanner next to it on the wall.

"Benten's grin, I wonder if she keeps them locked in," commented Mickie. "Her own human bloody zoo. You ready, lass?"

"Open it."

Mickie touched Feenk's key card to the reader, and the door slid open.

Relief spread through Mona Ripple like a flood.

Darien Vance sat at an ornate table against the left wall, brushing his blond hair in front of a curved mirror. Shirtless, he wore tight, cream-colored shorts, and his wrists sparkled with jewels. A thick gold choker set with more rubies surrounded the young man's thin neck.

Darien spoke without taking his green eyes from the mirror. "I don't recall putting in my breakfast order. Just leave it on the coffee table. If it's a greasy mess like yesterday, just know that I'll be ordering something different."

Mona floated into the room, her heart swelling. She removed her Deshi veil as she closed the distance.

"Darien, my love!"

The young man turned at the familiar voice, the brush falling from his hand to land loudly on the antique table. Mickie winced at the noise as Darien stood.

"Mona? Is that you? But how?"

Mona launched forward, burying Darien in a hug, followed by a passionate kiss, her rough hands gripping the sides of his face.

"Oh, my love! I'm so sorry that this happened to you. I'll never let you out of my sight again."

Darien ran his slender fingers through Mona's tangled hair as he spoke. "Benten's grin, Mona. How did you get in here?"

"No time for that now, my love. But it wasn't easy. Luckily, I had help."

Darien's gaze moved past Mona to find Mickie Brass standing by the door. The Space Cowboy removed his kasa hat.

"I see… Mickie."

"Darien."

The young man returned to Mona. "But what are you doing here?"

The Kisser's bright smile fell a bit.

"What do you think? We're rescuing you, my love."

"Rescuing me from what?"

Mona's smile vanished.

"From what?! From all *this*!"

Darien grinned and took a step back from Mona. He motioned around the room.

"Who would want to be rescued from this? Look around you, Mona. I have the best of everything."

Mona's face began to twist.

"Darien, my love… You're a slave."

The young man laughed. "Is that what they told you? I'm a paramour. That's a high honor around here. And not just any paramour. I'm the prime paramour, first among a select few." He began to pace on the thick carpet. "Look at what I've been given, Mona. A suite to myself—all the other paramours are two or even three to a room. And look at that view!"

"That's Karudera IV, mate," Mickie cut in. "They say that's where thousands of bodies are hidden. Many of them former paramours."

Darien waved Mickie away. "Only the ones that disappoint the Countess. I don't plan on doing any such thing."

Mona's hands clenched and unclenched.

"Darien, a gilded cage is still a cage, my love."

The young man's green eyes flashed. "Being poor is a cage, Mona. Having dreams but no means to reach them is a cage. Life is a cage. When you realize that, you'll see that living in a gilded one is preferable."

"She doesn't love you, Darien."

"You don't know that!"

"You're an object to her! Nothing more!"

"You don't know the conversations we've had! She likes my ideas about fashion. She's gonna take me to Tokyo eventually, introduce me to all the leading designers."

Mona stepped closer to the young man, her body starting to shake with rage.

"She's lying to you, Darien! She'll tire of you and then dispose of you! Look out your window, my love! That's where you'll end up!"

Darien offered a shrug. "I don't see it that way, Mona."

"You're not seeing things straight at all, my love!"

"I disagree."

"You're a *slave!*"

"I'm a *paramour*. The *prime* paramour."

"She's put a collar on you! You're property!"

Darien reached up to touch the metal choker. "Oh, this? This is 24 karat gold, I'll have you know. I'm sure I could get it off if I really tried." He held out his arms. "And look at all the jewelry she's given me. And this isn't all of it. Not by a long shot. I have a whole box full of the stuff. With more to come!"

"They're trinkets, Darien! Trinkets to control you!"

Another shrug. "For now. Until I can control her."

Mickie simply shook his head from the doorway.

"You can't believe that," said Mona, her words coming out in a whisper.

Darien moved to Mona and stroked her arms.

"Look, I've been given an opportunity. A golden ticket."

"To go with your golden shackles."

"I'm going to make the best of this, Mona."

"But… I love you."

"I know. And I appreciate that."

Something snapped in Mona Ripple, and she ripped herself free of Darien.

"Let's go! You're coming with us. You're not yourself. Who knows what kinds of chemicals or drugs you've been given?"

"Ambition's the only thing he's high on, lass," said Mickie.

"Shut up, Junker! You keep your mouth shut! Let's go, Darien!"

"I'm sorry, Mona. I like it here."

"You don't know what you like! What you need!"

"I'm staying."

"You're coming! And that's final! Junker, he's obviously been brainwashed. Grab him, and let's get out of here."

Mickie advanced on the young man, the look on the Space Cowboy's face leaving no room for discussion.

Darien, seeing the hulking brute coming his way, held up his hands in surrender.

"Ok, ok, I'm coming with you. Let me at least put a shirt on."

Darien moved toward his plush bed, touched something on the nightstand there, and then stepped to a massive dresser from which he removed a silk shirt and slipped it on over his head. He turned to face Mona and Mickie.

"It's time."

Mona let out a relieved breath. "My love, you've finally come to your senses. This time tomorrow, we'll have new lives, away from all this—"

"No. I mean, it's time for you both to leave."

Mickie's head cocked to the side as sudden tension filled the man. He glanced over to the nightstand to see a red light blinking.

"You little bastard," said Mickie, ripping off his kimono to reveal a skinsuit beneath.

"You left me no choice, Mickie."

"What's going on?" demanded Mona.

"We have to go, lass. The bastard triggered an alarm."

Mona's brown eye went wide. "But why?!"

"I told you why, Mona."

Mona Ripple fell to her knees, a marionette whose strings had been cut.

Mickie pulled a laz-pistol from his belt and pointed it at Darien.

"This is for being a slimy twat," Mickie stated coldly as Darien's green eyes slammed shut in terror.

"No!" screamed Mona from the floor. "No, Junker!"

"He's a rat, lass."

Mona scrambled to her feet and stood on wobbly legs. Her right hand went to her chest. Her heart no longer pounded. In fact, it didn't feel as if it was beating at all. Her shoulders slumped.

"Let's go, Junker."

"But, lass—"

"Let's go."

And with that, Mona slunk from the room, leaving Mickie and Darien alone.

Mickie tucked away the pistol and stepped forward.

"You just rejected the greatest gift, mate. You're a bloody slug, Darien Vance."

"I'd rather be a slug than a Maggot, Mickie Brass. Say hi to the Guntai for me."

Mickie nodded and turned to leave but spun back, delivering a left cross that connected cleanly with the young man's jaw, sending him sprawling onto the bed unconscious.

Mickie smiled. "By the way… thanks, mate."

Mona's mind reeled as she staggered down the hallway, red lights blinking everywhere along the walls and ceiling. She was numb, dead inside. It was a feeling she knew all too well, for far too long.

But as she passed the ornate double doors to her right, another emotion slipped in and swelled, filling the void.

And Mona Ripple gave in to cold rage.

Tearing off her Deshi kimono, Mona took out her own key card and touched it to the sensor.

The doors swung open, and the Kisser marched into the private quarters of Desma Ghool, the Countess of Kalderra.

Her laz-pistol leading the way, Mona marched through the massive suite, a hunter stalking the most valuable of prey. GLIM-patch swiveling left and right, Mona searched every corner—until she heard mechanical whirring coming from a room to her right. She made for it.

Mona Ripple stepped into the open doorway, gun drawn, prepared to take a life for the one that was stolen.

She froze.

Seated before her on a bizarre medical chair was not the highly decorated woman Mona Ripple expected to find. Instead, she discovered a ruined monstrosity.

Pink, scarred skin covered the Countess's face, stealing the natural curves of brow, cheek, and chin. Bejeweled teeth gleamed within a lipless mouth. A gaping hole stood where a nose should have been. Red, bloodshot eyes stared out, missing eyelids painting an expression of horrified shock.

Two arms of the machine swung over the Countess's head, coming to rest in front of the mutilated woman, an oval of rubbery material stretched tightly between them. The arms retracted horizontally, pulling the pale membrane against Desma Ghool's melted visage. Small instruments unfolded and traced the lines of the fleshy mask, surgical lasers smoothing out contours while microscopic needles secured the new face.

Within seconds, the transformation was complete, and the many arms of the medical chair retreated into their various slots.

Desma Ghool blinked several times, wetting her eyes, before licking her artificial lips and gingerly touching her now-smooth cheek. She noticed Mona in the doorway, laz-pistol pointed her way.

"Are you here to kill me?"

"I am."

The Countess studied Mona for a moment before recognition struck. She offered a red smile. "But that's not why you came, is it? You're that Maggot. The one from the yakai."

"I'm Mona Ripple. It's important that you know my name before I kill you."

Ghool's head tilted to the side, and she glanced at the red warning lights blinking outside in the suite.

"It must have been hard getting this far, *Mona Ripple*. What could I possibly have done to you to warrant such effort?"

Mona's outstretched arm trembled with rage, causing the gun to waver.

"You stole my one true love, you bitch. And now you're gonna pay."

Ghool's eyes widened in understanding. "Ahh, I see. So you came here to rescue Darien. Is that it?" Mona did not respond. "Well, if that's the case, then where is he? Surely you wouldn't risk your grand getaway for a little payback?"

When Mona only offered continued silence, the Countess slowly rose from her medical chair, careful to keep her hands out and to her sides.

"Where is your love, Mona Ripple?"

The barrel of the gun now shook.

"Mona? Why are you alone here with me?"

"Because he chose to stay!" screamed the Maggot, her brown eye beginning to fill with water. "The bastard chose to stay!"

Ghool's smile shifted, and the Countess offered a knowing, almost sympathetic look.

"Of course he did, Mona Ripple. He's a bastard, all right. They're all bastards. They use our love against us. It's a tool for them. Nothing more. They use it to get what they want. They use it to punish us."

"You don't know about punishment yet, bitch."

Ghool scowled in anger. "*I* don't know about punishment?! Foolish Maggot! Are you not paying attention? Has fury robbed you of your sight? How do you think I got this way?!"

"I don't care, bitch!"

"Well I'm going to tell you anyway. I fell in love once, too. To a Morishita. He was a prince of the most powerful family in the universe. He was kind and attentive and beautiful. Until he wasn't. And when I dared confront him about his behavior and endless discretions, you know what I got, Mona Ripple?" Now both women quivered with rage. "Acid thrown in my face! Acid!"

"I... I didn't know."

"Of course you didn't know! The Morishitas wiped the story clean. I'm sure they would have rather I died. Would have made everything so much simpler for them. But I'm not one to die, Mona Ripple. I'm one to fight, even when brokenhearted." Ghool began to pace around the room. "Even by Morishita standards, my husband's actions were considered reprehensible. So to save face—poor choice of words, I know—he was knocked down to some backwater province, and I was given jurisdiction over a mostly dead planet with unattainable resources. To stay quiet! To remain silenced!"

Ghool ceased her pacing and turned to face Mona once more.

"But look at what I've built. Look at what I've become."

"You've become a monster."

"How?! By treating men the way they've treated us for millennia?! They want to keep seeing us as property? Fine. But two can play that game."

"Your little game stripped me of the only joy I ever had in this world."

"I did you a favor, Mona Ripple! Your love wasn't real. *Love* isn't real."

The red lights continued to blink, casting odd shadows between Maggot and Countess.

"You know, Ghool, you're not the only one the Morishitas have hurt. My scars might not be obvious, but they run just as deep as yours."

"I told you, Mona Ripple, that we are very much alike."

"No! We're not!"

"Why?! Because you're still silly enough to believe in love, and I'm not?!"

"No, Countess. Because I'm alive, and you're about to die." Mona's arm steadied. "I'm sorry for your pain. But that doesn't excuse the pain you caused me." Index finger pressed against trigger. "This is for—"

"Mona! Mona!" called out a voice from the Countess's quarters.

Mona turned her head to see Mickie Brass racing toward her. Ignoring the man, she returned to Ghool, determined to complete her grisly task.

The Countess was gone. A door in the back of the medical room slid silently shut.

"Benten's grin, lass! What are you doing?!"

Mona began to respond, but something stopped her. She thought about chasing after the Countess, finishing what that Morishita prince started. But the idea failed to excite her anymore. The vision of Ghool's brains covering the marble floor provided no solace.

"Mona! In case you didn't notice, you daft sheila, we're in real trouble here!"

Mona shook loose of the confusing thoughts.

"I noticed, Junker! What do we do?! I'm paying *you* for situations like this!"

"Situations like this?!"

"Yeah! Emergencies!"

Mickie grabbed Mona by the arm, yanking her through the Countess's quarters and toward the main parlor.

"Your boy did a bloody number on us, lass. Triggered the bloody alarm and got everything locked down. I already tried the Red Lyft. Nothing doing. They must have overridden the bloody thing. It was heading down last I checked. It won't be empty when it comes back up."

The pair slid to a stop in the parlor.

"Fujin's ass! It's back up!"

The Red Lyft opened, filled with Guntai soldiers and deadlier ChoMM guardians. They began pouring out of the open doors.

"What now, Junker?!"

"I've got an idea. But you're not gonna like it."

"Does it beat getting killed?"

"Unsure."

"I'll take it! Go!"

Mickie pulled Mona back down the hallway leading to the paramours' rooms just as gunfire erupted in the parlor, leaving holes in the walls where the Maggots once stood. As they ran, Mickie fumbled for something at his belt.

"Where are we going, Junker?! This is a dead end!"

"Doesn't have to be, lass!"

The sounds of footsteps filled the corridor as the Maggots reached the circular mini-parlor of the paramours. Darien's door remained open, and Mickie sped toward it, Mona in tow.

Mickie opened fire upon entering the room, blasting holes in the massive window overlooking Karudera IV. The Space Cowboy continued to shoot, and the glass shattered completely, sending shards cascading over Darien Vance, who was just beginning to wake, the young man's jaw swollen and misaligned.

"Come on, lass!"

"This is insanity!"

"I know. Let's go."

Mickie moved to the window, now just an empty frame running from floor to ceiling, and held up the flutter square he'd taken from the fitting room. His finger found the button on its edge, and the item began to unfold. Mickie dropped the still-expanding flutter pallet to the floor, leaving it to hover a meter above the lush carpet.

More gunshots rang out, peppering the room with bullets as Mona rushed to join Mickie. She looked down from the top of Ghool Tower.

"This is suicide, Junker."

"Better than a public execution, lass."

"That it is."

Both Maggots stepped onto the flutter pallet, and Mickie gripped the edge of the window with both hands.

The weak, mumbling voice of Darien Vance caused Mona to look to her left.

"Mona. I'm sorry."

Two ChoMM guardians tore into the room, nano-edged katanas leading the way.

"No, you're not, Darien. But I have a feeling you will be."

Mickie pulled, and the Maggots disappeared as the flutter pallet plummeted to the ground far below.

Mona's stomach reached into her throat as she fell from the top of Ghool Tower. Too terrified to watch the ground rushing up to meet her, the Maggot instead stared out at the vast emptiness of Karudera IV, convinced that it would be the last view she ever took in.

Fitting that the final scene I look upon is one of nothingness. Ghool was right. I am a fool.

"Bend your knees, lass!" shouted Mickie next to her on the flutter pallet.

Stupid junker doesn't even have enough brains to be scared. To know that this is the end.

The flutter pallet's descent slowed a bit five meters from the ground, then more at four. At two meters, it seemed to hit invisible breaks, driving both Mona and Mickie hard into its metal surface. They collapsed in a heap, and the flutter pallet kissed grey rock before rising to hover at its usual half-meter height above the ground.

As Mona struggled to pull air back into her lungs, Mickie rolled off the flutter pallet, laz-pistol still in hand. Before she even had a chance to scramble to her hands and knees, two blaster shots could be heard, followed by the falling of bodies.

Mona collected her gun and crawled to the edge of the flutter pallet, tumbling from it to hit the rocky terrain. When she finally got to her feet, two Guntai lay dead between her and the Tower. Mona's GLIM-patch swiveled left and right, but only Mickie Brass could be seen, racing for a vehicle parked a short distance away.

Mona shook her head to collect her bearings. Quickly recovering, she realized it was the same imperial transport that had delivered the Maggots from Luxx Manor not thirty minutes prior.

Of the other Guntai, none were seen.

"Hurry, lass!" called out Mickie, almost at the shiny vehicle.

Just as the words escaped his lips, the Tower's rear entrance opened, and Guntai appeared. Mickie slid to stop and let loose a barrage with his weapon, forcing the soldiers back into the safety of the keep.

Mona rushed forward. As she did, the transport driver, invisible until now, dropped from the vehicle and aimed his weapon at Mickie, who was still keeping the Tower Guntai at bay.

Still running, Mona raised her laz-pistol without thinking and fired, leaving a neat hole in the driver's chest and sending his corpse to the ground.

Mickie offered the driver the slightest of glances before resuming his assault as Mona passed behind the Space Cowboy and leapt into the driver's seat of the imperial transport. Finger firmly on the trigger of his weapon, Mickie reached into his belt and tossed an item found there toward the rear entrance. Before it had a chance to land, the man was in the transport behind Mona.

"Benten's grin! Drive, lass!"

Guntai stepped out from the Tower to relaunch their attack, but an explosion ripped through their ranks, sending bodies flying in every direction.

A bloody arm landed with a thud on the transport hood, and Mona slammed the accelerator, giving thanks that the vehicle was already silently running.

The transport took off, outrunning the dust cloud that Mickie's grenade had created.

"Make for the karudera."

"I know the plan, Junker! Or what's left of it."

"Staying alive is what's left of it."

"Who cares at this point?"

"I do, lass. I care."

"Very well, Junker. Brace yourself."

The vehicle nosedived as it sped over the ledge separating Karudera IV from the rest of Kalderra. Luckily, Mona was able to find a section that descended less steeply into the crater. Still, they hit hard. Still, the transport bottomed out. But onward they went, crossing the sea of broken rock.

Mickie and Mona rode in silence for several long minutes, Mona watching for boulders to swerve around while Mickie stared out the windows, searching for signs of trailing Guntai.

"Anyone coming, Junker?"

"Not that I see, lass."

"So we got away?"

"I wouldn't say that. Not yet anyway."

Ten more minutes passed with only broken stone, bare ground, and weighty boulders to be seen. A short time later, the northwestern edge of

Karudera IV came into view, massive walls of the crater appearing to their left and right.

"Where do I go, Junker?! It's too steep!"

Mickie leaned over Mona's shoulder, studying the scene ahead.

"There should be a—there! Veer right a bit. You see that ramp?"

"I see it."

"Take it. There's a few of them on this side. The Mining Corps uses them."

"Then where?"

"If we don't see anyone, we'll head to Shonin Crossways. Successful plan or not, we still gotta get you off-planet."

"And what about you?"

"I'm not going anywhere. I'll be fine."

Mona thought to argue, but kept her thoughts to herself. Soon after, the transport hit the ramp and raced up it, leaving the desolation of Karudera IV in its wake.

As they crested the top, Mona's mind began to drift to a new life off-planet—alone and hunted, old and ugly. Loveless.

That's no kind of life at all. Loveless. Looking over my shoulder. With no—

"Fujin's ass!"

Mickie's curse brought Mona back to reality, and she slammed on the brakes, bringing the transport to a sliding stop. The woman let out a deep, resigned sigh.

"Well, Junker? What now?"

Before them, blocking their path on all sides, was a massive Guntai force, soldiers standing before lines of black armored cars with Howas drawn.

When Mickie didn't answer, Mona repeated the question.

"Well, lass, if they just wanted us dead, they'd have lit us up already."

"So, they don't want to kill us?"

"Oh, they do. Just not here and not now. There's no audience to entertain."

"Then what do we do?"

Despite her grim outlook on life, despite her fatalist views, Mona's voice quivered in fear. And in that moment, the Maggot Kisser came to a sobering realization.

I have nothing. I am nothing. But I still don't want to die.

"Stay here, lass. Keep her running. When the time comes, you floor it straight ahead. Don't worry about me."

"Junker?"

"Just do what I say, Mona! Please!"

"How will I know when the time comes?"

Mickie laughed. "Oh, you won't be able to miss it."

A voice boomed from the Guntai force. "Get out of your vehicle! Hands up! One wrong move and we open fire!"

Mickie dropped his laz-pistol to the floor and made for the transport's side exit. Mona grabbed him by the arm.

"You can't go out there unarmed, stupid junker!"

Mickie delivered a wry, gold-toothed smile. "Who says I'm unarmed, lass?"

The side door slid open, and Mickie stepped out, empty hands leading the way. He took several steps forward until he was a third of the way to the Guntai force ahead of him.

"That's far enough!" the voice called out again. "Now the woman!"

"I'm ready to parley!" Mickie announced and was met with laughter.

Mona could overhear Guntai talking to her left.

"Did the idiot say he's ready to party?"

"Benten's grin! He said *parley*, you moron!"

"Par-tay?"

"Oh, just shut your gob, and keep your weapon up!"

The megaphone-assisted voice resumed. "Look around you! There will be no parley. You're accused of identity falsification, trespassing, attempted theft of imperial property, and murder! And since this is Kalderra, with no court of law, it's within my jurisdiction to find you guilty! How's that for a parley?! Now, get that woman out of the transport, or we go in and get her! And neither of you will like how we do that!"

Mickie, hands still in the air, widened his stance before speaking.

"That's a crap parley, mate. I got a better one for ya. Move those vehicles. Let us be on our way. And I won't send you all to Takamagahara here and now."

More laughter started up but was quickly cut short as two compartments opened on the outside of Mickie's thighs. In a blink, two tech-revolvers were in the man's hands, pointing directly at the leading Guntai force.

"Last chance, mates!" declared Mickie.

After a tense beat, the voice returned, no longer using an amplifier. "And what are you gonna do with those?! Wound a couple of us?!"

Laughter, louder than before, assaulted the Maggots. Mona's scarred hands tightened on the steering wheel.

This is your grand plan, Junker? Go out in a blaze of glory, leaving me to suffer a stoning? Benten's grin, you're dumber than I feared. And I'm the one paying you! So, what does that make me?

"Just shoot him already," came a cry from the right side.

"No! The Countess wants him alive! Wants them both alive! Entertainment for the Sindo-Emperor!"

Mickie remained frozen, cover art from an old gunslinger novel.

"Alive! Not unharmed! Shoot the bastard in the knee or shoulder and let's—"

Metal unfolded from Mickie's thigh compartments in a blur until a metal arm—two meters in length—jutted out from each, arching up and away from the man. Before the Guntai could react, barrels of varying shapes and sizes sprang from the strange metal appendages.

"Parley's ended, mates."

Mona shielded her eyes, overwhelmed by the brightness that appeared at Mickie's sides as rockets and lasers shot forward, tearing into the Guntai and their vehicles. The metal arms moved like shokushu tentacles, swaying left and right, sending Guntai running and lifting black cars into the air on all three sides.

And in the middle of those writhing appendages of death stood Mickie Brass, taking helmeted heads from Guntai necks with every release of his tech-revolvers.

Pupils shrunk, Mona watched open-mouthed as smoke billowed around Mickie like a phantom cape.

One man against an army. And the bloody bastard didn't blink.

With the Guntai all hiding behind their vehicles or hugging the ground, Mickie concentrated his attack on those directly ahead of them. Missile after missile launched forward, knocking some cars back and sending others flying into the air to land atop retreating soldiers.

And then Mona Ripple saw it.

A gap had appeared in the line, just wide enough for the imperial transport to get through.

That's my bloody sign that the time's come.

Mona gunned the engine, and the transport spun its wheels before taking off.

At the sound of the transport advancing, Mickie's thigh-arms disconnected from the man, falling to the ground in a loud *clang*. Despite another shock, Mona kept her foot firmly on the accelerator, even as the vehicle came alongside the still-firing Space Cowboy.

Come on, Junker! Don't make me—

With surprising speed and agility for one his size, Mickie dove through the open side door and into the transport, crashing hard into the leather seats.

"Keep going, lass!"

"No shit, Junker!"

Mona made for the gap as smoked filled the battlefield, sending the Maggots blindly into a tangled mess of metal, flesh, and bone. She was jolted to the side after hitting the corner of a flaming Guntai car. Her head nearly struck the steering wheel when she slammed into back of an upturned vehicle. But she pushed her way past, the transport shuddering as it plowed into and over soldier bodies.

And then the smoke was gone, and the Maggots were free, speeding away from a Guntai force left wondering how things had gone so terribly wrong. And how they were going to tell the Crimson Lady that they had failed.

"Benten's grin, Junker! What the bloody hell was that back there?!" Mona's voice was unsteady, shaken by the recent adrenaline dump.

"What was what, lass?"

"Don't play stupid with me!"

Mickie chuckled. "Oh, *that*? Just a trick of a Space Cowboy."

"Fujin's ass. Sorry I asked." Mona thought it over. "You know, we could have bloody used that trick during the scav. You know, the one where we lost two good Maggots!"

"Sorry, lass. I didn't have it then. Teddy installed it when we were in the Laughing God."

"Installed it?! Where?!"

"At his place."

"That dirtbag room of his?!"

Mickie shrugged. "Teddy told you. The back's a lot fancier than the front."

"Oh just shut up, Junker."

"Ok, Mona."

The makeshift roadways of Kalderra were strangely empty, even given the still-early hour.

"Shonin Crossways still?"

Mickie glanced out of the windows. Behind them, a few of the undamaged Guntai cars could be seen following in the distance. To the west, Shonin Crossways rose from the relative flatness between karuderas. A thick line of vehicles was exiting the trade city, heading for the fugitive Maggots.

"Crossways is a no-go, lass. Word's out. We're officially Kalderra's most wanted."

"Then what, Junker? You got more tricks up your thigh?"

"Afraid not, lass. There's only so much room in there. I blew my bloody load back at Karudera IV."

"What a lovely choice of words. So now what?"

Mickie looked to the rear once more. The Guntai were gaining ground, the imperial transport no match for the engines powering the soldiers' cars.

"Well, Mona, back's no good. West is no good. They're obviously trying to press us north, where I'm sure another batch of bloody Guntai are on their way down from the upper base."

"Where does that leave us? I don't see us getting through another last stand."

"Neither do I. Which leaves us with exactly one final option. But I have to warn you, it's a shit one."

"It's all been shit, Junker."

"That it has, Mona."

"Give it to me. I'm numb to bad ideas."

"We can try and lose them in Mori Mangekyo."

"Entrance is going to be crawling with Guntai."

"Maybe. Maybe not. It's still early, right around the shift change. And who knows how the Sindo-Emperor's imminent arrival has mucked up the staffing plans. We might get lucky."

"We haven't been so far."

"No. No, we haven't. But I don't see any other way."

"Well, lucky for *you*, I don't either. Heading for the Maggot Trails."

"Take the closest entrance. The longer we're out here in the bloody open, the shorter our life spans will be."

"You need to work on your phrasings, Junker."

"Ok, Mona."

By the time the imperial transport hit the Maggot Trails, Guntai had closed in on two sides. Dust clouds from the North signaled a third contingent moving in fast. Mona cut along the main trail and took the first fork to the right, a path leading directly into Mori Mangekyo. Mona's GLIM-patch zoomed in.

"We got Guntai at the checkpoint, Junker!"

"How many?"

"Not as many as usual. No vehicles blocking our path, but the gate's down."

"Drive through it, lass."

"Will this transport make it? Not exactly a krawler we're working with here."

"Only one way to find out."

"Fujin's ass!" Mona spat, tightening her grip on the steering wheel.

Moments later, Mona called out again. "We've been spotted, and they know we ain't stopping! Got Howas pointed at us! I'm a bloody sitting duck!"

Mickie's thigh compartments opened and out came his tech-revolvers.

"You worry about the driving. I'm going topside."

"Where?!"

"The roof, lass. Don't take your foot off that pedal for nothing."

Before Mona could argue, Mickie had opened the side door and climbed his way to the top of the transport. Once there, he lay flat on his stomach, both tech-revolvers held out before him.

The Guntai fired first, peppering the transport with bullets. Several struck the windshield, forcing Mona to lower her head so that her eye and GLIM-patch barely peeked over the steering wheel.

They were the last shots six Guntai ever fired as tech-revolver slugs ripped through heads and chests. Above her, Mona could hear Mickie roaring in delight.

Bloody crazy junker! Benten's grin, who is this man?!

More rounds were exchanged, with Guntai falling to Mona's left and right as they advanced on the checkpoint gate.

"Brace yourself, Junker!" Mona yelled, hoping to be heard over the drum of artillery.

"I got eyes, lass!"

Fighting every urge to slow down, Mona kept her foot firmly planted on the accelerator, ignoring holes appearing in the sides of the transport and the metal barricade racing toward her.

The transport hit the gate in an explosion. Pieces of gate were thrown forward, to the sides, and over the transport. The vehicle jerked violently as it ran over twisted metal, and Mona prayed that a tire wouldn't puncture or an axel wouldn't bend.

And then it was over. The imperial shuttle dipped into Mori Mangekyo, and the shouts of Guntai and pops of gunfire faded into the distance.

When they leveled out on the mori floor, Mona finally slowed down as an unexpected fear came over her.

"Junker! Junker!" No reply came. "Junker! Junker, you bastard!"

A thick leg appeared in the open doorway, then another, before Mickie Brass swung back into the transport.

"Stupid move, Junker!" Mona screamed, surprised at her own anger. She turned to face him. "If you have a death wish, just tell—" She stopped, noticing the blood covering the man's face. "Benten's grin, are you ok?!"

Mickie wiped at his eyes. "Fine, lass. Eyes on the road, please."

Mona returned her look forward. "There ain't no road, stupid junker! What happened to you?"

Mickie continued to clear his face. "Wedge of gate hit me in the bloody noggin.'"

"Well, that's the safest place for you, Junker. Not much there to damage. What now?"

Mickie spun in his chair to look out the rear window.

"Now we wait and hope, lass."

Dozens of minutes passed. Then more. The subarashi trees pulsed and lightning streaked across thick, colorful limbs as the Maggots passed through Mori Mangekyo, heading west.

Mickie's breathing slowed, hope daring to creep in where desperation once sat. But then—

"Benten's grin, lass! They must want us really bad."

Between the thick subarashi trees, Guntai cars, monocycles, and battle taxis popped in and out of sight. Many followed, but others were beginning to flank the imperial transport.

"Don't tell me they entered the mori, Junker!"

"They did. And they're here. I suggest you speed her back up."

Mona hit the throttle, and the transport screeched loudly.

"Fujin's ass!" she cried.

"What?!"

"Bloody transport must have taken damage! She wasn't exactly fast before, but now she's really struggling."

Mickie watched as the throng of vehicles in pursuit drew closer, and his glimmer of hope vanished.

"Mona?"

"I'm listening."

"Just keep driving. I don't mind dying, but a car accident isn't what I had in mind. I'll do what I can back here. No matter what, just keep moving forward."

"I don't like the way you're talking, Junker."

"Neither do I, lass. Neither do I."

Mona cut hard around one giant subarashi, passed under the heavy arching roots of another. And on came the Guntai, some drawing even with the transport.

Mickie's thigh compartments opened, and out came the tech-revolvers, recharged and reloaded. He opened the doors on both sides of the transport.

"What are you doing?! It'll give them a clear shot!"

"Yeah, but it'll do the same for me. We can't let them get in front of us. One vehicle will be enough to stop us in the state this transport's in."

Mona glanced back to see Mickie kneeling on the floor, one outstretched arm pointing a tech-revolver in each direction. Battle taxis, topped with gun turrets, came along the transport's side.

"I'm not compensating you enough for this, Junker."

"Yes you are, Mona." A beat passed. "Mona?"

"Yes?"

Another beat.

"Never mind. Drive like your life depends on it, lass. It does."

And then, under the beautiful canopy of Mori Mangekyo, chaos reigned.

Mickie's guns roared in rapid fire. Turret barrels flashed, bombarding the transport with bullets until the men controlling them dropped from their speeding vehicles, dead from revolver slugs.

Monocycles sped forward, then were pushed back by the Space Cowboy. Guntai cars raced to take their places and were rewarded by Mickie with impossibly accurate shots that snuck through windows to strike shoulders and arms, necks and heads.

More came. Holes dotted the transport. The windshield shattered, cutting Mona's face and sending shards against her GLIM-patch. The woman did her best to use the subarashi to their advantage, putting them between the transport and its pursuers as often as possible.

But the numbers were too much.

Mickie screamed into the storm, firing both weapons to the left side, then the right. For every bullet given, five were received. One found purchase in Mickie's shoulder, spinning him to the floor. Another caught him in the ribs. A third cut across his face, slicing a neat line along his left cheek.

And still the Space Cowboy fought. Even with no path to victory.

The transport began to sputter and slow. Guntai vehicles surrounded the Maggots, some even racing ahead. Incoming artillery lessened before stopping entirely.

"Why have they stopped firing, Junker?!"

"Because they know they've won, lass. Next clearing, they're gonna block us in and take us. Alive, if possible."

"Anything we can do?"

"Try to go out in a blaze of glory, I suppose."

"Isn't that what we've been bloody doing?!"

Mickie chuckled despite the grim predicament. "I suppose—"

The man's words caught in his throat, and his grey eyes widened.

"Mona!"

"I see it! But I don't bloody understand it!"

Above the imperial transport, above the Guntai legion, in the canopy of Mori Mangekyo, a great show of shadow and light played out, greater than any witnessed since the destruction of the Morishita loggers years past.

Bolts of lightning criss-crossed in every direction between the subarashi, a mesh of power encasing the forest below. Heavy leaves pulsed with energy, and color swirled deep within massive trunks.

A palpable scent of ozone filled the air. Mona's hair rose to stand on end.

The world went white.

Lightning poured down from the canopy in thick ropes, striking Guntai vehicles and transforming them into balls of fire. Explosions rocked the transport from side to side as surrounding battle taxis detonated. Body parts rained down in a deluge of gore.

"Junker!"

"Drive!"

Wave after wave of lightning fell, quickly thinning the Guntai force. Mona held her breath as she weaved around charred metal, her jaw aching from clenched teeth, sure that the next strike would find the transport.

More lightning. More dead Guntai. More deafening cracks that threatened to rupture eardrums. More impossible brightness.

And then they were alone, the imperial transport loudly grinding through an eerily silent Mori Mangekyo.

"Junker, we made it! Benten's grin, I don't know how, but we made it! Junker? Junker?!"

Mona turned back to find Mickie sprawled on the seat, blood pooling on the leather beneath him.

"No, no, no!"

As Mona screamed, the transport sputtered and died, bringing the battered vehicle to a slow and final stop.

Mona jumped into the back and cradled Mickie's head in her lap. His hair was caked in blood, his breathing shallow.

"Don't you dare, Junker! Not after all this!"

"Wouldn't dream of it, lass," the man muttered, his eyes remaining closed.

Tears ran from Mona's lone eye.

"You bastard. Don't think this—"

Mona dove to the front of the transport, retrieved her laz-pistol, and jumped out of the vehicle. She raised her weapon with a shaky arm, terror stealing motor control.

"Don't take a bloody step closer!" she called out, her voice even less stable than her weapon.

The humanoid creature's head cocked to the side, its diamond eyes reflecting the colors of the forest. It smiled through clear lips.

"Your friend is hurt."

"You will be, too, if you try anything!"

The head cocked again.

"We can help him."

Mona glanced back at the unmoving form of Mickie Brass.

"How?"

The creature held a translucent arm out, indicating somewhere behind it.

"We will take him home. We will fix him."

Mona peered through the forest. Between the subarashi, she could just make out the outlines of an immense cave. Dim red light shone within.

"Sure, Crystals. Take us in there so you can kill us?! Nice try."

Another odd smile.

"We have no desire to kill you. We saved you."

"Saved us?! How did you bloody—"

Realization hit Mona like a thunderclap.

"We must hurry," said the creature.

Mona lowered her pistol.

"Help me with him, Crystals?"

The creature nodded. Together, they pulled an unconscious Mickie Brass from the transport, threw limp arms over their shoulders, and made for the cave that Mona knew to be Homusubi's Breath.

"Who are you, anyway?" Mona asked, struggling under Mickie's dead weight.

"You know who we are. We are the Kodama. And this is our planet."

"Well, Kodama, I appreciate the assist back there. And helping *him* now."

"You are most welcome, Mona Ripple." The woman stumbled. "We are happy to lend a hand. And perhaps one of you can lend yours in return."

"Of course," Mona muttered under her breath. "Always a bloody catch."

CHAPTER 5

LOVELOST

"You should be dead, Junker."

"You told me that already, lass," said Mickie as she shook himself awake. "Benten's grin, Mona. Where am I?"

"You wouldn't believe me if I told you."

Mickie pushed himself into a sitting position, grimacing as he did.

"Careful, Junker. You took a few slugs. Gonna be tender for a while."

"How long have I been out?"

Mona shrugged. "Surprisingly not that long. Half a day, maybe. Your wounds have already started to heal, which makes no bloody sense. But not much about you does, Space Cowboy."

Mickie's skin suit had been removed. His rough hand traced the lines of bandages.

"Who patched me up?"

"The Kodama."

Grey eyes widened. "The bloody who?"

"The Kodama. I said you wouldn't believe it."

Mickie looked around, his eyes finally starting to adjust. He had been laid out on a bed of clear, rubbery material in a small, rocky alcove. At the mouth of the makeshift room, a dull red glow emanated from the cave system beyond. Mickie thought for a moment, replaying the last moments he could recall from the imperial transport.

"Homusubi's Breath?"

Mona nodded. "Not bad, Junker. Venture to guess how we got here?"

Mickie rubbed his head, which throbbed as much as his other wounds.

"I remember lightning. So much lightning. But it… it only hit the Guntai."

"Which means?"

"Which means someone was helping us escape. I suppose that's where the Kodama come in."

"And who says all junkers are dumb."

"I think that was you, Mona."

"Well, I ain't saying it now."

"Why did they save us? Save me?"

Mona shrugged. "They haven't said much to me. They wrapped you up, stuck us in here, and we both slept. I just woke up a little before you."

Mickie sat up a little straighter. "Bloody warm in here."

Mona's brown eye and GLIM-patch studied her companion. "You didn't ask what they put on your wounds to make them heal so fast."

Mickie's gaze went everywhere but to Mona. "What did they put on them?"

"Nothing, Junker. I watched them simply remove a couple slugs, clean, and patch. The healing's all you."

The Space Cowboy waved her away. "Good genes, I suppose. Or just lucky. I've always been lucky. Except when I haven't been."

"Sounds like you're feeding me rotter shit, Junker. But fine. Keep your secrets."

Mickie was massaging his legs in preparation to rise when a look of desperation painted his weathered face.

"My guns! My guns!"

"Calm down! You'll rip your bloody stitches open. I grabbed your revolvers on the way out of the transport."

Mona tossed a wrapped bundle onto Mickie's lap, inducing another grimace. The man quickly removed his tech-revolvers, let out a sigh of relief, and placed them in his thigh compartments, which had opened to his silent command.

"Hopefully, we won't need those, Junker."

"Agreed. Any idea what they want from us?"

"Nope. But they want something."

"Nothing's free, lass."

"No. No, it isn't."

"Well, I'm sure we're going—"

"We are pleased to see you awake, Mickie Brass."

Mickie and Mona both jumped at the voice and turned to face the visitor to their alcove.

"Bloody hell, mate! Gave me a scare."

The Kodama offered a slight bow, its skin appearing to glow as it refracted the red light behind it. "Apologies, Mickie Brass. That was certainly not our intent. Your clothes were quite damaged. We brought you some replacements."

Mickie rose painfully to his feet and shuffled in his underwear to the Kodama. The native Kalderran held out a stack of clothes which Mickie accepted with a nod.

"Appreciate it, mate. And for saving our asses."

"It was our great pleasure, Mickie Brass." The Kodama's crystal eyes vibrated for a moment before settling on the two Maggots. "The Goddess would like to see you when you are ready."

"The who?" asked Mona.

Translucent teeth appeared behind clear lips. "The Goddess, Mona Ripple. Sakuya-hime. She is excited to meet you both. And we are excited to bear witness."

Mona's face twisted in confusion. "So this… goddess is here? In the caves under Kalderra?"

"She is, Mona Ripple. We will take you to her."

"Uhh, sure, mate. Just give me chance to get dressed?"

The Kodama bowed again. "Of course, Mickie Brass. We will be waiting outside to escort you to her chamber."

The Kodama left the alcove, and Mona hurried to Mickie.

"A bloody goddess?!" she whispered. "Benten's grin, what do think that thing's going on about?!"

"I don't know, lass. But nothing good ever comes from gods, goddesses, or those proclaiming to be such."

"I don't like any of this, Junker. What have we done?"

"I think we traded one sticky situation for another," said Mickie as he slipped into the strange trousers. After carefully pulling the cotton shirt over his bandaged chest, the Space Cowboy looked down at himself. "Benten's grin, these clothes are ancient."

"The Kodama don't wear clothes, Junker. So where do you think they got these?"

Mickie went to the corner of the alcove to retrieve his boots. "I don't know, Mona. But I think we're about to find out. About the clothes and much more."

"You mean like how an ancient Japanese goddess is apparently living in a cave on a dead planet?"

"Yeah, lass. That's what I mean."

"I hope you got more tricks up your thigh, Junker."

"Me, too, Mona. Me bloody too." Mickie glanced down once more and thought. "Just in case, help me cut a couple holes in these pants, lass."

Mickie and Mona were led by several Kodama through the sweltering cavern system beneath Kalderra. They passed large openings in the rock from which bright red light shone brightly. Along the passage walls and ceilings ran thick roots of translucent green, many carving their way through rock to head for the surface. Mona ducked under one and noticed that it swam with swirling tendrils of light that twisted like a helix.

On and on they walked in silence. Eventually, they reached a large chamber, where a natural bridge of stone traversed a massive chasm. Mona looked down as they marched along the bridge and through a curtain of uncomfortable steam. Far below the Maggots, a blinding river of magma bubbled and churned, angrily fighting against its rocky prison. The roots were even more plentiful here, with several especially thick ones diving over the chasm's edge and disappearing into the pool of liquid fire.

Mickie gently nudged Mona and nodded, and her GLIM-patch swung to where the man was indicating. To her left, sliding forth from the magma and up the wall, was a kameeba, its ticker swollen and pulsing with energy.

The Maggots shared confounded expressions as they exited the magma chamber.

Three tunnels later, the cave opened up once more. Thick roots covered the ceiling here, running down the dozens of corridors that dotted the room's jagged walls. Mona examined the roots, tracing their many paths, her GLIM-patch making it easier to follow the complex lines. Then her breath caught in her throat.

All the roots were emerging from a single opening at the far end of the cavern. And toward it they were marching.

More Kodama had gathered outside of this opening, more than five-hundred crammed together in silence. Strange runes had been painted in the spaces between roots, coded language not yet deciphered by human minds.

As Mickie and Mona passed through the throng of Kodama, their convoy broke off to join their fellow natives until only the lead Kodama remained. It stopped just before the opening and turned to face the Maggots.

"This is the Divine Hollow, resting place of the Goddess Sakuya-hime. She will see you now. She will judge whether you are worthy of the gifts of life we have bestowed upon you. She will judge whether you are friend or foe. Please follow us."

The Maggots shared another look—one of concern—as the Kodama vanished into the gloom. After a brief hesitation, they followed, turning to their sides to avoid the thick collection of roots escaping the opening.

The Divine Hollow was small and round, ten meters in both diameter and height. The air was cooler here, thick with the clean scent of flowers. Ambient light filled the room, a mix of green, purple, and blue.

And in the center of the room sat Sakuya-hime, the Goddess of Kalderra.

The Goddess sprouted from the stone, and endless roots reached out from its base, running across the floor, ceiling, and walls. The creature appeared nothing more than a fleshy spike standing three meters tall, her glowing skin gently expanding and contracting as if breathing.

The Kodama moved to stand before it and faced the human visitors.

"Goddess. We have brought those you wanted to meet."

Thick layers of the fleshy spike began to curl down, revealing a slimmer spire beneath the color of meat. This downward unfurling continued, and the leaves spread wide, creating a shroud surrounding the "neck" of the Goddess. Once fully opened, thin stems popped out from the base of Sakuya-hime, each tipped with fist-sized, heart-shaped fruits that glowed a deep red.

Once this was completed, the top of the spire began to quiver. From its point, a single flower bloomed. A meter across, its five petals released soft pink light. In its center, a yellow eye appeared, staring out at the Maggots.

As a stem-like tendril tenderly wrapped itself around the Kodama, Sakuya-hime's lone yellow orb locked onto Mona's brown eye, and an itching sensation assaulted the woman's brain. The Kisser slammed shut her eye, but still the feeling persisted, pulling at memories pushed deep long ago. Hidden, only to be discovered by a buried goddess.

Minutes passed in a nauseating wave of recollection, and Mona could feel Mickie's hand sliding into her own, offering strength where nothing but shame and weakness could otherwise be found.

And then the connection broke, and Mona was left looking once more upon the Goddess and her faithful Kodama. She shook her hand free of Mickie's.

"Mona Ripple," said the Kodama, "Sakuya-hime has seen you. We are empathetic to your pain. We share a wounded spirit. And our injuries point to the same cause. As will our wrath. The enemy of our enemy is our friend, and we were right to save you. You wish the same as us. The destruction of the Morishitas."

Mickie glanced over to Mona, who trembled under the words of the Kodama. The tendril caressed the Kodama's face as the native Kalderran turned its attention to Mickie.

"Mickie Brass. Sakuya-hime is most perplexed. The Goddess is unable to read your mind. It is protected by a strange cloud. Only one thing managed to leak out. Rage. Tell us, Mickie Brass. At whom is this rage directed."

"Same as you, mate. The bloody Morishitas."

The tendril tickled the Kodama's ear, eliciting a clear smile.

"Sakuya-hime believes you, Mickie Brass. You now have Her trust. You now have our trust. We shall be partners in this."

Mickie's face twisted. "In what, mate?"

"Vengeance for deeds most foul." The tendril retracted. "The Goddess thanks you. And dismisses you."

Mickie and Mona began to exit. Mona turned back one last time to find Sakuya-hime's yellow eye on her once more as the Kodama whispered unfamiliar words to its goddess.

Mona's head swam as she and Mickie reentered the cavern. They sped past the waiting Kodama and found a quiet corner away from natives and goddess roots. Mickie grabbed Mona by the arm and leaned in close.

"That was no goddess, lass."

"Yeah, Junker. It was no mere plant, either."

"Agreed."

"Then what did we just see?"

"That's an alien, Mona. And a bloody nasty one at that."

Moments later, the lead Kodama found the Maggots and approached with a smile.

"Mona Ripple. Mickie Brass. Are you ready to take the next step in our journey together?"

"I've been wanting to ask," said Mona. "How do you know our bloody names?"

The crystal eyes shook in their sockets.

"We have eyes and ears everywhere, Mona Ripple. We have watched you enter our mori. We have witnessed your work. Your bravery. And Mickie Brass. Well, Mickie Brass is known to all. All but those who need to know him most."

"Benten's grin, what in blazes does that mean, Junker? Junker?"

But Mickie Brass remained silent.

The Kodama continued. "Please follow me. You will now hear of the Kodama."

Mona couldn't help herself. "You mean how you slaughtered the human colonists sent to Kalderra."

The Kodama smiled once more. "Mona Ripple. We did not kill the colonists. We *are* the colonists."

They gathered in the largest cavern yet seen, thousands of Kodama lined up in neat rows. Although generally homomorphic, small differences could be spotted between Kodama—discrepancies in height, small outlines of breasts on some, indistinct mounds on others where genitalia once stood.

The right side of the cavern was dominated by an enormous pit, steam and the familiar glow of magma rising from its depths. Gripping the walls of the pit were dozens of giant kameeba, their tickers bright enough to damage any eye that looked directly upon them.

The lead Kodama stepped up onto a stone outcropping and cast its crystal eyes over to Mickie and Mona.

"Mickie Brass. Mona Ripple. You will now hear the tale of the Kodama. And you will know the why behind what has to be done.

"We were sent to Kalderra to build a new world. Promises were made. Freedom to worship for those wanting to spread the word of god. A second chance for those who had taken the wrong path. An opportunity of exploration for those thirsty for adventure. A better life for those labeled as destitute.

"These were the promises made by the Morishita Galactic Corporation.

"We were told that the air was breathable. It was. We were told that resources would be delivered to us. They were. We were told that the rays of the blue star Anohoshi would not harm us.

"Of this they lied.

"For two generations, we thrived. Despite our diverse backgrounds and callings, we built a community. Free from the bonds of the Morishitas, a society was born.

"And then the changes began.

"Mutations in our newborns. Bluish tints to our skin. Tumors that sprouted in our bodies. Growths on our eyes. Clouds of confusion that settled over our brains.

"The scientists among us determined that it was Anohoshi that was ravaging our people. So, we became creatures of the night, only venturing out under the violet gaze of Kuyomi. Things only got worse.

"Kuyomi did not protect. She merely twisted the rays of Anohoshi, making them more potent. More harmful. More sinister.

"Our people died. So much death. So many horrific scenes involving loved ones.

"We pleaded for evacuation. We pleaded for assistance. We pleaded to be saved.

"Morishita Galactic cut all communication. And we were left. To be forgotten.

"Those that survived the great wave of death retreated into the caves, away from the vile rays of Anohoshi and Kuyomi. Starving and afflicted with monstrous maladies, we resigned ourselves to a grim fate. But a voice was heard by some. It bounced off the rocky walls, sweet and caring and encouraging. It urged us on, and we delved deeper into the planet.

"And we found Sakuya-hime.

"She nourished us. By consuming the Goddess fruit, we became part of Her, and She part of us. We grew healthy. We grew hopeful. We grew to become greater than.

"We were transmogrified.

"We learned about our Goddess. How Her galactic seed became stranded on a dead planet. How volcanic upheaval buried Her deep within the world's crust. How She willed Herself to bloom. How She fed Herself with the hot energy of the planet's core. How She spread and broke free of her rocky prison. How She birthed the great forests of subarashi that you call Mori Mangekyo and Mori Hotaru, creating today's Kalderra. How She used the subarashi to attract galactic attention.

"And through that attention, fulfill Her godly mission."

"What *is* her godly mission?" asked Mona.

All the Kodama smiled as one.

"To create a shared kokoru under Her glory."

"I don't know what that means, Crystals."

"We will all be one, Mona Ripple. One body. One mind. One heart. One spirit. There will be unimaginable strength in our transfiguration. We will work together in perfect harmony. Uniting under the guidance of Sakuya-hime, all will flourish. None will be without. Collective well-being."

"That's ambitious, mate. Especially given that there's only a few thousand of you."

"But you are wrong, Mickie Brass. There are trillions of us, scattered across planets and systems and galaxies." The crystal eyes vibrated. "I can hear their thoughts, as they can mine. I can see what they see—worlds of peace populated by Kodama, unified under Sakuya-hime."

Mickie glanced at Mona, and although not Kodama, unsaid words passed between them.

"What's the plan you speak of, mate?"

"Using our now-ancient comms devices, the Goddess allowed us to strike a deal with the Morishitas. We will gift them our subarashi in exchange for a new world. One where we can spread the truth and love of Sakuya-hime."

"Sounds to me like you folded," Mona spat. "Making a deal with the Morishitas? Giving them the only thing they ever wanted? All you accomplished was making the Sindo-Emperor wait a little longer for his prize."

"Not exactly, Mona Ripple."

"Enlighten me, Crystals."

"Just as we are now the Goddess, the Goddess is now us. She knows of the pain the Morishitas inflicted on our people. She knows that they are not to be trusted. She knows that the galaxy is better off without them. So, She will be taking her planet back once we are free of it."

"I still don't understand."

The Kodama motioned around the cavern. "Sakuya-hime breathed all life into Kalderra. Not just the Kodama and the subarashi. But the forest creatures. And the butterflies that you, Mona Ripple, so enjoy visiting. And the kameeba."

"The kameeba?" asked Mickie. "But why?"

"This planet is angry. It lives a lonely life far from its blue star, bullied by its oversized moon. It wants to erupt. The karuderas it created were to be the first of many. The Goddess could not have this. She created the kameeba to calm the planet, to confiscate its rage, its power. Preventing Kalderra from destroying itself. Until the time comes."

Realization hit Mickie like cold water. "Benten's gin. The bloody Sindo-Emperor's visit."

"Very good, Mickie Brass."

"Well, mate, it sounds like you lot have everything figured out. What do you need us for?"

"We have received a starship from the Morishita Galactic Corporation. We find it to be… unsatisfactory."

"Then why don't you take it up with the Syndicate?"

"The starship is not *unworthy*, Mickie Brass. It is… restrictive."

"And you think I can make it less so?"

"We think you are resourceful enough to do so."

"Then I guess you better take me to this bloody ship."

"Rest first, Mickie Brass and Mona Ripple. The journey is not a short one. You have experienced recent struggles, and we need your minds sharp."

"I can wait if you can, mate."

"We will have water brought to you. There are pockets of it that we have found within the caves. I can have food brought, as well. Some fruit, perhaps?"

"No!" Mickie and Mona exclaimed in unison.

"Just the water, mate."

The Kodama offered a wry grin. "It will be done."

Mickie woke with a start, the heat of his rocky alcove-turned-bedroom conjuring dreams of a burning forest home. Looking around, he realized he was alone, Mona's resting spot empty beside him.

The Space Cowboy drank deeply from the old water container provided by the Kodama. The liquid was warm and tasted of minerals.

Standing with a groan, Mickie left the alcove in search of Mona, uncomfortable with the idea of her being alone with their transformed hosts.

After several minutes of searching, Mickie found the Maggot Kisser in an adjoining cavern, seated at the edge of a magma river. Although nothing more than a shadow, Mickie recognized the heaving shoulders of a sob, a woman in the throes of a breakdown.

Her attention no longer diverted by escapes, chases, and alien encounters, Mona Ripple was left to finally reconcile the fact that she was rejected. That the love of her life was her love no more.

"He's not worth your tears, lass."

"You don't know what my tears are worth, Junker," said Mona, her voice straining.

"I have an idea, lass."

"They're *worthless*! Just like me! Worthless!"

"Don't say that. It's not true."

"What do you know, Junker?! What do you know about me? Nothing!"

Mickie's shoulders dropped. "I know everything I need to know about you, Mona. The only thing I don't know is how a man like Darien captured your heart."

"Because he was beautiful! I finally had something in my life that was beautiful." She spun to face Mickie, shadows flickering across her tear-soaked face. "My life is ugly, Junker. Everything has always been ugly. And this was my chance. My one chance! My chance to have something beautiful to call my own. And he's gone! And now..." The woman sank lower to the stone. "And now I know."

"Know what, lass?"

"I'm an ugly woman doomed to live an ugly life. I should be used to it by now. After all these years."

"Your life's been tough, Mona. As has mine. That doesn't make it ugly."

"You know nothing, stupid junker! You don't know what they did to me! You don't know..." Her voice trailed off.

Mickie thought for a moment, knowing he was stepping across a field of hidden mines.

"The Kodama said that you hated the Morishitas as I do. What did they do to you, lass?"

"You don't want to know, Junker. No one should hear it."

"Please. Tell me."

Mona took several deep breaths as the steam swirled around her.

"My mother died in childbirth, and I've been paying for it ever since. My father was long gone by then, so I was sent to an orphanage in Tokyo to be raised. I don't remember much of those early years. But I remember this. Men in suits would visit. Those older than me would line up, and a child would vanish the next day. Gone to their forever home, we were told. But none of us really believed that.

"On my tenth birthday, it was my turn to join the line. I remember the house parent was more nervous than ever. She must have inspected each of us three or four times. My friend was hit on the thigh with a switch for having something stuck in her teeth. I was terrified.

"He came in wearing the fanciest suit I had ever seen. Middle-aged but handsome, he walked as if nothing could touch him, as if he floated above all others. His watch alone could have bought not only the orphanage but the whole block.

"He checked out each child in line as we stood there shaking, squeezing shoulders, parting lips to see teeth, checking for imperfections. Like we were bloody cattle! In many ways, I suppose we were.

"I remember his dark eyes lighting up when he got to me—I was quite cute as a child. He kneeled down and swept hair from my face. He smelled like sandalwood and smiled at me. He told me his name was Masami."

"Masami? Masami Morishita?!"

"That's him. One of the twelve princes. But I was made no princess. I was kept in a shabby hotel room on the edge of the city. I was fed three times a day. I was given a TV, books, magazines. When I was bored, which was almost always, I would tear pages from the magazines and fold them into shapes from my imagination. I filled my little room with those origami creations. Would fill the time between his visits with imaginary worlds, places where children weren't treated like playthings.

"Masami would talk to me sometimes in English, always complaining about his father or brothers or some off-world troubles. I liked it when he talked. It meant he wasn't doing other things.

"Time passed in a blur, pain followed by boredom followed by pain. One week, Masami didn't show up. Then another. And another. Perhaps he had grown tired of me. Perhaps I'd gotten too old for his liking.

"They came and took me one evening. They didn't say anything. They didn't tell me where I was going, but I knew it wasn't somewhere nice. But even my darkest fears couldn't compare.

"I traded one monster for many, a series of ugly men doing ugly things. Don't ask me how long I was there. I've blocked it out. But one man, an especially fat one wearing too much cologne, carried a knife in his boot. I waited until he slept and used it to slice open his throat. Then I threw myself from the window, hoping that would be the end of my story. I wasn't so lucky.

"I was never caught and never went back to that dreadful place. But things didn't get much easier. I lived on the streets, did what I must to survive. I dropped more bodies, took more beatings than I care to remember. When I was finally old enough, I started to get manual labor jobs. I didn't have dreams like other young people, so I was the perfect worker. I moved up quickly. As soon as I could get out of Tokyo, I did. As soon as I could get off-planet, I did.

"I made money. Stashed it away for no real purpose. I became old. And angry. Put one joyless foot in front of the other. There would be no blooms in my barren world.

"And then I met Darien. And something long thought dead came alive. Hope. There was something beautiful in my life, something to call my own. I wouldn't expect you to understand. But for a moment, a magical moment, I had a purpose. And now I realize that it wasn't taken from me. I simply lost it. If I ever had it at all. Maybe this was just the cruelest trick of them all.

"Life has no meaning to a broken person, Junker. That's what I was. And that's what I am. And there's no fixing what I've become."

Her story finished, Mona stood on wobbly legs, put her hands to her face, and cried.

Mickie, helpless and unsure, had no words to offer. Instead, the man walked over and took Mona into his arms, providing a home for her tears. And as the red river bubbled beneath him and steam stung his eyes, Mickie held on tight. And as Mona fell to pieces against him, the Space Cowboy felt whole.

Eventually, Mona pushed him away.

"I don't need your sympathy, Junker."

"That's not what you have, lass."

Mona wiped the wetness from her face, and Mickie couldn't tell if the fire in her lone eye was a reflection or something deeper.

"The Kodama are right to hate us, Junker."

"Hate who?"

"Us! Humans! Look at what we do to each other. Look at how little we care."

"That's not all of us, lass."

"The Morishitas have to pay, Junker."

"They will."

"Good. Now leave me alone, please. And stop trying to understand me. You never will."

"Ok, Mona."

Mickie turned to exit the cavern, hurt by the woman's words. For Mickie understood much more than Mona could ever comprehend. Like how magical moments could be brought to such abrupt ends.

The Kodama was right. The hike through the caves was long and twisting, with Mickie and Mona completing it in sweat-soaked silence. After several hours, the final natural corridor of their trek spilled into a massive chamber that also served as the cavern system's western mouth. A still-rising Anohoshi filled the room with murky light that revealed several ancient computer consoles pushed to one side, dim digital screens aglow.

The lead Kodama motioned to the units as the group passed through the open space.

"Sakuya-hime had us recycle these from our colonial vessels. We used them to access the galactic network and make contact with Morishita Galactic. Their false gifts will prove their downfall. Fitting."

Exiting the mouth, the Maggots entered more shadow created from the high peaks above. Cables connected to antiquated solar panels ran back into the cave from which they came. In the near distance, brightness filled the flat, rocky ground.

"This is the Kodama Plateau," said the Kodama. "And *that* is our starship."

Mickie squinted his grey eyes against the morning rays being reflected off the ship's shiny metal hull. It was a medium-sized starship, one capable of traversing the galaxy.

Looks like it could take these freaks anywhere they want. Benten's grin, they could make it to Chikyu in this thing.

Mickie studied the starship as the group drew closer.

"Looks like a class III cruiser, mate. Not exactly top of the line, but she's no slouch, either."

"Like we said, Mickie Brass, the starship is not unworthy."

"Then what's the problem, Crystals?" asked Mona.

"Let us show you."

Reaching the star cruiser, a code was punched into an exterior panel by the lead Kodama, and the boarding ramp folded down from high above, settling softly onto the plateau floor below.

Mona swung her arm toward the ship. "Crystals, first."

The group climbed onto the ramp and were whisked into the starship via its conveyor-belt floor.

Mickie whistled as they entered the bowels of the starship.

"The bastards even gave it a scrub for you before delivery." He looked around some more. "This is a bloody nice ship."

"We concur, Mickie Brass."

"Alright, mate. Let's see the turd in the punchbowl." The Kodama looked to each other quizzically.

"He means show him where the problem is. And don't worry, Crystals. No one knows what the heck he's talking about half the time."

The lead Kodama nodded. "This way, please."

They delved deeper into the ship, through the payload bay and cabins and into the winding maze of the engine room.

The lead Kodama spoke as it walked. "They must think us simple creatures, easy to trick and manipulate. At one time, this may have been true. But now, through our shared kokoru, we have the collective intelligence of trillions."

Trillions of brains and not one set of balls. What bloody good is that?

"We will not be deceived again, Mickie Brass. From now on, it will be us who executes the deception. We are here."

They had stopped at an especially complex section that housed the quantum drive.

"Ok, mate. What am I looking at?"

"We were able to download the schematics of this class III model from the Dark Tide. We painstakingly compared every drawing of every section to this craft. *That* does not appear in any of the diagrams. We need you to tell us what it is."

"Benten's grin, how would a bloody junker know that?!"

"He is Mickie Brass, Mona Ripple."

"What's that supposed—"

"I'll check it out," Mickie cut in.

The Space Cowboy moved to where the Kodama indicated. To the untrained eye, nothing seemed out of place—just a metal box bolted onto another metal box connected by a complex network of wires leading to a thousand other hunks of metal.

Mickie's fingers traced the wiring, moving meters to his left, then right.

His grey eyes scanned up and down before zeroing in on the device. Finally, he turned to face the Kodama.

"Looks like you got a bomb on board, mate. She's not a big one, but my guess is that as soon as the quantum drive is engaged, she blows. And given her location—*that* over there is the hyper core, by the way—she'll be enough to vaporize this entire vessel mid-jump. There'll be no remnants. It'll be as if you lot never existed."

"That was our fear, Mickie Brass. It seems that even when they get what they want most, the Morishitas cannot help but to take more."

"This your only concern?"

"No, Mickie Brass. There is one more… obstacle for you to see."

"Let's see it, then."

Back through the starship the group moved, all the way to the command center, an oval room of seats, digital displays, and control boards. A large, curved panel of fused silica, serving as a window to the stars, showed the Kodama Plateau spreading out into the distance. The great peak known as Kodama-san stood out like a dagger to the North.

The lead Kodama pressed several buttons on the main console, and a galactic map appeared, brightening the command center. A single dot, blinking a rapid succession, could be seen, denoting somewhere in the Norma Arm of the galaxy.

Mickie examined the digital map.

"What's that dot?"

"That is supposed to be our new home. It is a newly discovered planet called Nethelia-162. All indications are that it is inhabitable—water, oxygen, flora and fauna."

"What's the problem?"

"We have no intention of going there, Mickie Brass."

"Why not?"

"It is empty. There are no ears to hear the word of the Goddess."

"Go somewhere else then, Crystals," said Mona.

"That is the problem, Mona Ripple. Watch as I input another galactic coordinate."

The Kodama's clear fingers swam across the keypad, and a red message materialized on the screen above.

"Looks like they got the ship locked onto a single coordinate, mate."

"Exactly, Mickie Brass. The ship is worthy. But restricted. We need to travel freely. Sakuya-hime demands it be so."

Mickie thought for a moment.

"So, their plan is to detonate you on the jump, but if that fails for some reason, they still know exactly where you'll be. And then they'll just nuke the planet from orbit."

"You see our predicament, Mickie Brass."

"Oh, I see it, mate."

"We need you to assist. A small price to pay to see the Morishitas brought to justice. A small price to pay for saving your life. And that of Mona Ripple."

"Always a catch, huh, mate?"

My thoughts exactly, Junker.

"Can you remove these obstacles, Mickie Brass? Can you make this worthy ship worthy of the Goddess?"

Mickie rubbed his neatly trimmed salt-and-pepper beard.

"I think I can handle the bomb. But the coordinate restrictor is most likely embedded in the cruiser's core programming. Getting in there and cutting that out is beyond my skills."

"That is disappointing, Mickie Brass. And unacceptable."

"You didn't let me finish, mate. I can get in there but won't know what I'm bloody looking at. But I know someone who does."

The Kodama looked to each other with crystalline eyes.

"We do not have time to bring another here, Mickie Brass."

"You won't have to, mate. I can patch him in remotely with the ship's prefix code. I assume you have that, at least."

"We do, Mickie Brass."

Mickie nodded. "I'll need that. And I'll need to use your comm system back in the cave. With your permission, of course."

"Whatever you need, Mickie Brass."

"Then I'd better get to work. Bomb first. You lot should clear the ship."

The Kodama looked to each other once more.

"We hoped to observe your efforts, Mickie Brass."

"Look, mate, I'm good but nothing's for sure. There's a twenty-five percent chance that bomb detonates on extraction. You want to be here when that happens, or you want to be able to negotiate another star cruiser?"

The Kodama's eyes vibrated as it responded. "We will wait in the caves for your triumphant return, Mickie Brass."

"Good lads… or whatever."

"Mona, I'm gonna need your help with the removal."

"What?! I don't know a bloody thing about bombs, Junker!"

"Then let me rephrase that, lass. I'm gonna need that finger of yours. And that GLIM-patch might come in handy, as well. These eyes don't see as well as they used to."

So, that's why the bastards needed me. Benten's grin, they must know everything.

"We will leave you to the task at hand, Mickie Brass and Mona Ripple."

The Kodama left the command center. As soon as they had, Mona spun to face Mickie.

"You know they're gonna bloody kill us if you can't pull this off, Junker."

"I know, lass."

"I'd love to know how you're gonna reprogram a bloody class III cruiser?!"

"I'm not. Teddy Feenk is."

"Blinders can do that?! What does that old fart know about starships?"

Mickie laughed. "More than you know, lass."

"And the bomb?! A bloody twenty-five percent chance of it detonating?!"

"Well, I may have exaggerated a bit to get those hive minders out of our hair. Probably more like fifteen percent."

"Benten's grin! I don't know rotter shit about bombs!"

Mickie shrugged. "Sure you do. It's no different than a kameeba ticker. And you're pretty good with those. Let's get to it."

Mickie began to leave.

"Junker!"

He turned back.

"If we die before the Morishitas get theirs, I'm gonna kill you."

Mickie offered a gold-toothed smile. "Ok, Mona."

"Ok, Mona, just cut where I tell you to. Use your femtofinger to solder the wire as quickly as possible. Just like cauterizing a ticker. Zoom in with your GLIM-patch to make sure you don't touch multiple wires at once. If you do—"

"You already told me it's like a ticker, Junker! I know what happens, and I know what I'm doing. This might be the only thing I'm good at."

"You're right, lass."

"And who cares anyway? This whole planet is going to erupt, taking us with it. Whether here—now—or there—then—it doesn't make a bit of difference to me."

Mickie did a poor job of concealing a smile.

"What? What?!"

"I don't plan on going down with the ship, Mona. Or, in this case, planet."

"Well, I'd love to know how you plan on getting off-planet now that we're the two most wanted criminals in the history of Kalderra. Unless you've decided to travel with these freaks. Oh, don't tell me you're leaving with these hivers?! Cause if you are, you can count me right the heck out! In fact—"

"Mona! I'm not going with the Kodama. I have something else in mind."

"Another trick up your thigh, Junker?"

"One last one, lass."

Mona thought for a moment. "Is there any extra room in this scheme of yours?"

"For you? Always."

Mona waved Mickie away. "Not for me, you dolt! Well, I mean, of course for me. But for more than me? Like sixty or so more?"

Another coy smile from the Space Cowboy.

"I think I can manage, lass."

"Good. Then after we're done doing the dirty work for these alien worshippers, I got somewhere I need to go."

"Where's that?"

"Camp Karcass. I'm not leaving my Maggots here to die. And don't try and stop me, Junker! I don't care if—"

Mona's rant was cut short by Mickie's upraised hand.

"I would expect nothing less from the Kisser of Karcass Five."

Mona rocked back on her heels, unused to winning a fight before it started. Strange thoughts and feelings swam to the surface, but she pushed them back down.

"Well, alright then. Now let's rip this bloody bomb out and be done with it. And don't tell me how to do my job again!"

Mickie grinned. "Ok, Mona."

"Try it, mate."

The lead Kodama's finger typed coordinates into the command center's main console. A new dot appeared on the galactic map. He repeated the process. Another dot materialized. It did it once more.

"How, Mickie Brass?"

Mickie shrugged. "I told you. I know a guy who knows his bloody stuff. I used your comm system to give him a heads up on what I was doing. With the ship's prefix code, he was able to hack in and excise the restrictor programming. Took him a bit longer than he thought. Morishita Galactic definitely didn't want you lot going anywhere but Nethelia-162."

The group of Kodama smiled as one, and Mona sensed real excitement among them, the first human emotion she'd detected other than anger.

"You have kept your word, Mickie Brass. And you, Mona Ripple. Your debt to the Kodama is paid in full. When Sakuya-hime's shared kokoru blankets the universe, we will remember your names and sing songs in your memory."

"Then we're free to leave, Crystals?"

"The Goddess has looked into your soul, Mona Ripple. Your hatred of the Morishitas is unimpeachable. We have no doubt that you will do nothing to thwart Sakuya-hime's plans. And, Mickie Brass, we know you are the thorn in the foot of the Syndicate. You are both free to go. With our gratitude. And our friendship."

What are they bloody on about again? Mickie Brass is a Maggot like me. Nothing more. Nothing more.

"Then we'll be off, mate. We'll need a guide to get us back to Homusubi's Breath."

"And you shall have it, Mickie Brass."

The bizarre pairing of Maggots and Kodama exited the star cruiser and stepped onto the Kodama Plateau. As they did, a massive thunderclap crashed down, shaking the rocky ground beneath them. Heads tilted up to find that a starship had hyper-jumped into the atmosphere high above. It looked to be the largest in existence, long and angular and invulnerable to attack.

A strange look crossed over Mickie Brass's face as he stared at the fortress in the sky.

"I can't believe it. The bastard actually came."

"Who?" asked Mona.

"Sakuramachi Morishita, lass. The bloody Sindo-Emperor."

"How do you know that's him, Junker?"

Mickie's eyes found Mona, and the woman spotted a twinkle within the greyness.

"Because *that's* Ryugu-jo, the Dragon Palace. The bastard's galactic home when he's not in Tokyo."

The lead Kodama's crystal eyes shook.

"Things will move quickly now, Mickie Brass. And there are many tasks that require attention. On both our sides. I suggest we all be on our way."

"Bloody well said, mate. Bloody well said."

The group resumed their trek back to the cave mouth, passing the disarmed bomb that had been haphazardly left on the plateau. Mona watched as Mickie continued to glance up at the Dragon Palace, his hands dropping to finger the metal of his thigh holsters.

One more trick? I think this bastard still has several up those thighs of his.

Mickie and Mona did not stop as they made their way through the sweltering cave system, their Kodama guide showing them the shortest possible path. There were no goodbyes as they reached Homusubi's Breath; the Kodama simply nodded and spun to return to its goddess.

The imperial transport was where they had left it, bullet ridden and undriveable.

"What now, Junker?"

"I get this thing moving, lass."

"This hunk of junk ain't going anywhere."

"I can get her going. Not well. But going."

"*This* I have to see."

True to his word, Mickie got the transport running, although he did need Mona's femtofinger more than few times to cut away torn metal and weld patches onto the engine and axel. When he was finished, the vehicle no longer resembled an imperial conveyance. It looked like something from a dystopian sci-fi movie Mona had watched in the hotel as a child.

She liked it much better this way.

The transport sputtered and coughed, rocked and jerked, but progress was made across Mori Mangekyo. Other than the subarashi, no life was to be seen—rotters having retreated underground and Guntai having avoided the place altogether after their last ill-fated foray into the forest. After countless minutes of silence, Mona finally broke the tense spell.

"Are we already dead, Junker?"

"Why do you say that, lass?"

"You heard the Kodama. The Morishitas lied to us. That bloody star and that bloody moon have been microwaving us ever since we stepped foot on this cursed planet. I was so stupid. No wonder Karudera City and Ghool Tower have those field bubbles encasing them. No wonder the Guntai are covered head to toe. No wonder—" Mona paused as a sharp realization pierced her. "Junker, why was the Laughing God covered? Did your people know about this?!"

Mickie rubbed his beard. "Well, everyone knows the Morishitas lie about everything. I think it was a case of better safe than sorry."

"Fujin's ass! Are we gonna die, Junker?! Are we already dead?!"

Mickie thought for a moment before answering. "There were some secret studies circulating. Seems like the radiation needs extended time to build up in the tissue and cells before real mutations occur. That's why the colonists didn't experience anything for a couple generations."

"So, we're good?"

Mickie glanced over nervously. "Maybe some tumors later in life. But nothing a good medipod couldn't cut out."

"But not for you, I suppose, Junker. Not with your bloody magical healing powers that you still haven't explained!"

"I told you, lass. Good genes."

"Rotter shit!"

They rode on in more silence. Rounding an especially large subarashi, Mona finally decided to let it go.

"I guess it makes no difference, anyway," she said, more to herself than her companion. "What's gonna happen? I lose my looks?! Not like men are gonna be lining up to get with an old former Maggot with trust issues."

Mickie opened his mouth to speak but closed it, and the transport stumbled ahead, quiet once more.

***

Mickie brought the transport to a jerky stop at the southeastern corner of Mori Mangekyo. He slapped the scarred vehicle's side upon exiting.

"I can't believe it, but I'm actually gonna miss this old girl. She got us through a real ordeal."

"Never has the term junker fit so well, Junker."

"I like things with a little age and character, lass."

Mona rolled her eye. "Let's get going. These cliffs ain't gonna climb themselves."

Mickie nodded, and the pair began to scale the steep edge of Karudera III. Booted feet slipped on loose rock, but together they reached the top of the massive bowl, only to find themselves at the foot of a mountain ridge. Luckily, narrow paths wound their way through the cliffs, allowing the Maggots to avoid the more treacherous heights.

Day turned to violet night as they trekked through shadow, pushing through exhaustion and the tension of unasked questions. Eventually, they dropped down from a twisting trail onto flat land.

"There's Camp Karcass, lass."

"I'm not blind, Junker."

"We need to be in and out. Quietly. Tell them what's going on and load everyone up on krawlers."

"Where are we sending them?"

"The Laughing God."

"The Laughing God?! They need to get off-planet! We need to get them to the Spaceport."

Mickie shook his head. "The Sindo-Emperor's landed by now. The Spaceport is gonna be locked down. As is Karudera City and Ghool Tower. They'll be safe in the Laughing God."

"I don't see how! If the—"

"Mona. Do you trust me?"

Mona wanted to argue, but looking into Mickie's grey eyes, she found she could not.

"I do."

"Then let's get this done."

"Ok, Junker."

Mickie and Mona slipped into a quiet Camp Karcass. With the Sindo-Emperor's arrival, scav efforts had been paused, leaving the Maggots with little to do.

"What do you think, lass? The break room?"

"Yeah, heads probably swimming in whiskey by now."

"Good. Might help the news go down easier."

The raucous break room immediately grew quiet when Mickie and Mona entered. Jaws hung low on shocked, silent faces until—

"Mickie! Ripper! Benten's grin, we thought you were goners!" exclaimed Amos Bedford, who limped over to bury both in a hug. "The bastards are reporting that you died in Mori Mangekyo." Bedford stepped back to look at Mickie. "But I knew better." He motioned to the other stunned

Maggots. "I told *them* that Mickie Brass don't die. He just gets angry." Bedford looked the Space Cowboy up and down. "Benten's grin, Mickie, what are you bloody wearing? You look like something out of an old video feed."

Mickie offered an embarrassed smile and took note of weasel-faced Vasily Pappas slipping from the room.

Biggson Baft, standing silently in the corner, gave a knowing nod to Mickie.

Mickie placed a hand on Bedford's shoulder. "It's time, mate."

Bedford's eyes lit up. "After all this time, Mickie. We're finally gonna do it. I'll put out the word. The plan should be—"

"Plan's changed, mate."

"Why?!"

"Divine intervention. Someone's gonna do the heavy lifting for us."

"I don't understand, Mickie."

"And I don't have time to explain. You'll just have to trust me."

"Always, Mickie."

"Good lad." A pause. "Mona?"

"Alright listen up, Maggots! I can't get into the details, but this planet is cooked. Anyone who values their lives needs to get their stuff and get to a krawler ASAP. You'll be traveling to the Laughing God."

"We ain't welcome there, Ripper!" argued Ricksin Hinch, the man donning a new artificial hand.

"You are now, mate," said Mickie. "The gates will open for you." To Bedford, "I contacted Teddy Feenk already."

"But how?"

"You wouldn't believe me if I told you, mate. Get these guys and gals moving. You need to be on the road well before the Sindo-Emperor is ready to tour his new forests. The Guntai will have the whole bloody planet locked down shortly."

Bedford's shoulders slumped. "Everything we've invested, Mickie. All our planning. Just to run and hide?"

"The movie's different, mate, but the ending's the same. And there's still gonna be fireworks. More than you could ever imagine."

Mona stepped forward. "Five minutes, Maggots! And make sure you let anyone not in this room know what's going on. Go!"

"Aye, Ripper!" came the unified call, and Maggots poured out of the break room, leaving only Mickie, Mona, and the giant Baft.

Mona spun to Mickie. "What was all that about with Bedford? What plans, Mickie?"

"I'll tell you everything later, lass. I promise."

"I'm getting real tired of all the cloak and dagger, Junker?"

"Me, too, lass. Me, too. Biggs, you need anything from your room?" The large man simply shook his head. "Alright then, head for the Nest. You'll be driving one of the krawlers. Let Sadler and Bedford helm the others. Use the city's main gate. Teddy's got everything ready."

Another silent nod and Biggson was off.

"What about us, Junker?"

"Let's help round the Maggots up. The sooner we're outta here the better."

"Some might not want to leave. Especially from the other Karcass units."

"I'll convince them."

"How do you plan on doing that?"

"Simple. I'll tell them the truth. Kalderra's fixing to explode. And there's only one way to avoid going down with her."

"And if they don't believe you?"

The Space Cowboy's thigh holsters opened through the holes in his ancient trousers.

"Oh, they don't have to believe me, lass. But they *will* get on those krawlers. But first, I need to find a skin-suit. I'm tired of wearing a dead man's clothes."

"What is the meaning of this?!" roared Colonel Toro as he waddled into the Nest, the last of the Maggots cramming onto the krawlers. "Ripper! Mickie! You're supposed to be dead! But you're not! Therefore, you are enemies of the Imperium! Everyone get off those krawlers!"

"You're welcome to come along, mate," said Mickie in his new skin-suit, sleeves and thigh material already removed.

Toro's eyes grew large on his fat face. "I will do *no* such thing! Camp Karcass is under my command, and I *command* all of you to return to the barracks!"

"The Morishita empire is about to be drastically downsized, Toro," said Mona from the side. "If you don't want to be downsized with it, I suggest you come with us."

Toro fixed his froggy stare on Mona. "There is nothing you could possibly say to me, Ripper, that would get me on one of those krawlers!" Toro flinched as the barrel of a tech-revolver touched his temple. "Mickie Brass, however, makes a most compelling case. Let the record show that my compliance was given under threat to life!"

"Noted. For the record, mate."

"Very well, then."

Toro was helped onto one of the krawlers and settled into his seat with a sigh of resignation.

"That everyone?" asked Mona.

"All but Pappas," replied Kisser Colby Chambers. "I couldn't find him anywhere."

"Then he stays. We go."

"Never liked the bastard anyway," commented one of the Maggots from Karcass Two.

Mickie and Mona hopped onto the back of the lead krawler.

"Biggs! Get us out of here, mate!"

The giant man nodded, and krawler one sped from the Nest, four other rovers in tow. Camp Karcass flew past, and the open world lay just beyond, bathed in violet moonlight.

Mona slapped Mickie on the shoulder and smiled brightly for the first time in days.

"We're gonna make it, Junker! Benten's grin, that went about as well as possible!"

Krawler one slammed to an abrupt stop, sending packed Maggots crashing into one another. Mona craned her neck to see what lay ahead.

"Fujin's ass!"

"My thoughts exactly, lass."

An entire regiment of Guntai and their vehicles sat blocking the path to the Maggot Trails. Nearly two hundred blasters, Howas, and battle taxi turrets were leveled in the Maggots' direction.

So bloody close. What a shit way for it all to end.

"Step out of the krawlers with your hands up," called out the Guntai commander at the head of the soldiers.

The Maggots complied.

"I was taken against my will!" shouted Colonel Toro as he fell from the rover. "Against my will, I say!"

"Shut your gob, Toro, you slug," spat Betsy Sheppard, offering a swift kick to the Colonel's plump side.

"That's them!" screamed another familiar voice, and Mona's face twisted as Vasily Pappas stepped out from the collection of Guntai and closed on the Maggots. "That's who you want! Mickie Brass and Mona Ripple! They're not dead as has been reported! They live, and they're right there! They're dangerous traitors of the Imperium! I suggest you shoot them now!"

"The Countess wants them alive, if possible," responded the Guntai commander in a distinctly accented voice.

"You really want to take that risk?" asked the weasel-faced Kisser. "What will be the repercussions if you lose them, Guntai? Or do you want to cash in now? I'm sure their heads on sticks will still greatly please the Countess."

The Guntai commander looked around to his fellow soldiers before nodding.

"Very well. Mickie Brass. Mona Ripple. Step forward."

As the Guntai commander advanced, Vasily Pappas delivered a wicked smile before speaking. "I never forget, Mickie. And never forgive. And Ripper, it looks like I'll be getting the best scavs from now on. Perhaps they'll even elevate me to colonel. Toro won't be missed."

Mona began to shake as the Guntai commander approached, blaster in hand.

"Junker?" she whispered, her voice quaking. "Is this it?"

The Guntai raised his weapon, pointing it directly at Mickie's forehead.

I need to tell him. I need to tell him now.

"Junker, I'm so—"

Mickie glanced over. And offered a sly wink. "Easy, lass."

Pappas giggled from the side. "And so ends the great Mickie Brass. You will be forgot—"

A light flashed from the blaster muzzle, and Mona jumped as the shot ripped through Kisser Pappas's temple, leaving a neat, cauterized hole in the man's head. Pappas stared out dumbly for a moment, turning to face the Guntai commander and his smoking weapon, before collapsing into a dead heap.

The Guntai commander then raised a fist in the air and gunshots rang out across the Guntai regiment. Mona watched in shock as one in three Guntai turned their weapons on their fellow soldiers. Terrified screams erupted and bodies began to fall. Maggots, including Mona, dropped to the rocky ground in horror as a fog of blood and smoke enveloped the Guntai army.

Mona looked up to find Mickie Brass still standing, arms crossed over his chest, calmly taking in the chaotic scene.

After thirty seconds of carnage, all went quiet save a few audible moans from the mass of Guntai.

The Guntai commander returned his blaster to his holster and removed his helmet, revealing shoulder-length blonde hair and striking blue eyes looking out from a handsome face.

"Well met, Mickie," said the man in his odd accent, reaching for the Maggot.

Mickie clasped the man's forearm in greeting. "I recognized that Slavic lilt immediately, mate. Good to see you, Urek. And great timing, lad."

Urek brushed back his blonde hair with a gloved hand. "Yeah, Teddy said he spoke with you. I'm all caught up. He called us all back to the Laughing God but said we might want to stick around Camp Karcass. Said he doubted you'd leave the Maggots behind."

Mona scrambled to her feet.

"What in the bloody blazes is going on, Junker?"

"Looks like we've been rescued, lass. Again." Mickie called out over his shoulder. "Maggots! You can get up now. Reinforcements have arrived." As the Maggots rose, Mickie returned to Urek. "You managed to get everyone together, mate?"

Urek nodded. "I did, Mickie. It wasn't easy, but I was able to convince my Guntai superior to let me handpick some of my regiment."

"Was this a female superior, Urek?"

Urek smiled and shrugged.

Mickie laughed. "Handsome bastard. Always good to have one of you around."

Amos Bedford limped up from behind.

"Urek! Benten's grin, am I glad to see you here!"

Urek exchanged forearms with Bedford. "Amos! It's been too long, friend. And Biggs! Gypsy! Betsy! Glad your Maggot days are at an end?"

Ellis Sadler slapped Urek on the back as he spoke. "If never see a forest again, too soon!"

Betsy Sheppard slapped Urek on the rear. "Urek, have you gotten more beautiful, or have I spent too much time with these ugly lumps?!"

"I'm right here!" complained Bedford, and everyone shared in a laugh.

Moments later, the sixty-plus surviving Guntai pushed forward, helmets coming off.

"We'll catch up in a bit," said Urek as the crowd surrounded Mickie, Bedford, Baft, and Sheppard—welcoming them back.

Back to what? What the heck is going on? Why is everyone celebrating a junker?!

Mona found herself nudged to the edge of the bizarre reunion, observing the scene in total bewilderment. After several minutes of staggering around in confusion, she found Urek, who was directing some of the unmasked Guntai. She waited for him to finish before approaching.

"Now I know why that lady Guntai was willing to divulge so many secrets."

Another shrug. "We work with what we are given, Miss Ripple."

Together, they watched as a line formed to shake Mickie's hand, some even bowing before the man.

"Urek? You're gonna have to fill me in because I don't understand any of this. Why's everyone flocking to the junker?"

Urek's head cocked to the side as he studied Mona, a puzzled look etched onto his handsome face.

"Because he is Mickie Brass."

"That doesn't help, Blondie."

Urek began to say something but clipped it back. He restarted.

"Who do you think he is, Miss Ripple?"

Mona thought for a beat.

"He's just a Maggot. And a junker. You know, a Space Cowboy."

Urek chuckled, as if a child had just made a ridiculous claim.

"Miss Ripple. Mickie Brass is not *a* Space Cowboy. He's *the* Space Cowboy." A pause. "He's the Honcho."

Mona's head swam.

"Ok… so he's the head junker for a group of junkers. I still don't see what the big deal is."

"Miss Ripple. The Space Cowboys are no mere junkers or pirates. We haven't been for quite some time. Since Mickie took over, actually. But our power resides in letting everyone—especially the Syndicate—think that we still are. In truth, we are a complex network of talented dissidents. Our numbers are vast, spread across every planet in the galaxy." Urek noted Mona's dumbstruck face. "Miss Ripple, the Space Cowboys are the second most powerful entity in the known universe. And *he*," pointing to Mickie, "is the second most powerful man, behind only the Sindo-Emperor." Urek grinned knowingly. "For now."

Mona felt her knees growing weak.

"Then what in blazes is he doing here on Kalderra? Acting like a Maggot? For years?!"

"Mickie knows the Morishitas. He knows that they want most what they can't have. He knew that they would eventually come here for the subarashi. He couldn't get to Sakuramachi Morishita in the Sindo-Emperor's stronghold in Tokyo, so he waited for the bastard to come to him. Here on Kalderra. Mickie spent years stationing Space Cowboys as Guntai, traders, hoteliers… Maggots. All hiding in plain sight. So when the Morishitas finally set down on the planet, we'd have the numbers to take them down." Urek sighed. "Despite all the planning, it still would have been a messy affair, one that most of us never would have made it out from under. That's why these recent developments have been most encouraging, to say the least. I, for one, am happy to avoid dipping my toes into a bloodbath."

Mona grabbed onto Urek's arm for support as a flood of memories rushed to the surface—admiring nods in the Laughing God, Shivantae Tong's warning, offhanded remarks about plans. Mona shook her head.

"No, no, no. This doesn't add up. All these years of planning. The Sindo-Emperor's visit. Everything was falling into place. Why would he offer to help me rescue Darien? It could have ruined everything!"

Urek removed his gloves and took Mona's hands in his. She saw that three small stars had been tattooed atop each.

"Miss Ripple. You might want to get that GLIM-patch checked."

"Why's that?"

"Because you can't seem to see what's right in front of you. Now, if you'll excuse me."

Urek returned to Mickie, around whom a space had formed. The Space Cowboy spoke to his enraptured audience.

"It's bloody good to see you all!" A cheer rose up. "And to the Maggots who have no clue what's going on…" Mickie's grey eyes found Mona in the distance. "…we are the Space Cowboys! And we're bringing an end to the murdering Morishitas!" Mickie's gaze drifted to the gathered Karcass units. "I consider you Maggots dear friends and capable comrades. You're more than welcome to join our ranks. But that is no bloody order! Not how we do things around here. It is an invitation! Nothing more. Regardless of your decision, you will all find sanctuary within the Laughing God, where we'll ride out the events that'll shake the pillars of Takamagahara. Who's bloody with me?!"

Another great cheer erupted, and Mona watched as Kisser Colby Chambers grinned beneath his well-trimmed mustache.

This is a dream. It has to be. And what was that pretty fool Urek going on about?

"Urek!" shouted Mickie. "How're the Maggot Trails to the Laughing God?"

"Clear, Honcho! Every other Guntai on Kalderra has been called to the Spaceport, Karudera City, or Ghool Tower."

"So we'll be unbothered?"

"Yes, Honcho! Especially with the Guntai escort I'm about to provide you!"

And everyone laughed. Except for Mona Ripple, who felt drunk as strange feelings threatened to take her from her feet.

CHAPTER 6

LOVEBOMB

The Laughing God had become a city of contradictions. While there was a frenzy of activity, with residents sprinting to and fro, shouting unclear orders and hauling goods into nearby buildings, Mona noticed that the population seemed to have decreased dramatically. The street hawkers and food stalls were nowhere to be seen. Shops stood empty of both customers and owners.

Boots pounded loudly off the city's metal roads as Mona, Mickie, Urek, and the rest of the Space Cowboys dismounted from their vehicles in Yorokobi Square. Gone was the festive atmosphere, replaced by heavy tension despite the returning Honcho and his band of infiltrators.

Teddy Feenk was there to greet them, his visor a kaleidoscope of digital light.

What's going on behind that old codger's metal eyes? What does he see that I can't? What does he know that I don't? That everyone seems to understand?

"Mickie," Teddy greeted, "better late than never. I thought you were a goner until I received your communication. It took me a while to process it all." His visor dropped a bit. "I'm ashamed to say that I feared you had ruined everything, Honcho. Even if for a good cause."

Mickie tenderly raised the old man's head with a finger under his jaw.

"You were right to doubt and fear, mate. I nearly did. But it seems that Izanagi is on our side, at least this time. Is everything prepared?"

Teddy smiled, his conscious now clear.

"Not yet. But it will be. We're tracking."

"Good. And that other thing we spoke about?"

Teddy nodded. "I'm still in there, Honcho. It's ready when you are."

"Not until I give the word, mate. Timing will be critical on this one."

"Understood, Mickie."

"Alright. Teddy, I'm sure you have somewhere more important to be. Urek, get these krawlers and Guntai seizures secured somewhere. They might come in handy at the next stop. We'll want to—" Mickie noticed two massive objects in a hauler hitched to one of the battle taxis. They were strapped down and covered by thick plasteen tarps. "What are those?"

Urek swung his pretty face to where Mickie was pointing.

"Benten's grin, I nearly forgot. I was able to procure two Guntai Skeeters for your capture."

"How'd you swing that, mate?"

Urek showed his perfect white teeth in wide grin. "Something about you potentially taking off on foot or escaping into the cliffs. I also may have insinuated that I'd sleep with the Equipment Management Officer. Anyway, I'll get them inventoried and—"

"No, mate. Unload them here."

"But why?"

"Just do it, mate."

"It'll be done, Honcho."

"Good lad."

Urek spun on a heel and called out orders. Space Cowboys began offloading the Guntai Skeeters as Mickie turned back and saw that Teddy was still standing there.

"I thought you had somewhere to be?"

"Why do you need the Skeeters, Mickie?"

"Just had an idea, Teddy."

"Don't do it, Mickie. We're too close. *You're* too close. And you're the Honcho. You have responsibilities larger than yourself."

"So I do, mate."

Teddy began to argue but closed his mouth after seeing the man's face. Instead, he simply sighed.

"Very well. Here, I brought you something. I have yours as well, Miss Mona."

Teddy pulled two bags from the metal ground and offered them to Mickie and Mona. Mickie took his with a gold-toothed smile.

"You beautiful, bastard. My pack!" Mickie immediately removed two items, placing one on his head and another in his mouth.

Mona groaned. "Not that bloody hat, Junker."

"It's an Akubra, lass."

"I know what it's bloody called! You've only told me a hundred times. And how old is that cigar? Aren't you some kind of big shot? We can get you a fresh one."

"I don't want a fresh one. I want this one." Mickie bit down on the mangled cigar and placed his fists on his hips. "How do I look, lass?"

"Like a backwater bumpkin."

"Perfect. Just what I was going for. Thanks, Teddy. And now—"

"Yes, yes. Now, I have somewhere important to be. Miss Mona, I'm glad things worked out."

"They didn't, Teddy," the woman responded.

"Oh, sure. Sure. Well, I'm off. Honcho?"

"Yeah, mate. I'll fill you in shortly."

Teddy nodded, visor blazing, and scurried toward a nearby building.

Mona watched the old man go. "He's gonna bust his ass hurrying like that, Junker."

"Teddy will be fine. He sees more than you and I combined."

"Well, that's not hard. Especially since I don't seem to see anything as it really is and have no idea what's going on. What *is* the plan, anyway? Just ride out the world's end under this bloody dome?"

"Oh, I think we can do better than that, lass."

"Do you ever give a straight answer?"

"Not if I can help it, Mona."

"Great. So now what?"

"I need to chat with Urek again. There're some things I want to bring with me."

"Bring with you where?!"

But Mickie had already moved off to speak with Urek.

Bloody idiot junker with his secret idiot plans! And I'm just the idiot along for the bloody ride!

Mona hung around on the periphery as the Guntai Skeeters were uncovered and unloaded before the battle taxi hauling them was driven off into the distance and around a bend in the metal road.

As she waited, a few Space Cowboys offered to take Mona into one of the many buildings, but the former Maggot chose to remain close to Mickie, unsure of her place in this foreign world.

The Guntai Skeeters, now fully revealed under Kuyomi's glow, were single-seat aircrafts with folding rotors and unenclosed cockpits—ideal manhunt vehicles for Kalderra's insect- and bird-free environment. Mona watched as a plasteen bag and one large cloth-wrapped bundle were carefully placed into the back storage compartment of one of the Skeeters.

Once the Space Cowboys had completed their task and exited to perform other duties, Urek approached Mickie, who had been anxiously observing the Skeeter's loading.

"You sure about this, Honcho? Sure seems like an unnecessary risk."

Mickie spoke around his old, unlit cigar. "I promise you, mate. It's very necessary."

"It's just that…" Urek struggled to find the words. "It's just that we've come so far… We can't afford to lose you now. I don't know—"

Mickie silenced the man with a starred hand on his shoulder. "I'll be fine, lad. Time to see things through."

Urek swung his blonde head as if to shake away the doubt.

"Benten's grin, Honcho. Sometimes I forget who I'm talking to. We all know Mickie Brass can't be killed."

"Bloody right, mate. Finish things up here for me?"

"Of course, Mickie. Of course, I will."

"Good lad."

Urek began to leave but surprised Mona by stopping to offer her a small bow on his way to the nearest building. He disappeared inside.

Mona marched up to Mickie, who was looking over the Skeeter. "Want to tell me what in blazes is going on, Junker?"

"I'm heading out, lass," he replied, tossing his pack into the bottom of the cockpit.

"Heading out where?!"

Mickie smiled. "To bear witness."

"Bear witness to what?"

"Justice, lass. Sweet justice."

"Urek was right. You *are* an idiot."

"He never said that!"

"Well, he was thinking it! Just as I am now!"

Mickie sighed. "Look, you have no idea how much I've put into this moment, Mona. How much I've sacrificed. How much I've changed myself. And now that it's here, I'll be damned if I'm gonna watch it on some video feed!" He pointed to his face. "These eyes! These eyes, Mona! The same ones that saw my family burn! They're the ones that are gonna record the event! And finally—"

"Where are you going, Junker?" Mona asked calmly, ending Mickie's tirade.

The Space Cowboy straightened. "Kodama-san, lass." A wicked grin appeared. "Best seat in the house."

"Fujin's ass! Kodama-san, Junker?! You'll be shot down before you get there!"

Mickie waved her away. "Nah, you heard Urek. All the Guntai are tied up around Karudera City and Ghool Tower. I'll be far from there. Plus, it's a Guntai aircraft. Even if I'm spotted, it won't arouse any suspicions. You know how disorganized they are on Kalderra."

Mona could feel her anger begin to swell.

"So let me get this straight. Everything you've planned. All the lives you've put at risk. All the death you've dodged. You're gonna risk it all to watch the show?! With *your own eyes*?!"

"Mona—"

"No, shut your gob, Junker! I'm coming with you."

"Mona—"

"I said shut it! You think you're the only one who's suffered? The only one who deserves to watch these bastards die?!"

"Mona—"

"No! I've suffered! You haven't heard the half of how I've suffered! All because of the Morishitas! All because of the Sindo-Emperor and his Syndicate! And now you think that I'm not gonna see this through! That I don't deserve to—"

"Mona!"

"What!"

"The other Skeeter is for you, lass. I wouldn't dream of doing this without you."

Mona fell back a step, struck by Mickie's words. His grey eyes bore into her, and her GLIM-patch glitched momentarily.

The Kisser fumbled for words. "Well, ok, then." A beat. "But I don't know how to fly a bloody Skeeter."

"But I do, lass. I can fly anything. I'll simply lock your Skeeter controls to my own. You can just sit back, relax, and enjoy the view."

A thin smile split Mona's lips.

"When do we leave?"

Mickie motioned to the second Skeeter. "How about now? Throw your pack in and buckle up. Press that green button on the collective lever to fire her up, and I'll take care of the rest. You don't even need to touch the cyclic stick."

Mona placed her bag on the cockpit floor and fastened the belt around her waist and chest. She went to push the ignition button but stopped and turned to look at Mickie.

"Junker?"

"Yes, Mona?"

"I'm going to bear witness, just like you. But it won't be justice I'm looking to find. It'll be vengeance, pure and simple."

Mickie shrugged. "Vengeance is just justice misspelled, lass."

"I like that. Then let's go see this misspelled justice."

Mickie nodded, started his Guntai Skeeter, locked Mona's controls onto his own, and pulled back on the collective lever.

As a pair, the Skeeters rose into the air, through the Laughing God's protective dome, and into the Kalderran night, whisking away two Maggots from different worlds, each sharing hope that old wrongs could be righted. And deep wounds could be healed.

The Guntai Skeeters came to gentle landing on a wide ridge just under the peaked summit of Kodama-san, their rotors folding neatly down as they ceased spinning. The former Maggots exited their small aircraft, and Mona's breath caught as she stared out at the view, one encompassing the Kodama Plateau, Mori Mangekyo, and the northern part of Mori Hotaru before things shrunk into the horizon, only Ghool Tower visible in the distance. The massive eye of Kuyomi hung heavy overhead, bathing the planet in her violet gaze.

"It's beautiful, Junker."

"I told you, lass. Best seat in the house."

As Mona admired the landscape, Mickie moved to the rear storage compartment and unloaded his Skeeter, placing the bag and long, wrapped bundle onto the hard ground. Unlit cigar still hanging from his mouth, he rummaged through the bag and took out two pairs of digital binoculars, handing one to Mona.

"These are gigantic, Junker."

"Yeah, SkyMaster 5000s. Best in the galaxy, lass. Can spot a squirrel's nut sack from twenty kilometers away."

"Is that what you do in your spare time?"

Mickie shrugged. "If the sack's interesting enough."

Mona laughed, and Mickie smiled.

Mickie pointed to a red button on the goggles.

"Best part? We can record everything we see. And I have a feeling we're gonna run this back any time we get down."

"*We*, Junker?" Mickie, always the coolest head in the room, stammered for a response before Mona let him off the hook. "Relax. I'm just teasing."

Mona lifted the SkyMaster 5000 to her eye and GLIM-patch, and the world far below her came into focus. She swung the goggles from Mori Hotaru to Mori Mangekyo and zoomed in. The forest's thick canopy blocked much her view.

"How're we supposed to see anything? The bloody mori is too bloody thick."

As Mona continued to peer through the SkyMaster, Mickie approached and gently moved the digi-goggles, his rough hands gently touching hers. For the first time, Mona noticed that he smelled of wood and spice.

"There, lass. That's where I think they're gonna stop. That's where the Sindo-Emperor is gonna tour his spoils."

Mona sucked in as everything came into focus. In Mori Mangekyo, just east of center, was a wide clearing known by Maggots as The Lone Nipple.

Mona spoke as she continued to study the clearing. "What makes you think it will be Mori Mangekyo and not Hotaru?"

"You know subarashi grow a bit bigger in Mangekyo. I think the bastard wants to see the full possibility of his new acquisition."

"I think you're right, Junker. And The Nipple will give them the space they need for all their bloody pomp and circumstance." Mona continued to look out. "So, when do you think they'll move?"

"Not until these bastards are gone, lass."

Mona removed the SkyMaster to find Mickie using his own to search the Kodama Plateau.

"What's over there?"

"Take a look."

Mona joined Mickie and aimed her digi-goggles down into the plateau. The starship was still there, a long line of Kodama making their way up the boarding ramp and into the vessel.

Mickie commented from the side. "The Morishitas know that the Kodama control the subarashi. They won't move the Sindo-Emperor into the mori until the Kodama are gone, their connection to the trees severed. Only then will they officially claim their prize."

The former Maggots watched as the line of Kodama continued to fill the starship.

"Benten's grin, Junker! What is that?!"

Near the end of the alien line, a large, square load skate was being pushed and pulled by a dozen Kodama, its oversized rubber wheels leaving marks in the dusty plateau floor. Six Kodama rested on their backs atop the conveyance. Pressed closely together in two neat rows of three, their bodies quaked, clear hands clenching tightly.

And atop the six Kodama sat Sakuya-hime, the Goddess's roots delving deep into the chests of her sacrificial lambs.

"Fujin's ass! What am I looking at?!" asked Mona, her mind refusing to process what was playing out far beneath her.

"Makes sense, lass."

"None of this makes sense."

"From a human lens, you're right. But that... *thing* obviously needs to feed. It started by feeding on the core on the planet. Then it fed off the light of Anohoshi and Kuyomi. Now that they need to move it, another source of sustenance had to be found. And it looks like they found one, pretty close to home."

"It's grotesque, Junker."

"Alien shit usually is, lass."

Mickie and Mona zoomed in with their goggles. Sakuya-hime was in full bloom, its yellow eye panning left and right. Apparently it, too, was without trust in the Syndicate's seemingly magnanimous deal. Suddenly, the Goddess's eye shifted up, lining directly with the former Maggots high above. Mona took a reactive step back as the yellow orb settled on her, the itchy sensation on her brain commencing anew.

"Fujin's ass!" the woman cursed, and Sakuya-hime, seemingly contented with what it read within Mona, lazily drifted its eye away.

Once the Goddess was safely loaded into the starship and the trailing Kodama entered the craft, the boarding ramp finally slid up to seal the vessel. Mickie and Mona held their collective breath, waiting for—

"And we celebrate, for Sakuya-hime's voice will now be further spread throughout this galaxy."

The unexpected voice ripped the former Maggots from their spying, forcing them to drop their SkyMasters and spin abruptly. A Kodama had appeared on the far side of the ridge and began making its way toward them.

"Benten's grin, Crystals! What the bloody heck are you doing up here?!"

The Kodama smiled through clear lips.

"We are here to bear witness, Mona Ripple."

"Funny, Crystals, that's exactly what we're doing here."

The Kodama nodded. "What we see here today will be recorded in the collective mind and integrated into the shared kokoru."

"You're gonna die here, Crystals."

"Sacrifice is often necessary for the greater good, Mona Ripple. Our sacrifice will prove the power of obedience for generations that follow the Goddess." The Kodama's crystalline eyes began to vibrate. "It is time."

Mickie and Mona looked once more into the plateau. Gases hissed from the many vents of the starship and dust swirled from beneath the craft, enveloping it in a grey cloud. The sounds of engines roaring to life reached the spectators just as the vessel began to lift from the rocky surface.

The Kodama spoke from the side.

"Humans are a virus. They eat away at planets, poison all that they touch. They're a rare strain, one that is most malignant to each other. The Morishitas are not unique in this. Rather, they are the embodiment of the human condition. The human need to dominate and destroy. To inflict pain. We know you share in this view, Mona Ripple, for we have seen the damage done to your soul. We know you share in this view, Mickie Brass, for we have followed your exploits across the galaxy. You will both be known as forever heroes in the shared kokoru. Sakuya-hime wills it. And so it shall be done."

The starship continued to rise, escaping the Kodama Plateau and climbing toward the stars. Mickie moved to his Skeeter as the Kodama held out its clear arms, a look of ecstasy on its typically stoic face.

"Trillions of us are sharing in this triumph," said the Kodama. "Across the universe, we observe through these eyes and celebrate as one."

The starship grew smaller as it raced through Kalderra's atmosphere. Once through, the quantum drive would engage and the Kodama craft would disappear, free to roam the galaxy.

Mona glanced back to find Mickie pressing the comm button on his Skeeter.

"Teddy. Do it, mate."

Several seconds passed, the Kodama still staring up in euphoria, before the night sky lit up as the starship exploded high overhead, sending flaming debris to arch and scatter against Kuyomi's violet backdrop.

The Kodama's crystal eyes went wide and its mouth opened to release a piercing scream. Mona covered her ears as wails, moans, and shrieks— too many to count—joined in a chorus of anguish, a trillion Kodama voicing their distress through a single mouth.

Just when Mona thought her eardrums could take no more, the intense noise ceased, and the Kodama spun to face Mona, rage burning in its crystalline eyes.

"Why?!" the Kodama roared. "Why?! You know better than anyone the evil that humans do! You have to know that there is no salvation for your kind! You have to know that a shared kokoru is the only way forward! You have to know that the Great Transmogrification is the only way to start anew! To clean the slate of sin!"

Mona looked to Mickie and unspoken words passed between them. She then returned to the Kodama.

"You're right, Crystals. Humans can be the lowest form of life. We take from planets, from nature, from each other. Benten's grin, you don't have to tell me about the vile things humans can do to one another, especially to the weakest and most vulnerable."

"Then why?!"

Mona glanced Mickie's way again.

"Because there is good among us. And there are people willing to fight against the powers of evil. Against the Morishitas and the Syndicate. We have to be given a chance to clean up our own backyard."

"You never will!" the Kodama hissed. "You are incapable, for you know nothing of the shared kokoru! The glory of the hive mind! Humans do not evolve! You are the same pathetic, selfish creatures that crawled from the oceans millions of years ago! Humans deserve extinction!"

Mona chuckled. "I can't argue your point. Humans as a whole are a dreadful bunch. But they're *our* friends and family, lovers and colleagues. They might be terrible, but they're also our kin. And you ain't, Crystals."

"Junker, send this alien bastard home."

Mickie's thigh holsters sprang open, and a tech-revolver appeared in the man's hand in a blur. The Kodama's hands went up in protest, just as a bullet ripped through its head, sending a spray of clear brain matter into the air behind it.

The Kodama's eyes went still, and the creature stumbled backward, tumbling from the ledge to plummet to the rocks far below.

Mickie returned his weapon to his thigh holster, which immediately snapped shut.

"Never did like bloody aliens, lass."

"They're the worst." Mona laughed and shook her head. "How'd you swing that, Junker?"

Mickie shrugged. "Pretty simple, really. Once I had the prefix code, Teddy could override any system remotely. Even the Flight Termination System. With full autonomy over the starship, Teddy just had to input the command."

Mona thought for a moment. "And the Morishitas will just think that the bomb they planted worked. They won't imagine that anything else is amiss."

Mickie offered a gold-toothed smile. "That's right, lass. Sorry I couldn't tell you, but those bastards can read your mind."

"But not yours, huh, Junker?"

"No. Not mine."

"And why's that?"

"Being Honcho has its perks. Including access to certain... enhancements."

Mona's brown eye searched the unusual man before her.

"You thought of everything, didn't you? You saw all the angles. You anticipated every move. You foresaw it all."

"Not everything, Mona."

Mona started to respond, but the question caught in her throat. She switched gears.

"What now, Junker?"

"Now we wait."

"How long will it take?"

"No idea."

"So you don't have *all* the answers?" Mona teased.

"Sorry to disappoint you."

"I'm beginning to think that's impossible. How will we know when it's started?"

"Oh, lass, I don't think we'll be able to bloody miss it."

***

Below the surface of Kalderra, the departure of Sakuya-hime was felt, the connection with its creations severed. Hundreds of giant kameeba, tickers swollen with energy, lined pit and chasm walls, clung to ceilings above magma rivers, awaiting orders from their goddess.

But none were to come.

Instead, a vast emptiness assaulted the glowing blobs, robbing them of purpose, stripping them of a reason to exist.

Gelatinous bodies began to melt away. Clear material dripped into magma, sizzling and popping as it touched the superheated rock. Massive tickers, free of their meaty prisons, plunged into red liquid, where they floated momentarily before even their protective casings evaporated, returning Kalderra's stolen power to the heart of the wrathful planet.

Rivers surged, spilling over their rocky banks. Magma raced up craggy shafts. Caverns shook as chasms within erupted, filling the rooms with heat and steam.

And the planet known as Kalderra woke after a long, forced sleep—restless and angry and vengeful.

Mickie and Mona, standing on Kodama-san, had nothing to do but wait. As Mickie continued to search Mori Mangekyo through his SkyMaster 5000, Mona's thoughts raced. A faint tension had fallen over the former Maggots—too many questions yet unanswered, too many words yet shared. Finally, Mona had enough.

"Junker?"

"Yeah, lass," Mickie responded, his grey eyes still locked onto the forest below.

Mona waited for a moment before continuing. "What was the plan if the Kodama hadn't thrown a wrench in the works?"

Mickie kept the digi-goggles to his face as he answered. "Well, we've been placing Space Cowboys in positions across the planet for years. When the Sindo-Emperor came to Kalderra, which I knew the bastard would, we'd attack. We'd be vastly outnumbered, but with the element of surprise, I still liked our chances. Plus, I'd put a Space Cowboy against any five Guntai any day. It would have been bloody, to be sure, and we'd have lost a lot of good people. But the Morishitas would have fallen. And our sacrifice would have been worthwhile."

"Sounds like a solid plan."

"About as solid as any galactic upheaval can be."

Another long pause from Mona followed. She took a deep breath.

"So why?"

"Why what?"

"Why did you agree to help me? No, that's not accurate. Why did you *volunteer* to help me rescue Darien?"

Mickie hesitated, so Mona went on.

"Years of planning. Potentially millions of lives on the line. The future of the galaxy at stake. One man seemingly at the center of it all. And he risks it all to help a love drunk woman save an idiot from a monster? Help me understand it."

Mickie slowly lowered his SkyMaster. His grey eyes found Mona. For one of the very few times, a veil of uncertainty shrouded the man's face.

"You… you were paying me."

"Benten's grin, junker! *Paying you*?! Urek told me that you're the second most powerful man in the galaxy! The last thing you need is money!"

Mickie shuffled from one booted foot to the other, looking nothing like the critical galactic chess piece he was.

"Mona… I…" he began, trailing off.

"Unbelievable! Always a step ahead except when you're tripping over yourself! Here, let me help you."

Mona stomped over to Mickie's Skeeter and retrieved his pack from the cockpit floor. She rummaged through it.

"What are you doing, lass?"

"Shut up!" she yelled as she rifled through the pack. And then—"Here! Here it is!" She thrust an object at the Space Cowboy. "Care to explain this?!"

In Mona's hand was the origami heart she had given to Darien. Mickie took it with trembling fingers, stared at the contours and sharp creases.

"It didn't belong in the trash."

"Why not? Darien certainly thought it did."

"Then he's the most foolish man in history."

"That makes it even worse! Why help me rescue a bloody fool when there was so much to lose?! *Everything* to lose?!"

"I… I…"

"Answer the bloody question!"

Mickie's eyes rose from the paper heart, locking onto Mona.

"Because I love you."

And there it was, the long unsaid laid bare between the former Maggots. Mona felt her knees grow weak, her anger and frustration washing away like sweat in a rainstorm.

"I still don't understand," Mona said softly. "If you love me, then why help me save another man?"

"He seemed to make you happy. More than I ever could, anyway. And that's more important to me than anything else… including my own bloody feelings."

Mona's mind reeled in a swarm of memories. Mickie assisting her with the kameeba ticker despite having taken a fatal hit from a shokushu. Mickie saving the scav with his quick thinking. Mickie refusing to allow Mona to assault Ghool Tower on her own. Mickie leading their escape, killing dozens of Guntai while accept grievous injuries. Mickie holding her in his arms in the Kodama cavern. Mickie ignoring the concerns and objections of his fellow Space Cowboys.

Mickie doing all this for Mona.

"Mickie. I—"

Something in the distance caught Mickie's eye, and the digi-goggles sprang back to his face.

"Mona! The Sindo-Emperor!"

Mona rushed to the edge of the ledge and brought up her own SkyMaster, running it over Mori Mangekyo until she reached The Lone Nipple. Into that massive clearing rode the imperial convoy, hundreds of Guntai vehicles bracketing the oversized golden carriage of the Sindo-Emperor.

The carriage slowed to stop in the middle of The Nipple as a tight perimeter was established around the clearing. A regiment of ChoMM guardians took up positions, nano-edged katanas drawn and ready. Several attendants in gaudy kimonos rushed to the carriage, helping an ancient man step down into the mori.

"Is that him?" asked Mona, her heart racing.

"That's the bastard. Sakuramachi Morishita. The bloody Sindo-Emperor."

Mickie continued to watch the scene unfold. "And it looks like he's got company."

Several more men were helped down from the royal vehicle, four in total.

"Who are they, Mickie?"

"Morishita princes."

Mona's heart raced faster.

"Mickie? Is… Is Masami Morishita there?"

Mickie studied the faces of the princes.

"I'm sorry, lass. He's not there."

Mona blinked away the tears that had formed in her eye.

"Good. I want the bastard to see my face when I carve him up. I want to remind him of everything he did before he begs for his life. I want—"

Kodama-san shook beneath the former Maggots' feet.

"Mickie!"

"It's beginning, lass. Keep looking. You don't want to miss this."

Mickie and Mona watched as soldiers swayed on the suddenly unstable ground. The Sindo-Emperor fell to his knees as attendants and princes hurried to his aid. Helmeted heads swung to the subarashi, terrified that lighting would rain down at any moment.

But their fears were misplaced, as retribution would not come from above but below.

Mona grabbed Mickie for balance as the planet began to quake, her digi-goggles firmly pointed at Mori Mangekyo.

Soldiers ran back and forth, unsure what to do amidst the chaos. The circle around the imperial family tightened, weapons searching for threats, anything concrete that could be fired upon.

Attendants began pushing the Sindo-Emperor and his sons back toward the golden carriage, but it was too late. It was too late for all of them. Kalderra had already decided their fates.

Massive fissures opened up across Mori Mangekyo and Mori Hotaru, lava erupting from each like blood from an open wound. Subarashi disappeared into cracks and collapsed under waves of molten rock.

Mona blindly reached for Mickie's hand, found it, and squeezed tightly.

The Sindo-Emperor fell back as a geyser of lava shot forth from beneath the imperial carriage, liquifying the gold. Sakuramachi Morishita screamed under the torrent of superheated metal, clutching his burned face with smoldering hands.

Mona chuckled, the symbolism not lost on the woman. "You can't make this shit up, Mickie."

Together, Mickie and Mona stood, hand in hand, bearing witness as The Lone Nipple was ripped apart, sending Guntai soldiers, ChoMM guardians, and imperial attendants into the planet's raging core. The Sindo-Emperor shrieked in horror, his sons holding him upright, as a surge of lava poured out from one of the fissures, a wave of unimaginable heat sweeping across the clearing and clawing at Morishita legs. The princes' panicked howls joined their father's as bodies were swallowed by flame.

"That's for my family, you bastards," said Mickie.

"That's for a little girl who was stripped of everything," added Mona.

As Mona continued taking in the carnage, Mickie reached into his waist pouch and removed a lighter. With an audible click, the end of his old, chewed up cigar began to glow a deep red. The Space Cowboy took a long pull, sending a cloud of smoke to soar above the destruction.

Mona lowered her goggles.

"This was my father's cigar," said Mickie. "One of the few things I was able to scavenge after the fire."

"How is it?"

"Tastes like shit, truth be told. But nothing's ever been sweeter."

Mickie turned and began moving away.

"Where are you going?"

"I forgot. I have a present for you."

"After what we just saw, I have need for nothing else."

Mickie shrugged. "Let's see."

The Space Cowboy returned to the area behind his Skeeter and collected the large bundle he had carried from the Laughing God. After removing the cloth covering, Mickie brought it to where Mona still stood. Unfolding three metal legs, he placed it beside the woman.

"Is that what I think it is, Mickie? A bloody rocket launcher?"

The man nodded. "But not just any rocket launcher, lass. That's the Starstreak 9000, capable of taking down anything smaller than a class V starship. All you have to do is lock it on and fire."

"What do I need it for?"

"Take a look through the tracker. Aim it at Ghool Tower."

Mona hesitated but did as instructed, swinging the launcher's canister toward Ghool Tower before placing her eye and GLIM-patch to the visor displaying the tracking and locking system.

"What do you see, lass?"

"I just see the Tower. And people scrambling around it. But nothing— wait! There's a small spacecraft taking off from somewhere nearby."

"Just as I thought."

"Care to share, Mickie?"

"*That* is the Countess Desma Ghool, making her escape. I knew she'd want to remain behind to oversee preparations for the Sindo-Emperor's grand celebration. That's if she was even invited to accompany him into the mori. It's no secret that Ghool is not exactly popular among the Morishitas."

"Desma bloody Ghool," said Mona, lining the Starstreak's sights with the ascending aircraft.

"And, lass, I doubt she's alone in there. My guess is that she's taken her paramours with her."

Mona lifted her head from the visor to glance at Mickie. "You mean..."

"That's right. If you want your revenge, it's yours to take."

Mona returned to the Starstreak and looked through the visor once more. A message flashed as the circular crosshairs turned red: *Missile lock ON. Fire when ready.*

Mona thought of Desma Ghool's mocking smile. She recalled Darien's cold rejection. She remembered an origami heart folded with love, only to be discarded in the trash. Moments in time, painful and heartbreaking, played out behind her GLIM-patch. And Mona found herself surprised.

Because she didn't care.

Mona stepped away from the Starstreak, and Mickie raised an eyebrow.

"Let the bitch have him. They deserve each other. And I couldn't give less of a shit."

An explosion rocked Mori Hotaru, the northernmost part of the forest vanishing in seconds.

"You sure, lass?"

Mona slid toward Mickie, her acid-marked hands finding the man's waist.

"I'm sure. I got everything I need right here. Even if it took me too long to realize it. Apparently, Darien's not the only fool."

Mona plucked the cigar from Mickie's mouth and took a long drag.

"There, now we both have cigar breath. Come here, Mickie."

"Ok, Mona."

The former Maggots fell into each other's arms, mouths meeting like two perfect folds, and the planet shook violently.

When they finally separated, Mona stared up into Mickie's grey eyes.

"You got me feeling off-balance, Mickie."

"Well, the mountain is shaking beneath us, lass."

"Don't shortchange yourself. It's got nothing to do with the bloody world crumbling." Mona placed her head against Mickie's chest. "And if this is the end, what a bloody wonderful way to go."

"Why would you say that, Mona?"

Mona took a step back and motioned around her. "Am I that stunning, Mickie, that you didn't notice that Kalderra's on fire? And I don't see anywhere safe to go."

Mickie shook his head. "Such little faith, Mona." He walked to his Skeeter and pressed the comm button. "Teddy! Come get us, mate."

"Oh, I'd love to see this! Old man Blinders driving through an ocean of lava to—"

Mona's words were cut short as something unbelievably massive broke free from the range of cliffs to the southeast. As large as a city, it rose above the mountains and fiery death consuming Mori Hotaru, carving a neat line to Kodama-san.

"Mickie?"

"Meet the Laughing God, lass. The most cutting edge starship in the galaxy. And home of the Space Cowboys. It's also our ticket out of here."

Mona cackled as she slapped her hands together.

"Mickie bloody Brass! The man with endless tricks up boundless thighs. Get over here. Now."

Another embrace. Another deep kiss.

"So, Mickie Brass," said Mona, her fingers tracing the Space Cowboy's weathered face. "The Sindo-Emperor's dead. I guess that makes you the most powerful man in the galaxy."

"I suppose so, Mona. But it's not really an official title."

"So… you're basically royalty now. What will I be? A queen? A consort? A mistress?"

Mickie raked his hands through Mona's wiry hair. "I'm no king, lass. I'm just the Honcho."

"Which would make me?"

"I was thinking Honchess. The first Honchess in Space Cowboy history. Together, we'll traverse the galaxy, fixing what the Syndicate has broken. Honcho Mickie Brass and Honchess Mona Ripple. The scourge of the bastard Morishitas."

"I like that Mickie. I like that a lot. But what about Honchess Mona *Brass*? I think it has a better ring to it. Wouldn't you agree?"

"Aye, lass. I would agree."

The Laughing God appeared overhead, and large bay doors slid open.

"We can take the Skeeters up, lass. You ready?'

Mona shook her head, refusing to look away from Mickie's face.

"Let's stay here for a while longer. And watch the world burn."

Mickie pointed his chin over Mona's shoulder. "All the action is behind you, lass."

"I can see it reflected in your eyes well enough, Mickie. Now, let's see if you can keep them open and kiss at the same time."

"Ok, Mona."

Finally. Something beautiful to call my own.

Mickie Brass and Mona Ripple stood intertwined atop Kodama-san as the planet known as Kalderra erupted around them, signaling that a new power had arrived on the galactic scene. The tale would spread far and wide—of how a Space Cowboy and a Maggot fell in love… and brought down an empire.

EPILOGUE
LOVESTRUCK

Colonel Toro paced around his office as Maggot Mickie Brass stood just inside the doorway, Akubra hat in hand, head down in a show of contrition.

"Fujin's ass! What were you thinking, Mickie?!"

"I was thinking of protecting the unit."

"How?! By slugging Vasily Pappas in the face?! He's your bloody Kisser!"

Mickie raised his head as he responded. "Look, Colonel, the bastard was insisting on unnecessary risks. I had to—"

"No, no, no! Don't give me that, Mickie! You know bloody well that Pappas's orders fell well within acceptable risk limits! So why'd you do it?!"

"Maybe I don't like the bastard. Or how he runs his unit."

Toro ceased his walking.

"Of course, you don't! No one does! That's why I made you Second Kisser of Karcass Two! The plan was to get you some reps, so I could replace that weasel! With you, you fool! But now?! Well, now you've gone and mucked it all up! That's what I get for putting my trust in a bloody Space Cowboy!"

Mickie dropped his head again.

"Sorry, Colonel."

"Pappas wants you out of here, you know? He has every right to formally request your dishonorable discharge. And I'm expected to approve it without question. For striking your commanding Kisser?! I *should* approve it!"

"I understand, Colonel."

"Oh, I know you understand, Mickie. Because that backwater twang of yours does a shit job of masking how talented you are. Benten's grin, you're the best I've ever seen with a weapon, with balls and brains to boot! Oh, you really screwed up my plans! Might as well have kicked me in the berries while you were at it!"

"Sorry, Colonel."

"Shut up!" Toro resumed his pacing. "You're too good to let go and too defiant to get your own unit. And protocol dictates that I have to knock you down. No more Second Kisser for you. And I can't keep you in Karcass Two. Pappas would shoot you in the back the first chance he got. I see only one way out of this."

"What's that, Colonel?"

Toro pulled up next to Mickie. "Look, I'm sorry."

"For what?"

"You give me no other choice. I gotta ship you back to Karcass Five. Now, now, I don't want to hear it. I know Ripper's a major ballbuster, but she's the best Kisser we got. You've worked together before without killing each other, so I'm assuming you can do so again."

"If you think it's the best option, Colonel."

"It's the only bloody option!"

Toro began to spin away, but something gave the fat man pause. Looking past Mickie's mask of remorse, something was hiding within the man's thick salt-and-pepper beard—a thin smile.

Toro's frog-like eyes narrowed. "Dismissed. Report to Ripper and Karcass Five. And stay away from Vasily Pappas!"

Mickie placed the black Akubra hat back on his head, his thin smile becoming a wide, gold-toothed grin.

"Thanks, mate. I won't let you down."

"Get out of here, Mickie."

When the office door slid shut behind Mickie, Colonel Toro snickered to himself and moved behind his desk, dropping his girth into his leather chair. He reached for his bottle of whiskey and poured himself a glass. Toro downed it in one giant gulp and helped himself to another, shaking his head the entire time.

"As if I don't have enough on my bloody plate," the Colonel muttered to himself. "Quotas going up, the bloody Countess up my ass, and *now this!*"

He drank again, thought for a moment, and chuckled. "The things they don't teach you in officer school.

"Like how to deal with a lovestruck Maggot."

LIKE THE BOOK?

Thanks so much for reading Lovestruck Maggot. Your time is valuable, so I truly appreciate you spending some to explore the worlds I create.

If you enjoyed the novel, please consider leaving a rating or review on your platform of choice. As an independent author, they're the fuel I need to restart the storytelling engine.

With gratitude,

Jarrett

ABOUT THE AUTHOR

Jarrett Brandon Early is the author of genre-bending science fiction and fantasy novels. He lives in Virginia Beach, VA USA with his wife Natthi and daughter Alex Beam. Lovestruck Maggot is his fifth book.

ALSO BY
JARRETT BRANDON EARLY

Children of Madness

The Station Trilogy: The Complete Collection

Station

The Rott Inertia

Ill Messiah